the PRIVATE LIFE of
ELDER THINGS

Adam Gauntlett has loved horror ever since reading Stoker's *Dracula*, given as a Christmas present. Thank you Santa, whoever you were! It was part of a packet of cheap paperbacks that Santa happened to be giving away down at Sandys Boat Club, but only *Dracula* captured any kind of attention. Santa must have noticed because for years afterward copies of Armada's *Ghost Book* series turned up, regular as clockwork, each Christmas.

Born in Bermuda, Adam has spent about half his life in the United Kingdom, with small snippets here and there in the States. His writing encompasses history, architectural history, games journalism (The horror! The horror!), and horror fiction of all stripes. Among his published credits are more than a few RPG titles, including many for Pelgrane Press' *Trail of Cthulhu* line. Among his scenarios are: "Hell Fire", "The Many Deaths of Edward Bigsby", "The Long Con", "Soldiers of Pen and Ink", "Not So Quiet", "Millionaire's Special", the *Dulce Et Decorum Est* collection, "Suited and Booted", "Remember, Remember", and many others. His short fiction has appeared in *The Bermudian* magazine, as well as a collection of Bermudian speculative fiction (due 2016).

Keris McDonald discovered H.P. Lovecraft in the local library at seventeen and started running *Call of Cthulhu* games at college. The *Horror on the Orient Express* campaign she ran decades ago is still one of her proudest memories – judge her as you wish. She turned to horror writing during a miserable year as a library assistant in the south of England, but nowadays lives a disappointingly pleasant life in the not-very-grim North. Her short stories have appeared in three Ash Tree Press anthologies and the magazines *Weird Tales, Supernatural Tales* and *All Hallows*, as well as the Hic Dragones collections *Impossible Spaces* and *Hauntings*, and Paul Finch's *Terror Tales of Yorkshire*. Her story "The Coat off His Back" was chosen for reprint in *Best Horror of the Year: Volume 7* (ed. Ellen Datlow) and her scenario "Master of Hounds" appeared in *Worlds of Cthulhu*.

However, she now spends most of her writing time under the name 'Janine Ashbless', spinning stories of paranormal erotica and dark filthy romance for publishers such as HarperCollins and Ebury/Random House. Her ninth novel, *Cover Him with Darkness*, an uncompromising tale of fallen angels and religious conspiracy, is out now from Cleis Press.

Adrian Tchaikovsky was born in Woodhall Spa, Lincolnshire before heading off to Reading to study psychology and zoology. He subsequently ended up in law and has worked as a legal executive in both Reading and Leeds, where he now lives. Married, he is an eager live role-player and has trained in stage-fighting and historical combat. He maintains a keen interest in history and the biological sciences, especially entomology.

Adrian is the author of the acclaimed ten book *Shadows of the Apt* series starting with *Empire in Black and Gold* published by Tor UK. His other works for Tor include standalone novels *Guns of the Dawn* and *Children of Time* and the new series *Echoes of the Fall* starting with *The Tiger and the Wolf*. Other major works include the short story collection *Feast and Famine* for NewCon Press and novellas "The Bloody Deluge" (in *Journal of the Plague Year*) and "Even in the Cannon's Mouth" (in *Monstrous Little Voices*) for Abaddon. He has also written numerous short stories and been shortlisted for the David Gemmell Legend Award, the Arthur C Clarke Award and the British Fantasy Award.

the PRIVATE LIFE of ELDER THINGS

ADRIAN TCHAIKOVSKY

ADAM GAUNTLETT

and

KERIS McDONALD

THE ALCHEMY PRESS

The Alchemy Press, Staffordshire, UK
www.alchemypress.co.uk

Contents

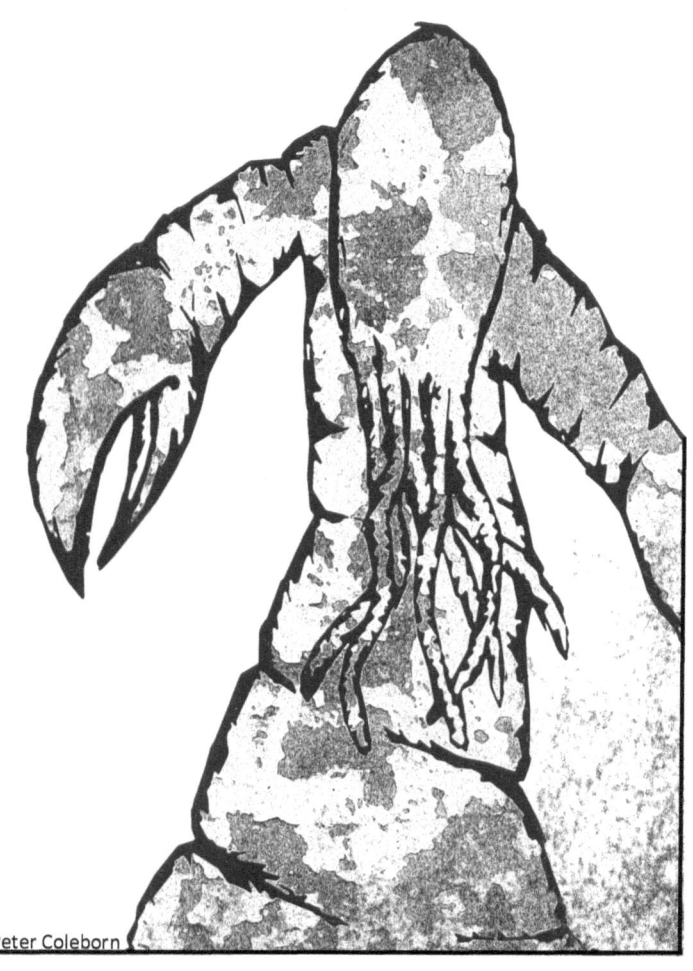

Donald

Adrian Tchaikovsky

Donald Toomey, yes. We were always good friends, which is surprising given what you and I both now know. I remember thinking when I first saw him – well, there's a man who's not going to win hearts and minds just by smiling at them. Yet he had a following, because he was keen, and topical, and he knew what he was talking about. A lot of young and dedicated people had time for Donald back then, despite his personal disadvantages.

Oh, it was a conference, where I first saw him. I knew the name from somewhere, but our specialities were different enough that I don't think I'd read anything of his, and vice versa. Seeing him up on the podium was an education: stooped, gangling, with a teenager's bad skin carried over into his mid-twenties. Still, he had made his mark by action, not by looking pretty, and not by toeing the line either. I hadn't really given a damn about sustainable fishing or all that sort of thing until I heard him talk about it. He had an energy about him, no mistake. I find that most of the time the people with that kind of drive to them know pitifully little about the subject, and those in the know are too jaded to get very excited, but Donald had the facts and the fervour, all in one package. You barely noticed the physical deficiencies, even the eyes.

I very nearly failed to talk to him because of that. It's small of me, but it's hard to know where to focus when the man's so wall-eyed that he's looking two directions at once. But we got to talking – he on marine conservation, me on my beloved ichthyological taxonomy – and let me tell you, he was one of the few people who would sit still for it – and we kept in touch after the conference, simple as that.

Oh, I found out soon that his reputation as a troublemaker was more than just hot air. Something of an activist, in his youth, chaining himself to this and sabotaging that. It meant that no serious research post would touch him. And yes, I had my own doctorate and a decent-sized grant, and because my life was very safe and slightly dull I did indulge in some vicarious rebellion and get him an assistant's place under me for a year, just to kick-start his CV. So you might say I played some small role in what was to come.

My demands on his time were small enough, and he devoted the rest to his own marine ecology research, with my blessing. It helped him build his professional reputation and start angling, if you'll forgive the pun, for another position. He gave a few talks while he was with me, too – all very green stuff, and this was just when green was becoming fashionable – all about responsible use of resources, sharing the planet, you know. Quite the darling of the smart set in those days, appearances notwithstanding.

The year after, he secured that place in Hull, doing what he wanted. Sad to see him go, really, but I knew that taxonomy was never his interest. Still, he didn't forget that he'd got his start from me. Every four or five months would come a package and a letter in his somewhat unruly handwriting – always the personal touches – and I would get the pleasure of some new specimen for my collection.

Yes, my pride and joy, as you see all around. Partly it's my own acquisitive nature, partly it's Donald's gifts, but as you can see, I've pretty much walled my office in glass cases and jars now, every specimen remarkable in its own way. If only you were in the field, you'd be all over them with magnifying glasses and reference books. I guarantee there are fish here which … or perhaps you're not really interested. Such a pity, but I suppose that ichthyology is not one of the areas you pride yourself in being so well informed about. But surely, this juvenile *Xiphactinus* must at least excite ... no, nothing? "That's an ugly fish," you say. Ah well.

Where were we? Well yes, it must have been the best part of a decade then – or longer, I think – and Donald and I would write to one another, he in his scrawl, me with my dictation and my secretary; believe me, my own handwriting isn't fit for a five year-old. Even later on, Donald's was better.

Yes, I have the letters still. If you go through them, you can see the change, but it was only the calligraphy that suffered. Once I could untangle it, the content was as educated and incisive as ever; more, perhaps.

And then I went to visit him, as you know. I was in Hull to meet with a potential co-author, and I thought, why not drop in on Donald? All very short notice and unannounced, but I was sure he would be happy to grab a sandwich and talk about old times.

Well, you can imagine my confusion when they told me he was gone. Missing for some time, actually. His colleagues at the institute were cagey, but I had the distinct feeling that they thought he might have, you know, topped himself, just walked into the sea. I did a little digging, and it was plain that, beforehand, his relationships with his peers had degenerated. He had become erratic, very conscious of his awkward appearance, seldom seen in public. I wondered at the time if there was not some sort of broken relationship or the like at the heart of it. Everyone was agreed, though, that my friend Donald had dropped off the map *three years before.*

I had received five letters from him, complete with specimens, since his supposed disappearance. I had written to him, too. The address was just a PO Box, it's true, but that had always been the way, because he did tend to move around a bit. Obviously I dropped him a line straight off asking what he was playing at, and whether I could help.

Of course, that was when I first had a visit from your lot. All those questions, all that suspicion. Well, obviously I thought that Donald had gone back to his old activist ways, perhaps with a more radical agenda than before. He always did care so much about the future of the oceans. He got so angry about the pollution, the overfishing, well... You'll forgive me if I wasn't very sympathetic to your interrogation, back then.

I'm sure you've kept tabs on me since, and those letters I got started looking as though someone had opened them before me. No doubt you examined the specimens he sent, too, and just saw, oh, another ugly fish. Or perhaps you have a tame ichthyologist on hand, and I'd have liked to have seen his face. Ever since Donald left his job, his gifts have been more and more fascinating, harder and harder to classify. I've stopped trying to publish about them. A man's professional reputation can only take so much eccentricity. Now they're just for me, to look at, to gloat over. It's enough.

And you'll know I tend to travel more these days – seaside resorts and old port towns my speciality, the dingier the better, rubbing shoulders with maritime folk off foreign ships, hanging out at the docks like, hmm, a woman of negotiable affection. Yes, of course I had word from Donald that way, information he didn't want to send by the old, compromised channels. And of course I lied to your colleagues when they asked about it. A man's got to stick up for his friends, hasn't he?

I've become aware that there is a history involved here, a sort of clandestine war fought between certain little branches of the intelligence agencies and ... the Donalds of this world, shall we say. I've seen some reports and I've spoken to some witnesses – wouldn't you have liked to be there for *that*? – and I know that in the past there has been all sorts of nonsense: cults, apocalyptic prophecies, new age mysticism, the sort of occult business that Crowley would probably have thought twice about. You've had your differences, you and the Donalds.

Charges? Against me? Well, no doubt you'll do what you

must, but I'd advise against taking any hasty action, what with the recent news from Portsmouth and all.

Now we come to the reason for this little tête-à-tête, or *my* reason. Your reason is to pry from me my knowledge of Donald's whereabouts, which I don't have in any event. My reason is to tell you his demands.

I have it written out here, not in the rather disturbing script his writing has become, but in my own somewhat halting typing. Not something I'd trust to the secretary this time, after all. Take it, take it all, and pass it on. You're just the messenger, and you'll see this needs to go to the top. After all, *you're* not going to be at that big environmental summit they keep talking about, but the man in charge is, or at least the relevant cabinet minister.

I think you'll find that our representative there will spontaneously propose a rather broad-ranging raft of environmental reforms concerning fishing policies: dramatic reductions in quotas, a new ethical directive on overfishing, fines and penalties for those who won't listen. Pollution, too: cleaning up the oceans, preserving our planet. It's the politician's dream, after all. The green lobby will love it, a sure-fire vote-winner, and if the fishermen and the industrialists complain, well, what's more important than the future of the world?

And you'll be amazed at the number of other countries that jump on the bandwagon, because believe me, ours isn't the only conversation of this sort that's going on.

And if saving the world doesn't motivate you, small-minded thug that you are, I would hope that the rather curiously specific tidal wave that swamped Portsmouth yesterday might give you pause for thought, or why else have you come? How many was it, are they saying on the news? Only, I heard some sensationalist saying somewhere around forty thousand – drowned or crushed by the water or just … taken. Sorry, 'missing' is the word they used on the TV, but you and I both know better, don't we. And, oh, the property damage, the buildings broken like eggshells, the insurance companies wringing their hands. Maybe that's what concerns you most. But I can assure you, Donald and his friends are far more interested in the people. Donald's kind like people. They have all sorts of uses for them.

So let's just take a moment to think about Portsmouth, and the way they're going to have to redraw all the maps of the shoreline after what's happened there. You can be sure that there's more where that comes from – imagine if that had been London, hmm? Have you ever thought about just how *coastal* rather a lot of our civilisation actually is?

Because they may have a rather different view of the world, the Donalds, and not just because they're seeing it from the other side of the meniscus – and they may have their crazy religions, and would you really say that we don't have a few of our own? – but it's like Donald used to say right at the start. We have to look after the planet, because we're sharing it with such a wealth of life.

And if we don't take care, some of that life may decide they don't want to share it with us.

Pitter Patter

Adam Gauntlett

This statement (consisting of ….. page[s] each signed by me) is true to the best of my knowledge and belief and I make it knowing that, if it is entered into evidence, I shall be subject to prosecution if I have wilfully stated anything which I know to be false, or do not believe to be true.

Well, that's me fucked, I say to myself. There's not a cat in hell's chance they'll believe this, but I can't think of a better lie that will explain the facts. So I put pen to paper and start writing, my signature and the date up on the top of the first page: PS Johar MPS, October 18th.

So let's get started.

*

The targets we were meant to be keeping an obbo on had a garage across the way from a Territorial Army base. The TA building was pretty impressive, all heavy Victorian with lots of crinkly bits, none of which had been maintained in donkey's. God knows what they did if ever they had to carry out a rapid response to any threat that breached the perimeter since trees and tall grass were growing up right to the walls of the place, and from the ground floor you couldn't see much. We didn't care about the ground floor. We cared about the third, south-western corner, which had a brilliant overlook on our target.

It took a bit of blagging, our boss talking to their boss, but the TA blokes were willing to help. It wasn't long before the sector surveyor was driving me over to examine our new accommodations. I forget his name. Sounded like Geffrey, but it wasn't. Big, fat bloke. You couldn't picture him going up a ladder, never mind poking his head in a roof void.

"What's the unit like?" I asked, more to make conversation than anything. I didn't really care who the neighbours were, so long as they stayed out of our way.

"Oh, you'll have the place to yourself. It's an artillery company, but this hasn't been their real home for a long time. They're out in Kent, now. But since this used to be theirs, and since they don't want to let it go, it's still on our books. To be honest, if this were a different part of London we'd have sold the bloody thing. We sold Holloway, after all, and the money's snug deep in the MoD's pockets. Of course, we had people wanting to buy Holloway. Not a cat in hell's chance any developer would want this one, not to build new homes, anyway. Maybe a crematorium."

"So there's nobody on site but us?"

"Oh, I wouldn't go that far. There's a caretaker, Barker, former RSM. Retired. He lives on site, but not in the main building. He's got his own accommodation in one of the ancillaries. We used to have a cadet unit here, ACF, kids, you know, but they shut down a few years back."

The way Not-Quite-Geffrey let the conversation die off made me wonder a little bit, and then I made the connection. Rape and murder. Nasty business. They'd caught the bloke who did it, one of the cadet instructors. Not that he'd put up much of a fuss, easiest collar any PC ever had; found the slag wrist-deep in the victim. This far back I couldn't remember what the sentence had been but it didn't matter, since he topped himself about a month after we put him in. I couldn't remember where, exactly, that had happened, and I didn't like to ask Not-Quite-Geffrey. I had a sneaking suspicion it was on base, here. No doubt the stigma had put paid to recruitment. No wonder he didn't want to talk about it much.

So we drive through the gate, park the car, and walk to the main building, giving me a chance to get a proper eyes-on.

It's one of those buildings you figure has got to have a past.

You know how you can walk by a block of flats and, even if it's been there since Queen Liz's daddy was a twinkle in his daddy's eye, it doesn't look like anything ever happened there? Oh sure, it might be pretty, might have a blue plaque on the wall, but you think to yourself, nah, boring. Snore, snore. If walls could talk, these wouldn't, you know what I mean?

But this place, it had a past, all right. I could just picture all those sweating kids, uniforms and full pack, marching off to get butchered in the trenches, or shot up in North Africa. You could smell the years. God knows what you'd find if you poked around the garages or in the empty rooms. Hidden treasures.

Not-Quite-Geffrey sighed. "It's a bloody shame. We need more money to maintain places like this but really, what's the point? Nobody wants it. Nobody even wants to buy it, so here it sits."

We go trumping along the drive to one of the smaller buildings. There were a few of these on the site. One of them was plainly the former cadet barracks, now a bit seedy with neglect. The rest were probably accommodation for the married blokes, back when the Territorial Army Centre was full up. Former RSM Barker lived in one of those. The front path was groomed within an inch of its life, and the place looked as if it had seen a coat of paint sometime this decade, which is more than could be said for the rest of the TAC.

Barker opens the door to Not-Quite's knock, and there's a bit of explaining. Then Barker takes a long look at me, leads Not-Quite off for a private confab, and there is much confab to be had, apparently, 'cos I can see arms waving about like semaphores and Barker's face going redder by the minute. Not that it made a quiet fart's worth of difference to me, since we had the go-ahead from higher up, but I was left with the impression that friend Barker was less than enthusiastic about the presence of yours truly. Either someone hadn't bothered to tell him we were coming, or they had and he'd hoped it was all bollocks.

We leave Barker to his little slice of heaven and cross to the main building. Barker's eyes were on me all the way as we left him. It's nice to be loved, isn't it? Not-Quite doesn't bother to fill me in, and I'm in no hurry to be filled, so that's where we leave it.

It's bigger on the inside. I'm pretty sure of that.

That's the thing with big buildings, isn't it? Especially if you don't know them very well. At least with a hotel, say, if you're on the fourth floor, room 414, you can be pretty sure that room 314 looks a lot like it, and the corridor's the same, and so's the carpet. A place like this, though, older than old, with addition after addition built onto its central mass like extra chambers in an ant mound, you couldn't be sure that turning right down this particular corridor would put you in the kitchen for a brew -up, or in the office, or somewhere else again.

It didn't help that the electrics were as wonky as fuck. I mean, if you're standing at one end of the corridor, with a light switch close to hand, and at the other end there's another switch, you're justified in thinking that the two switches operate the same set of lights, aren't you? And that those lights are in the corridor you want to traverse? No chance. I was only in the place a few days, and I never really mastered the set-up, but I think you'd need a PhD in bloody stupidity to make sense of it. Again, one of the perils of decade after decade of incremental changes, until what probably was a sensible design to begin with becomes an electrician's nightmare.

"This is the older part of the building," says Not-Quite, as he leads me through some grand hall or other. God knows what it was originally. The arty blokes were using it as a regimental museum now. Me, I'd have put the silverware somewhere a bit less tempting, but I suppose if you have command over three battalion worth of light cannon you stop thinking some council estate chancer with a brick and a sack is much of a threat. Or maybe they just forgot it was there.

"How much older?"

"Oh, several centuries. The original building dates to the reign of James the First, but there's precious little left of that, now. This bit's a little more modern, probably 1760 or thereabouts, though there's no way to be certain. What records we did have went up in the Blitz, and as you can imagine the TA isn't that keen on exploratory archaeology. There's our esteemed founder on the wall there, if you're interested."

The pic was of some plonker in his best Biggles costume, complete with what I took to be a Sopwith Camel, though it could as easily have been a Concorde for all I know about planes.

"Died young, poor chap. Left us the place in his will. This is back when we had the money to keep it up, you understand, or at least keep it vertical rather than horizontal."

By now we were headed to the stairs, and from there to the part I was most interested in. The digs were perfect from our point of view. The targets couldn't twitch without us knowing about it. Not-Quite helpfully pointed out that the nearest crapper was well past its sell-by, so unless we wanted to use buckets – an option Not-Quite put to me in all seriousness, God help him – we had to go down a level, along a bit, and then some stairs. However there was a place nearer than that we could use for a canteen, even if the cupboards hadn't been cleaned since the War.

"This will do nicely," says I. "Where do you keep the rat traps?"

Not-Quite twitched as if I'd goosed him.

"Ah. Not on site, I'm sorry to say. I mean, it's not the kind of thing we keep on site, if you follow me."

Now, I'm no girly girl, but I don't much like the prospect of Mickey's fucked-up cousin Bob paying me a visit in the wee small. And judging by what I was seeing, it was a sure bet Bob was familiar with the premises, and would become more familiar if we started leaving food about, as doubtless we would.

"Not to worry. I'll bring in some when my team come back with the gear."

Not-Quite's face lengthened.

"What?"

"Well, it's just ... it's Barker, you see. He's not very happy about this and I'm just concerned ... that is, it's not his place to interfere, I quite understand that, but Barker's been here a long time and he'll be here a few years yet, so I really don't like to upset him if I can avoid it."

"Don't you worry, sir." I patted Not-Quite on the shoulder. "We'll use the humane ones. No fuss, no muss."

Like I gave a hairy shit.

*

Now I suppose it's time to mention the other members of the crew. You don't need to worry about the day shift: they don't enter the picture. On nights, it was me, PC Gordon and PC Phillips, on rotation.

You won't see Gordon again. If you do see Phillips, check the eyes. I'm pretty sure you can tell by the eyes.

Gordon's one of those blokes who never takes a drink, never takes a crafty fag break, and always, always, always, complains that, as a nice guy, women don't give him the time of bloody day. No jacket, though if we were splitting hairs he's come close to a sexual harassment charge once or twice. There's nothing really bad about him, to be honest, but he's not my cup of tea.

Phillips is the kind of bloke you'd like to see promoted one day, if he doesn't screw himself first. Good job he's not a criminal, or he'd clean out the district and leave my boss in tears. He seems to sniff out all the angles ahead of time, and plans accordingly; if he ever did top someone, which I would not put past him, it'd be a stone cold whodunit with no clues or witnesses. For whatever reason, he and Gordon got on like a house on fire.

First two nights pass without any incident. Our reports were dead boring, to be honest, but at least the targets weren't doing anything unexpected. They were being so obliging that, I reckoned, we wouldn't be long on this nest at all. Small mercies.

In fact, it was just long enough to get jaded, so I was not surprised when I arrived one night to find nobody in observation. The two tits had wandered off, probably to the makeshift canteen, so off I go like a good sergeant, hoping to wring their little necks.

I find Gordon sat there with his tea in his hand and his feet well off the floor, the prat.

"Bloody big one, sarge," says he. "Ran right across the floor in front of me, like. Made me jump, I can tell you. Phillips gone for the traps."

"You're telling me, you idiot, that you're doing the dance of the seven veils over one little mouse?"

"Rat, sarge. Big as a bloody cat, I swear."

Just at that moment we hear him. Well, I say him but it was more like them. You ever heard it? We hardly ever think about it, how close they are to us all the time, I mean, but in those big houses, with those hollow walls, you can really hear them. Pitter patter, pitter patter, all in one quick movement. Bob does not slow down. When he wants to go somewhere, he moves rapid, and when he stops, he stops dead. Then, when he's satisfied, he moves on again. Pitter patter, pitter pat, and that odd dragging sound … you guess is its tail following it along the floor. That, and its piss trail. Little fuckers.

"See what I mean?"

I take a deep breath. "Gordo, you want to get yourself back on post, you hear? Get."

Which he does, and I go looking for Phillips, because it shouldn't have taken him five minutes to find those traps. Less, in fact, since I put them in the cupboard right by that plonker

Gordo's head, where they should still be.

Remember what I said before, about how confusing the building could be? It was even worse at night. The place felt like one great jumble, dipped in darkness, and you had no more idea of where you were than the Man in the Moon. But more by luck than judgement, I find Phillips, who had heartlessly abandoned his colleague in his time of crisis and gone looking for trouble.

Phillips was in the museum, and while he might have gone there for a dekko at the silverware and the like, that's not what had his interest and attention when I found him. No, he was much more interested in a pile of clothing that had been abandoned on the floor.

"Here, sarge," he says, and he points at what looks like a mask. "Get a look."

I examine it. I was expecting rubber, but that's not what it was. I don't know what it was, truth be told. I put on gloves to pick it up. It felt like, I don't know, candle wax, maybe, but soft, and flexible.

"I think I've seen that face," I muse. "In fact, I'm bloody sure I have."

"Bit early for Halloween, eh?"

"Not by that much. Anyway, what the hell are you doing here? Leaving your fellow officer in the lurch, shame on you. Anyone would think he deserved it."

"I was looking for the rat traps, sarge." He gives me that little-boy grin.

"And you didn't think to look in the cupboard where I put them?" Heavy sarcasm, but needs must.

"Of course I did, but they weren't there."

That got me. "What do you mean, not there? You looked all around, right?"

"Yes, sarge. I checked every cupboard up there, but someone's nicked 'em. I figure it was day shift having a laugh."

It could have been, sure. I wouldn't put it past them, but

right about then I remembered where I had seen that face before. Angry, red, lots of arm waving. It was Barker, to the life.

Now, at that point I do not leap to any bloody silly conclusions. I definitely did not conclude that someone was having a laugh and walking around in a caretaker suit of his very own. But it did occur to me that Barker, miserable old sod that he was, might well have stolen our gear, out of spite if for no other reason. I'd made a point of staying out of the geezer's way, but the few times our paths had crossed since Not-Quite had introduced us, Barker had given me the evil eye. I hadn't bothered to respond in kind, since he wasn't worth it, but if I could catch him in the act I'd have his bosses tear him a new one. Or so I promised myself, anyway.

"You go up. I'll be with you in a moment."

It was a pretty neat little suit, actually. The clothes weren't Barker's, or at least they weren't clothes I remembered him wearing, but they were about the right size and, as I say, the mask was dead on. Enough to make me shiver a little, if I'm being honest. No identifying marks, of course, and nothing in the pockets. Boots were worn, but not broken down, and they were military issue.

I'd brought a duffel bag with me, for my spare kit, and there were evidence bags in it. I put the mask in one and took it away. I figured I could at least find out what it was made of, and if it happened to belong to Barker, and he wanted it back, tough titty. He would have to make nice, first.

*

So of course the very next day I get a call from Not-Quite, who's very apologetic and doesn't want to cause a fuss, goodness knows, but he's just had an earful from your friend and mine. Former RSM Barker has in fact been quite eloquent on the subject of things being nicked, and how dare they, and what's the world coming to, and so forth.

"I don't know what he's talking about, sir," says I. "Did he mention anything specifically?"

No, of course he didn't. In fact, Not-Quite is rather puzzled on that score as well.

"Well, I'll go and have a word, shall I?"

Not-Quite's a bit anxious, but he agrees. I found out later that he also went to see the TAC himself, perhaps thinking that the Regimental silver had gone walkies. But that's by-the-by.

Off I go, and I'm knocking on Barker's door. This is just before day shift's due to wander off to the pub. It's a nice area up there, really. You forget how close London is to the country in places like that, until nightfall, when the birds settle in, the sun dips low, and everyone puts on the telly and has a cup of tea.

Barker's not answering, so I wallop the wood a few more times. Then, narked, I figured I'd do a walk-round, see if he was hiding in the back garden or something. Not only is he not there, but I get a look in the windows as well, and it doesn't look as if he's been here for a while. The place is a bit of a pigsty, frankly, which surprises me, since from the outside you'd think Barker was a neat freak. I push on the back door, and it opens, so in I go. After all, the man might have been lying hurt in one of the back rooms or something. I don't bloody think.

"Mister Barker? You about?"

Not a sound, and up close, the place is in worse shape than I'd have figured. The stink'd clear your sinuses for good and all. Friend Barker, it turns out, is a bit of a hoarder, and everything's everywhere. What sounds like a telly is going in the front room, so I head there, and it is a telly – black and white, would you believe; I didn't think those things existed any more – but nobody's watching. Someone had been, though, since a cigarette was still glowing in the tray.

"Mister Barker?"

Now there's a noise from what's probably the bedroom, upstairs, so off I trot like a good Samaritan. Stick out, mind you. Good Samaritans who don't take care get the shit kicked out of them.

Just as I'm halfway up, someone comes out of a back room upstairs. I shine the light, and who do I see but Gordo, large as life and twice as ugly.

"Jesus! You made me jump!"

"Sarge? What are you doing here?"

"Better yet, what are you doing here? Aren't you supposed to be going on post?"

"Yes sarge. But I heard something in here, like, and I figured I'd better check, but when Barker didn't answer I almost went off, except I found the back door open, and…"

"Christ, shut it, all right? I don't suppose you found him up there, did you? No, thought not. Right, sod this for a lark. If you see the caretaker, let him know I want a word, and in the meantime, off you go."

Which he does, and I take the opportunity to look round the place one last time. Nobody's upstairs, nobody's downstairs. Maybe Barker stepped off to the corner shop, or went for a curry or something. Not my business, anyway, and I did what I said I would, so Not-Quite can't complain. Which is just as well, since I see his car when I go up to the post, and I figure I'm going to be talking to him too. I don't. Not sure where Not-Quite ended up, but by the time I leave post, in the wee small, his car's gone. So I figure he found what he was looking for, or didn't feel the need to hang around.

Wouldn't blame him, really. The countryside loses its charm after the lights are out, the weather turns cold, and you're stuck in a great draughty tomb of a place, listening to Bob on the prowl, wishing the heating worked.

*

There were mice, mice, eating up the rice, in the stores, in the stores; there were rats, rats, big as blooming cats, in the Quartermaster's stores.

Can't get that out of my head. You know how you want to

think about something else, anything else, but that one thing's there, again and again and again?

Rats, rats, big as blooming cats, in the Quartermaster's stores...

They sung that in the War. It was up on one of the walls of the TAC, along with a bunch of other stuff. I remember seeing this documentary once, saying about the rats in the trenches, how they ate the corpses, grew fat on them. One bloke, his abiding memory was going to his new digs, hearing noises, shining a light on the bed and seeing two of the shits on his bed's blanket, fighting for possession of a severed hand.

They went for the eyes first, you know that? If they found a corpse, they'd chew right through the eyes, then get into the head. After that they did as they pleased. Fuckers.

Rats, rats, big as blooming cats, in the Quartermaster's stores. My eyes are dim, I cannot see, I have not brought my specs with me...

*

So the next day I remember I have something in my duffel that I wanted someone with more brain cells than me to have a look at. There's a bloke in Evidence Recovery who owes me, so I pass it on to him to have a butcher's at, when he gets a spare moment. I don't give it another thought.

Then he calls me up, fizzing like a firework, wanting to know where the hell I'd found it.

"Never you mind," says I, wittily. "What's got you so bloody ecstatic, then?"

At which point I get a lecture on the joys of what he calls anthropodermic art, blithering on about shoes, waistcoats, drum skins – honestly, some of 'em should just stay at home and drink milky tea, avoiding excitement of all kinds – and all the wonderful things that leather can do. Which is nice enough, I suppose. I like leather. I have a leather jacket.

"Is it made out of human skin, your coat?"

"You what?" I say.

"Human skin. Because this thing you gave me, that's what it

is, and if you'd told me someone could handle material as delicate and tricky as this, and somehow make it work, I'd have called you a liar. Yet I'm standing here with the thing in front of me, and what I want to know is, what kind of sick bastard are you hunting, that they go taking this kind of trophy?"

I put him off, I don't remember how, but I promise him I'll let him know as soon as I can, and he accepts that, for the moment. He won't accept it for long, I know that much.

For me, I'm thinking, no way. He's fucked it up somehow. I mean, would you believe it? I'd had the damn thing in my hands, and not known. I still could feel it, slick, like and yet unlike candle wax. But human skin? Do me a favour!

Besides, how the hell could anyone make a perfect Barker out of anyone except Barker? And it couldn't be his. I mean, we'd seen him, hadn't we? Since I'd taken the mask?

Had we? I couldn't remember. I remembered paying a visit to his house, sure, and I didn't find him then. Gordo and Phillips, though, had they seen him?

*

"So where's your partner in crime, then?"

Phillips twitched, guiltily. "You what?"

I settle in, grabbing a tea. "Gordo, you twonk. Where is he? I want a word."

It was a little more than an hour after shift start. The targets were going about their business across the way, and we were taking diligent observation of their movements. Anyone who says otherwise is misstating the facts.

"He's about, sarge."

"Oh ho. You usually aren't that bad a liar. What's the story?"

"Look, sarge, honest, he clocked in…"

He checks my face. He sighs. "I don't know where the bugger is, and that's flat."

"So when did you see him last?"

"Couple nights back."

That got my attention. "What the hell do you mean? He's supposed to have been here, he's on the bloody sign-in sheet. Why, I saw him myself…"

I was about to finish with "just yesterday" but didn't.

"I dunno what to tell you, sarge. First night, I figured he was shacked up, you know? Or maybe sleeping it off."

"Bollocks. Not our saintly Gordo. When was the last time you saw him drinking? And as for finding a girl, God help him, they aren't making snowballs in Hell just yet."

He grinned. "All right, I figured it probably wasn't that, but what the hell, it could have been, right? Except that he doesn't turn up again the next night, so I give him a call – by now I've got about three messages on his phone, none of 'em he answers – and all I get is voicemail. Again. But he's not signed off sick, and I didn't want to drop him in it, so I sign off on the sheets and keep eyes on."

I'm thinking at a pretty rapid rate, I can tell you. The last time I'd seen Gordo, it was at Barker's place. Then I'd said he should go on post, and off he went. Then I picked around at Barker's for a while, then I went up as well. Except I couldn't remember seeing Gordo after that. I don't know why, and I didn't think much on it because I had other things on my mind. I guess I figured he was bunking off, if I thought about him at all, which I didn't make it my habit to do.

"Right, come with me. We're going to have a look for Gordo."

"You think he's here, sarge? Why?"

"Never you mind why, you just follow. And don't let me out of your sight, you hear?"

*

It is bigger on the inside, I swear to God.

So here we are, we've gone through the museum, and we're poking around in what might be an officer's mess. It was a room we hadn't seen before, and I thought we'd seen them all.

It was put together on the cheap, whatever it was. There was what looked like it wanted to be a fancy candelabra hanging from the ceiling, as assembled by some colossal idiot who didn't know the first thing about electrics, so when I flip the switch there's a hasty fizzle, a brief flash, and a nasty smell. I take out my flashlight instead, not wanting to burn the building down.

"Who's there?"

I throw the light around. "Sir? Could you step into the light, please?"

It's Not-Quite, his great moon face all done up with worry. "Sergeant Johar? What's going on?"

"Sir, why are you here? Did someone call you?"

"No, not at all." He fumbles in the half-light. "I was hoping to find Barker. I came earlier looking for him, but he wasn't in; and after the phone call I was worried, especially since he didn't pick up when I called a second time. I thought something must have happened."

"But you haven't seen Mister Barker?"

"Not tonight, not yet. Why? Look, what is going on?"

A very good question. "Tell me, sir, how well do you know the building?"

"Very." Touch of professional pride, there.

"If you wanted to hide something, somewhere where most people aren't likely to go, where would you?"

That didn't take much thought at all. "The cellars. We used them for storage, but nobody's been down there in a long time, not after the unit moved all its records to Kent."

So that's where we head.

Not-Quite's chattering all the way down, about the history and whatever, but my mind is elsewhere. I'm wondering where the hell Gordo ended up, because I'm pretty sure by this point that he's not at home in front of the telly.

There's just too much mess. You know how a place can get, when nobody looks after it? It's a look, more than anything else: that neglected, nobody-cares look. Somehow a paperback or a broken bit of kit ends up on the floor, and nobody picks it up. Pretty soon the filth is thick, and you can't move without getting it on you. But with nobody to move things about, stuff tends to stay where it's put, you know?

Not this place. There's old bits of God knows what all over, and you can see trails in the mess. Something comes through here, often. Making its nest in the garbage.

We're passing steel doors now, and I reckon this is probably where they used to store the munitions, when this was a working building. I stop in front of one of them because I see a shadow and I want a closer look at it.

With Phillips backing me, I enter, and find it wasn't a shadow at all, it was a reflection in a tall mirror. Phillips laughs, nervous, but I'm not in a laughing mood. There's a table across one wall, with a set of mannequin heads on it. Along the other wall there's a rack of what look like costumes. All sorts, men and women both.

"Sarge?"

Phillips has his light on one of the mannequin heads, towards the end of the row.

I look and see Gordo's eyeless face staring back at me.

The mannequins almost all have faces, except for two at the other end, both empty heads.

Heads carefully taken, carefully preserved. Besides Gordo's, I don't recognise any of them. I think one of the ones next to the empty heads must have been there a long time, it was too badly stretched, flaking, but I don't know how long is too long for those things.

I can hear Bob. He's all around us, him and every cousin he's got, and Bob's family is large. They're rattling away underfoot, under the floors, behind the walls.

"We could go deeper," says Not-Quite.

"You what?" says Phillips.

"Deeper. This is just the upper cellar, dug out in, oh, 1820, I think. The building's much older than that, and there are levels below us, many levels. Would you like to see?"

I move to Not-Quite's left, as if to go past him and out the door, but he's large, and he puts himself in the way. He's got a good two inches on me, easy. He's smiling.

I reach out and grab his right wrist. Without giving him time to react, I strike at the inside of the elbow, bending the arm, and then I swing round beside him, twisting his arm behind him. Now he's bending forward, because if he doesn't his arm will snap, and I'm leaning all my weight on that right arm of his, grabbing forward at his collar.

"Get that thing!" I tell Phillips. Bright boy that he is, he goes for Gordo's mannequin head. My duffel's on the floor, with the bags in it, so he reaches for that.

Not-Quite doesn't feel right. Too soft, not enough angles. He's looking back over his shoulder at me.

"You should have left it alone," he says, and then he dissolves.

Dissolves is the only word I can think of that fits. It's like he comes in bits, breaking up, grey bodies escaping from the bulk, crawling out the arm holes, the mouth, the eyes. Hundreds. Maybe thousands, I can't tell, scrabbling over each other, over me, swarming up my jacket, hairy muzzles at my face.

They're going for my eyes. They're climbing up me, biting and clawing at everything they can reach, but not my face. That they leave alone, unmarked, as they swarm up, digging only for my eyes.

I let go of what's left of Not-Quite and I'm banging away, getting them off, but there's too many, too many, then Phillips is swinging, stick out. I get a breathing space. I run for the door.

If only I'd brought that bloody duffel. I know none of this will sound right, I know it won't make sense. If I had that mannequin head, if I had Gordo, it would make you believe me, I know it would. Or perhaps not. Perhaps it would have just gone missing, like the Barker mask. Maybe nothing I could have done would change things.

I don't get the duffel. I barely get out.

I don't know what happened to Phillips. I thought he was behind me, swear to God.

*

So I sign the statement. It's eighteen long. I hand it over, knowing it won't be believed.

Soon I'll leave. I'll go home.

People keep saying you're never more than six foot from a rat at any time. That's bollocks. But there are millions of the bastards, all over the city. There are some in the block of flats where I live. I've seen them in the bins, in the back alleys. I've seen them at crime scenes. I've seen them at the takeaway.

At night, will I hear them?

How far are they away from me?

Special Needs Child

Keris McDonald

My beautiful baby boy was born nearly three weeks after the levees broke.

We were checking out a street in the North Ward, just Austin and me, looking for bodies. It was over eighty degrees and seventy percent humidity and it stank. You have no idea how bad that city smelled. I had menthol gel smeared across my upper lip and it still felt like that stench was crawling down my throat. Mud and rotting weeds on fucking everything – on the smashed houses and the fallen trees and the tossed cars – and the mud was half sewage because the drains were fucked, and all mixed in with the smell of rotted garbage and dead fish and dead pets, and sometimes dead people.

We'd come in with the Louisiana State Guard. We both had experience in civil order establishment, though as search-and-rescue for the living was over by this point and the National Guard had been evacuating the last inhabitants since September 6th, we weren't expecting to be dealing with anyone living and we were even pretty chill about leaving the Hummer parked out in the open. The die-hard hold-outs were gone, and the Ward was silent. Not even any birds. I guess the winds had killed all those. Just the fucking flies for company. Flies everywhere, even trying to eat my Vicks VapoRub.

We'd been told – the details were sketchy – that there'd been a corpse reported out back of one of the houses down this street, so we'd gone out with a body-bag and were searching the whole row. Some places in the city the wooden buildings had been wiped clear off their concrete bases by the waters, but here they were standing, sort of. A lot of trees had come down, so we had to pick our way through the tangle of branches and planks with their crusty curtains of silt and shit. We split up to cover more ground, and moved slow and cautious.

I kept my Glock out as I worked my way through to the back of another house that'd never be a home again. In two tours in Iraq I'd never killed anyone myself – I'm a medic foremost – but though I'm not making any such claim on Austin's part, it wasn't humans we had to deal with that week. Austin had put a lot of dogs out of their misery by that point. Dogs starving on chains in yards, trapped on garage roofs, wandering the streets injured and hungry. There was nowhere to take them, no way of feeding them, and nothing for them to eat but each other and the bodies. Austin – two hundred pounds of muscle and beard and tattoos – is soft when it comes to dogs.

I found the corpse in the back yard, as reported. They're sometimes more difficult to spot than most people'd think. Once they stop looking alive they can just sorta merge into the background, the familiar human outline blurred by decay. But this one was pretty obvious, even under the shade of a sagging lean-to roof that had once been a barn of some sort, back before it was crushed by a toppled live oak.

The flies around here were thick and persistent and the ground for yards around was crawling with maggots.

The body's pelvic area had been completely eaten out by insects but I assumed, based on the filthy remnants of a flower-sprigged dress rucked around her shoulders, that she was female. She'd been swept in and dumped over a metal frame that I think was the support structure of a fallen table. Ass-up; there was no dignity in death for her. Her head and arms, which were flat against the ground, were skeletonised. Her lower legs, which hung in mid-air, were in contrast sort of mummified, the skin shiny and pitch black, even the soles of her bare feet.

It was the bits in between that bothered me. Her abdomen was hugely distended.

Now, there's not much about dead bodies that worries me these days, and even less that surprises me. I've seen a fuck-ton of corpses in my life, and they do not always act the way they are supposed to. The dead will at times fart, and vomit, and groan, and bleed. They get hard-ons. They'll occasionally move around – and it's all to do with gas pressure building up inside. They'll shed their skin to reveal bright pink layers of sub-dermis. They'll inflate and then pop, like water balloons.

That was what I was worried about here. This lady had a severe case of bloat and if we tried to bag her, chances were that swollen belly would burst and spurt rotted innards all over us. It's yellow, by the way, like chicken soup. I've seen that. I don't eat chicken soup any more.

I had white paper overalls on over my guard uniform, but that wouldn't help a whole lot.

I sighed, and considered calling in Austin on the walkie-talkie, but reckoned I should deal with the immediate problem. Puncturing her with a gunshot was a possibility, but seemed cruel. Finding a long slat of wood, I duct-taped my clasp knife to the tip to make a crude spear, and – standing as far back as I could – I gave the belly a prod.

The knife-tip was sharp, and made its hole. Skin split. Nothing slopped out. There was no *pfrrrt* of escaping gasses. She was dry.

I withdrew the spear point, surprised.

That was fucking nothing to what I felt when a tiny white hand emerged through the rip.

"*Shit!*" I'd thought I was immune to corpse-related shock, but I nearly fucking wet myself at that moment. I took a step back and shook like a spooked horse, suddenly drenched in sweat. It hadn't occurred to me that the dead woman had been pregnant. Poor bitch. Poor -

The hand clenched and flexed.

No! I thought

The tear in the blotched, putrescent skin widened. The little arm thrust out through the gap and waved around. I stood frozen as very slowly, almost gracefully, the entire child emerged through the tearing flesh and slithered onto the maggoty floor, the stretch of its umbilical cord saving it from hard impact.

It was pale as the Pillsbury Dough Boy. It kicked its legs and rolled its head.

This could not be happening, I told myself.

I staggered closer. It was a little boy, quite whole and sound under the fatty gunk that slathers newborns. He opened sleepy eyes that were the most beautiful clear green that I'd ever seen, and he yawned.

His mother's ruptured belly hung like an empty sack.

Okay. Let's be honest here. I never, not even in those first moments, thought that this was right or normal. Corpses do weird shit but one thing they don't do, *cannot* do, is incubate a live baby without blood flow or oxygen for three weeks, while they rot around it.

But there he was. And he was perfect.

I couldn't bear to see him lying there in that filth. I scooped him up with shaking hands. He looked up into my face with his huge wise eyes, and gave a hiccupping giggle.

By the time I made it back out to the Hummer, Austin, summoned over the walkie-talkie, was waiting there for me. He frowned at the bundle in the crook of my elbow.

"What the fuck is that, Gina?" he asked, puzzled.

"It's our baby."

*

You'll think I'm crazy.

But what was I supposed to do? Hand him over to the authorities? A *newborn* – what the hell chance would he have of survival if I did that? They wouldn't know where his family were or even if any of them were alive; the evacuees were scattered all over the country by now. Hey, I'd seen our care systems in action, and I had no faith in human nature. I'd seen people left dehydrated and starving on bridges and in the Superdome while officials pretended ignorance and washed their hands of all responsibility. I'd seen those motherfuckers at Gretna turn back refugees at gunpoint. I'd heard stories about the director of some nursing home who'd fucked off and left all ninety of his elderly charges to drown.

There is no substitute for a mother's love.

So we took off. Austin was sorta reluctant, because he was enjoying the work. Don't judge him; I know exactly how he felt. For maybe the first time since Iraq we'd both felt we were doing something useful, something we were trained for and no one else could do.

But Baby's needs come first. That's what it's like when you become a parent. Austin understood.

Getting away was surprisingly easy. The hard part for the first few days, of all things, was finding baby formula, since the supply chains were fucked and the shops emptied by hoarders. In fact by the next day I was so frantic I was ready to check in at an emergency shelter just to get my hands on supplies – even though that would have meant records being taken and the risk of a postpartum examination that would have found me out.

But Austin solved it. He suddenly pulled over to the side of the road and dodged out, and when he came back from the scrubby verge he had a dog in his arms. A skinny little bitch with dangling teats. She didn't struggle – she looked too dispirited for that.

"Here," he said, loading her into the back seat and climbing in beside her. He gave her the stub of a Slim Jim from his pocket, which she snapped up ravenously. "Pass him over."

"Fuck's sake – that's dirty, Austin! Look at her! She could be carrying anything!"

"You got a better idea?"

The bitch didn't like the smell of baby at first – she whined and flashed the whites of her eyes and tried to kick free – but when Austin held her firmly down and stroked her ears with his thumb she seemed to resign herself. The baby latched on to a leathery canine dug as if it was exactly what he was waiting for.

We kept the dog, and called her Lady. We fed her high-protein foil-wrapped survival rations and crackers, and she fed the baby. You know, he never cried during those first days, not before we found him his milk and not afterwards. I am not shitting you here, he never cried, not once, as a child. When he was distressed he'd sometimes make this high-pitched meeping noise, but he never bawled like most kids. He was one in a million. A real little soldier.

We called him Preston, after a buddy who'd bought it in Baghdad.

Our apartment in Monroe took less than an hour to clear. We're both used to living light. Neighbours who'd known us might be suspicious, so we weren't sticking round. Once out of Louisiana, we just kept heading West. The chaotic aftermath of the hurricane helped. Lots of people were on the move, lots of families were uprooted. People accepted that story, and to my surprise some helped out when they saw we had a baby with us. Moms gave us formula and diapers in grocery store lines. We were even allowed to stay free in a garage room for a few days.

For the first few years of Preston's life we travelled around a whole lot. Texas, New Mexico, Arizona, even California – but not the touristy bits. Just hick little towns where government was not expected to stick its nose into private family business, and sprawling arid suburbs filled with immigrants where no one gave a shit about more incomers. I worked. With my background and willingness to do some heavy lifting, it was easy enough most places for me to get a job. Paramedic, ambulance driver, morgue attendant, hospital orderly. Austin mostly stayed home to look after the kid and smoke weed.

He didn't like Preston much, though it's not like he was a difficult kid. I don't think they ever bonded. I guess it's harder for men, if it's not their biological child. It's not like they want or need kids the way we do. I'd been waiting years for this, praying in my desperation to a God who'd stopped listening when I was twelve and Pop got cancer. Maybe He'd heard me at last. Maybe He just got sick of me bugging him, and gave me what I wanted to shut me up. I was there, in the right place at the right time, for my miracle baby to be born.

Preston was my whole world.

Funny kid, though. I mean funny ha-ha. He liked to laugh, even though his loud hooting chuckle got on Austin's nerves. "He sounds like a fucking chimpanzee," he'd complain, popping another can of beer. Preston liked to play tricks, hiding in unexpected places and jumping out to startle you. Lady was always pretty nervous of him and stuck to Austin's feet all day, safety in numbers I guess. She was a real submissive dog.

Preston never seemed to notice that Austin and Lady weren't so keen on his company. He just loved to goof around. And physical contact – climbing, clinging, swinging on our arms, tugging Lady's tail – was how he interacted with us.

It took him ages to learn to speak, you see. He was healthy in most every other way, so even though he never got over that anaemic-looking pallor and I had to slather him in sun-block to stop him blistering, he would spend a lot of time outside climbing trees and digging in the dirt, like any normal boy. Well, except he preferred to do it at night. With Preston, the switch was either on or off. Ever since he was born he slept a lot during the day, and woke up burning with energy around evening. I guess it was just more comfortable for him, since we lived in sunny places Mid-West and West, what with his skin and his eyes. Those beautiful big green eyes of his were sensitive to bright light. I bought him his first pair of shades – oversized green plastic with frames in the shape of stars – when he was six months and he never went out without them after that.

There was no question of registering for a public school. We didn't have the paperwork and besides, he'd have been bullied, what with the mutism and the weak eyes and the white down of his barely-there hair. So homeschooling was the obvious solution. Austin was about during the day and I'd do my bit at night. He wasn't what you'd call a scholar, but that's nothing to be ashamed of. There are a lot of children with special needs out there. I've seen worse than Preston. And I relaxed a lot once he started speaking.

Oh yeah … the speech thing. He hit the babbling stage early on, chattering away to himself, but it took until he was four until it morphed into English. That's a long time to think that there's something wrong with your child. He understood us alright – he wasn't deaf or anything – but he just didn't talk back in anything but gibberish. Sometimes I thought he had his own private language – you hear about that, don't you? Twins, mostly?

I just know I was so pleased when he called me "Mom" at four that I cried, sitting in the kitchen, and he stared at me from behind those star-shaped patches of plastic in confusion, and then patted my face and hugged me and scampered off.

He was affectionate. That was the sweetest thing about him. Even when he grew up he never grew out of hugging. He didn't have school friends to teach him it wasn't cool. He didn't have a peer group to bully him and tell him how to think and how to act, so he didn't care what others said about him. In his quieter moods, during the day, he'd sit and talk under his breath to himself for hours, maybe rolling a die-cast truck back and forth, or turning a piece of wood over and over in his hands like it was the most fascinating thing in the world. At night he was full of such spontaneous joy and energy that sometimes he'd go climb out on the roof and sing wordlessly to the moon. He was a true free spirit.

So okay, the speech thing was worrying, but that all worked out. And the eating did too, eventually. Preston was always a slightly-built child, not like so many kids nowadays, and I guess that was because he had feeding issues. I don't think it was Lady's fault – he soon took to normal formula and milk well enough – but he was picky with solids. No bread or pasta or rice or anything that'd build him up. He flat-out refused vegetables of any sort, even baked beans, so I had to give him vitamin tablets. In fact the only vegetables I ever got him to eat in his entire childhood were sauerkraut and – when we moved to LA – that stinky Korean stuff, kimchi. He liked hot dogs straight out of the packet, chicken nuggets (as long as they'd been left to cool), cheese and bacon.

Lots of kids are fussy eaters.

I came down early one morning when he was three, and able to walk and get into any cupboard he could reach or climb up to. I found him with the refrigerator door open, sat in the pool of light, chewing with obvious delight on an open pack of bacon rashers. He looked up at me and burbled happily.

After that he ate all his bacon raw. It never seemed to do him any harm. I reckon we mollycoddle kids too much these days.

*

We were renting on the west side of Fresno and Preston was seven when Austin lost his cool. I came home one night after my shift to finding Preston huddled in the lean-to den he'd made in the basement, nose to the angle of the drywall. He didn't want to look at me. He wasn't crying precisely – like I say, he never cried – but he was so subdued that even my hugs couldn't raise much reaction. Austin was kicking angrily about the back yard, beer can in hand, popping off shots at empty bottles. Even in our neighbourhood that was not the sort of behaviour that let you go unnoticed.

"What the hell d'you do to Preston?" I demanded, standing under a sky without stars, everything bleared by the glow of city lights.

"Me?" he laughed. "Ask your shitty little kid what he did."

There was shouting then, and – after we got the shouting mostly over – a conversation where it finally emerged that he'd taken Preston out to shoot rats with the BB gun on the vacant lots round here, because I'd been nagging him to do something with the boy, find some common ground, teach him some of his own skills. They'd passed a raccoon, dead and flattened on the road, and Austin had told Preston to come away and stop poking it.

Now I knew Preston had always been fascinated by roadkill, ever since he was old enough to toddle out of the gate. Some kids are a bit morbid like that, it's perfectly normal, and I hoped it meant he had a leaning toward science. He had a collection of bones in his bedroom – desert-dried lizards, the sun-bleached skulls of rabbits and gophers and coyotes, and even a steer skull complete with horns that we'd found when we stopped on Route 66 that one time. I bought him picture books on biology and encouraged his identification skills.

That day they'd shot a few rats, and then Austin stopped for a smoke and when he looked round the boy was missing. He searched right round the waste ground where they'd been stalking, and then set off home, and on the way he'd found Preston hunkered down over that stinky old raccoon, pulling the dried-out flesh apart with his nails and chewing it down.

He'd marched the boy home and whipped him with a belt.

"You did *what*?" I hissed.

"There's something wrong with that boy! You know there is – he's not right in the head! Like that time he tried to bury that little Olsen girl in the back lot..."

"Austin, that's just the sort of dumb shit stuff kids do – the tunnel fell in! He didn't mean anything by it."

"That's not the way the Olsens saw it. He's not right, Gina.

He's a creepy little fuck and he turns my stomach."

"So you *hit him with a belt*? What sort of a pussy does that to a kid?"

There was a big argument that night, and Austin ended up sleeping on the couch while I tucked Preston into bed with me. I was only thankful there were no marks on his poor little body. Austin hadn't hit him that hard, it seemed.

Two days later I got home and found Austin had gone – taken the Hummer and his weed and half the cash from the box hidden behind the furnace. Only half though, I'll say that much for him.

Lady was distraught for days. She mourned more than I did. And way more than Preston.

I tried making it on my own, as a single mom. It was hard work. I had no school to leave Preston at, and didn't know any homeschooler families I could trust him with. I ended up doing late shifts and taking him with me into work at the funeral parlour. Luckily my boss liked me enough to turn a blind eye. Giving Preston a colouring book and crayons, or a few comic books, was usually enough to keep him quiet for a few hours. Then I'd set him sweeping, or counting stores, or throwing out old flowers or something.

That came to a halt when I glanced up one day after inserting the trocar into a client's abdomen and found that Preston had snuck into the embalming room. He'd pulled the cadaver's arm over the edge of the embalming table to where he crouched, and he had her fingers in his mouth and was chewing on them. There was an expression of pure ecstasy on his face.

I gave up then, and rang my mom in upstate Maine.

*

That conversation wasn't the easiest one of my life. It was the first time I'd spoken to her since I'd enlisted and, so she reckoned, joined the ranks of the Big Government plotting to take away her guns and her Bible. And when, two weeks later,

I drove up the dirt track and in through her gate to find her sweeping the crispy yellow fall leaves off her porch, she didn't exactly light up with pleasure at the sight of me, or the child she'd known nothing about until now.

Preston and Lady piled out of the car and ran round in circles, astounded by the sight of so many leaves, so many tall trees. Mom folded her arms and stared at us.

"What's his father's name then?" she asked.

"Austin."

"We likely to see him?"

I shook my head.

"Thought not." She seemed satisfied that I'd lived down to her expectations. "You weren't married then?"

"No."

She looked at Preston, who'd stopped in his tracks and was gazing up at her. "I don't approve, you know."

"I know."

"He's a funny-looking thing. Come on in then."

She never took to Preston much, any more than she'd showered affection on my brothers or me. But she let us live under her roof, and it was the ideal place to bring up a boy like mine, one who liked to run and climb and dig, and was best off on his own. Our lot backed on to woodland without any fence to show where one ended and the other started. There were miles of damp forest and scrubby fields and tracks mostly used by felling machinery. The nearest town was a faked-up colonial -era hamlet besieged by tourists during the blaze of fall and almost deserted the rest of the year round. Mom went in twice a week, once for groceries and once for the service in the white-painted church that stood in its lumpy overgrown graveyard where Pop was buried.

I didn't go to church, though Mom's disapproval was icy. I wasn't sure I could cope with any more of God's answers to my prayers. Besides, my Sundays were precious. I found work further down the valley at a turkey-packing plant in the next town, but it was a long drive and long shifts, six days a week. Not the best job, but there were perks in the form of raw wings and feet and bits not fit for human consumption, which the foreman let me take home in a plastic bag to feed my dogs, as I told him.

Preston throve on the fresh air and the good food. He put on a real growth spurt. The dried turkey bones became the centrepiece of a new art project – a wire and Krazy Glue conglomeration that started off as an attempt to reconstruct a whole skeleton and then morphed into a complex mounded thing with towers and buttresses that put me in mind of that weird cathedral in Barcelona. You know the one. Preston called it his More Digyon but couldn't explain to me what the words meant. He found more bones for his collection too, out there in the woods where he wandered at night. Most of a porcupine, and the jaw of a bear, and then the whole head of a moose, its bone green and furry with moss – Christ I hope it was just moss – which he proudly hauled in to the house by its antlers and his grandma screamed at him to take back outside. After that he had to move his collection to an outhouse. That wasn't the first or the last argument he had with her, though. She thought he was "kinda creepy for a boy his age" because he didn't want to go play with the other kids in the area. Telling Mom he was used to his own company and making his own amusements cut no ice with her.

But he was always waiting for me when I drove in, no matter how dark or wet it was. Sometimes the shine of his green eyes in my headlights was my first sign that I'd reached the narrow turn off the road. He'd climb up on the roof of the car and ride back that way to house, laughing at every jolt.

There were two disquieting episodes after we moved in. The first was quite early on, the day of the first snow. I remember the clouds were so heavy that it felt like night was falling, and the breeze raw and wet, flicking the slushy flakes in my face. Preston had been sent out to collect from the mail box at the roadside, and when he didn't come back I started to worry at the failing light. We'd only been here a few weeks, after all, and he was just seven.

I set off down the track to find him, bundled in my coat. Lady had taken one look at the weather and refused to follow me, retreating back to the fireside instead with her tail between her legs.

Preston was down at the mailbox – but he was talking to a man. That sight put my hackles up so fast you'd think I was a bitch-dog myself.

"Preston!" I called sharply, straining my eyes to make out what the guy looked like. He was broad-shouldered but hunched, covered up in a hooded coat that I could somehow tell was shabby and not clean, even before the wind brought a musty unwashed stink to my nostrils. He looked up sharply at the sound of my voice and then backed away behind the fence and jogged off into the shadows of the road. *Loped* might be a better word for it. By the time I reached the intersection he was nowhere in sight.

Preston looked up at me, puzzled by the clamp of my hand on his shoulder. "What's wrong, Mom?"

"Who was that man? What was he saying to you? Are you okay?"

The poor kid was confused by the interrogation. "I dunno. He said … he said he was a relative."

That threw me. I didn't know of any relatives left round here. "What was his name?"

"He didn't say. He just asked me a bunch of questions about where I came from and stuff."

"What sort of stuff?"

"I dunno." He had that bored-with-the-conversation-now look that kids do so well. "Is dinner ready?"

"Soon. Come on. I'll ask Grandma if she knows any relations of hers here."

"Not Grandma. My dad. He said he was from my dad's

side."

I didn't know what to make of that. He couldn't mean Austin, could he? Austin hadn't made any attempt to get back in touch with me – and why should he? We walked back to the house talking about Thanksgiving, and how we might get enough snow this winter that we'd have to dig our way out, which Preston was thrilled by.

*

The other incident was years later, and much worse. It signalled the start of the end.

Lady died. She was an old dog by then, stiff with arthritis, and since the woods were too wet and cold for her southern tastes she never went further than the yard, keeping indoors whenever she could. She had a convulsive attack one evening and died in the night as I sat up stroking her ears. Preston mourned quietly, and we dug her a grave right under the tree line. He made her a cross out of planks and went out to sing his croony little songs over her grave every day for a week.

Mom was in a worse mood than usual, her belly griping with pain. She snapped at Preston more often than usual, and when we heard the back screen door bang late at night she forced herself scowling to her feet, complaining that she wanted to lock up and what was he thinking of going out at this time, shouldn't he be in bed?

I volunteered to go fetch him, grabbed the flashlight and headed out into the dark. He wasn't with his bone collection in the outhouse so I circled the yard boundary, picking out the white trunks of birch with my beam. "Preston? Time to come in!"

A glint of emerald green gave his eyes away. He was over by Lady's grave again. I stomped through the long grass calling his name, but the closer I got the more misgivings crowded into my belly, and by the time I could see him clearly I was cold all over.

He was crouched over the grave, digging at the bare soil

with his hands. He glanced up at me and his eyes flashed like blank green suns over the shine of his bared teeth.

"What are you doing? Stop it!"

"I've got to get her out!" he gasped. His face was contorted, his eyes narrowed against the flashlight.

"What? No, Preston!" *He wants her for his collection.* "She's a pet – we buried her, remember?"

He seemed confused. "She's all alone and I want her back!" Drool slicked his chin – I thought I'd badly underestimated how upset he was at his loss. "She can't dig herself out and she wants to be with me!"

"Preston no, baby – she's dead. Just leave her be."

"But she can't get to Heaven if she's buried in the ground! She can't get out!" His hands never stopped gouging at the earth and I was really alarmed now – I could smell the week-old contents of the grave.

"She's not going to Heaven, she's just dead," I snapped.

For a moment his eyes seemed to glow like lamps. "But Grandma said!"

I could see fur in the bottom of the hole. His filthy fingers scrabbled about, tugging at the loose hairy skin.

"Grandma's talking horseshit," I snapped. Okay, so I lost my temper. It was the horrible memory of Pop's funeral, where the preacher and Mom conspired to tell me I shouldn't be mourning, that he had gone to a better place, that if I cried then I would make God angry. "There's no Heaven. We all die and we rot and that's it, we don't go anywhere, we don't do or think anything – she's gone Preston, STOP THAT NOW!"

He lunged forward at me, snarling. I grabbed him, dropping the flashlight. He was wiry as a lynx and much stronger than I'd expected, and I was shocked as I felt his teeth close on my arm, tearing my sleeve. Not shocked enough to drop him, though. There ways you learn of subduing people and as we struggled I got his neck in a pinch that overwhelmed his nerves with so much pain that he went limp and all but stopped breathing. I grabbed him up, half carrying him on my hip, and hauled back indoors. Dumping him on his bed, I tried to cuddle him, but Mom was standing at the room door demanding "What's wrong? What's he done?" and Preston was starting to thrash his legs, so I rolled him tight in the blanket, pushed her out of the room and locked the door.

"Don't let him out!" I ordered.

Then I went back down into the yard and built a big bonfire there. Once it was roaring I dug Lady up, flipped the fetid sodden mass of her onto a black plastic sack, dragged it to the pyre and stood over it until I'd burned everything to good clean ashes.

When I turned round at last, and my eyes adjusted to the night, I saw Preston crouched on the roof watching me. He'd climbed out of his bedroom window.

His howl was wordless and guttural.

*

After that, things began to change. They'd already been changing for a while I guess, but I had to acknowledge them now. Preston was growing, but this wasn't some kid thing. At nine, ridiculously early, he was hitting puberty. And hitting it *hard*. I watched over the following months as he put on bulk around the shoulders and neck – wiry still, but getting much stronger. His face was changing too, his delicate little-boy features swallowed up in new masses of bone as his brows beetled over his eyes and his jaws rushed to catch up with the dentition that replaced the last of his sweet baby teeth. He seemed self-conscious of his new height because he started to walk with a slouching stoop and turn his face away from me, answering my conversation with more grunts than words.

So far, so normal, right? He did all the usual boy stuff, which didn't bother me because I'd lived with army men and they aren't sugar and spice. And everyone knows that teenaged boys stink. Within the year I couldn't bear to walk past the open door of his bedroom. I nagged him daily into bathing, but it never seemed to make much difference.

He stopped wearing shoes. Plagued from infancy with corns and calluses that made wearing anything but trainers uncomfortable, his feet started to look twisted and lumpen, and his toenails were disgustingly yellow and horny. I thought about taking him to a podiatrist, but had to admit that he seemed to manage alright once his calluses toughened. He moved with a weird, limping gait, but boy could he go fast – even over the roughest ground.

He stopped eating anything but raw meat. And he insisted on storing it until it was grey and greasy.

He didn't grow a beard. Instead his light blond fluff all fell out, leaving him bald. I wept.

By ten, he looked like a fourteen year old skinhead. He acted like a teenager too – grouchy, secretive and inarticulate. I figured he'd come out the other side just fine if I kept my cool and didn't pick any more fights. Wasn't it just a matter of time? The petty dramas and agonies of my own adolescent years were memories that clung to this house, still fresh, and I'd be damned if I tried to control my son the way mom had tried to crush the rebellion out of me. Fuck that shit.

Mom was changing too. She lost muscle as Preston gained it, like he was eating her somehow. Her arms and legs shrank to sticks, though her belly still sagged from the cradle of her hips.

Eventually I took her to the hospital. Tests revealed she had stomach cancer, which her meagre insurance wouldn't touch. I drove her home.

That was my life, for a period that seemed like forever at the time but looks terribly short now when I glance back. I worked shifts to feed my surly introverted son and buy painkillers through the internet for my dying mother. I delegated Preston to look after the house, but he was useless at most tasks, like any teenager, and I had to quit my job in the end to give Mom her personal care round the clock.

Poor Preston. Too young to drive, no friends in the neighbourhood, no money, no girls to meet, no dad to take him hunting the way fathers in the area were supposed to. It's not much of a life for a boy, stuck in a house with a dying woman and a mom too busy and too tired to pay him any attention.

And then one night his grandma died. I was there, half-dozing despite my tears and my anxiety. Death can be so very boring and so very long, sometimes. I'd seen plenty of the other kind of course – and honest, I don't know which is worse. Whichever hurts the most as you go, I guess.

I think I'd rather bite a bullet, myself, than fight cancer they way my parents did.

She died late one night when the summer bugs were banging against the windows and the owls were calling. When it was all over I tucked her under the counterpane and came downstairs to the kitchen, poured myself a large glass of Jack and sat down at the table. A few tears leaked out. I knew I should ring the doctor but it was the middle of the night and my head was swimming with exhaustion. The thought of letting anyone into our home right now seemed unbearable. The house was silent, and I wished Lady was there to lean against my leg and nose at my hand.

I'd get a new dog now, I decided. I put my head down on the scratched Formica and let it all just wash over me.

What woke me up, hours later, was a bumping from the ceiling overhead. That house is pretty creaky – you can always tell if someone else is moving round in a room upstairs. I looked up, bleary eyed, and worked out that I was directly under Mom's bedroom. I could hear her headboard rattling.

Preston.

He'd gone into her room and I could hear him.

Shit no. Not my mom!

I was up those stairs and in the doorway in moments. Maybe he didn't hear me coming, maybe he was just too engrossed to care. It wasn't precisely the scene I was expecting to see.

I screamed. Preston uttered one wordless snarl, then hit the window at full pelt and burst through it out into the night.

Now here I sit, in the kitchen, nursing my whiskey and trying to ignore the smell seeping down through the ceiling. I still haven't called the doctor. I'm really not sure how I'm going to manage the situation this time. I need to think things through.

I wish I could get the picture of Mom's thin bare leg, her foot waving grotesquely in the air, out of my head.

I've not seen my son since that night. But I am looking forward to the arrival of my grandchild any day now.

Irrational Numbers

Adrian Tchaikovsky

Numbers have always been friends to me.

When I look at numbers, I see familiar faces, well-known associates of predictable behaviour that I can – excuse the pun – count on. I understand them, and they do what they can to oblige me.

I could never have been anything other than a mathematician. Pure mathematics, the highest and most true realm of thought, that's where the beauty and the wonder is. That's where the code of the universe is acted out by the numbers I grew to know when I was still a child: my friends, my playmates, my companions.

I have never had the same facility with people. People do not do what I want, nor have I ever been able to rely on them. They are unpredictable and difficult to work with. Not like my numbers.

And I know now that there is nothing but numbers.

Mathematics is competitive. There are some answers out there that are like a … "holy grail" is the cliché usually trotted out. It's a poor simile, holding up mouldy old superstition as a substitute for the ultimate truths. The greatest minds have devoted their whole lives to demonstrating the proofs of certain things such as Yang-Mills theory or the P vs. NP problem – that every problem with a solution a computer can easily verify can also be easily solved. Little things, of interest only to mathematicians, except they would transform the world just as we transform our numbers.

Numbers can do more than people. Numbers can merge

and combine, split and divide. Numbers can act on others in precise and remarkable ways. What we mathematicians can do with our friends the numbers bears as much relation to the algebra you learned in high school as a star to a guttering candle.

Which brings us to the Rigolo Transformation.

I am Rigolo; Doctor Anne Rigolo of the Faculty of Pure Mathematics at Hart Gilman College, Providence, and the operation to which I gave my name was my greatest triumph and, shortly after, my most dismal disgrace. And now may be something else.

Just what it may be, I cannot say. I would say it might be one more cruel prank from my colleagues, but I saw Schochtauer's body. I saw the expression on his face. Fear, yes, but fear because he was confronted by something he had opened his mind to understand, and failed. I've seen that look on my students' faces every time I try to teach them the true beauty of numbers. Schochtauer didn't love the numbers enough. That was all. Schochtauer underwent one of the limited set of transformations a human life is capable of.

Soon it will be my turn, and I will take refuge in my numbers and I will live. Because all the universe is numbers. There is nothing that cannot be described and commanded if you understand the numbers well enough.

*

I had been working on the same great mathematical problems as all the rest. Everyone at the top of our profession tried: some just once, so they could say they had put a toe in the water; others with a consuming obsession. I was of the latter camp.

And then I had a dream. In my dreams, numbers speak with me and try to explain how I can make use of them. All too often I cannot understand them, and I wake disappointed with the limits of my subconscious. But this night they spoke to me in words like crystal chimes and flutes, and showed me how they slipped from one dimension to the next, and when I woke,

I *knew*.

I did not go to work that day. I stayed at home with the phone turned off and wrote and wrote, covering every piece of blank paper I could find with my equations. They blazed in my mind, each one leading to the next. I scrawled them until my hand cramped, and then I wrote with my left. I had stumbled onto a new way of dealing with numbers, a way of twisting them through ninety degrees into a wholly unsuspected space. The Rigolo Transformation. It would be the greatest mathematical discovery in the world for just short of two weeks.

Simply transform an existing set of numbers into the hypothetical Rigolo space that I was constructing, and the gloves were off. Suddenly, the logical limits that had frustrated decades of mathematical proofs could be circumvented. I can still remember my tears dotting the original handwritten sheets because the equations were so *beautiful*: deeply true and satisfactory in a way even regular numbers were not.

And that is another thing Schochtauer never understood. He just thought they were something to *use*. He did not see that they were there to be loved and worshipped, as perfection should always be worshipped. And that is why his fate will not be mine.

But I must focus. There is movement in the next room. I can hear the metal of their tools clatter and scrape. I can hear their voices.

At first I thought the Rigolo Transformation was just some oddity, a curious oubliette into which numbers could be thrown. But when I had the equations written out, I wondered what might be done with the numbers I had so transformed. After three distracted days at the faculty I found myself at home again, applying my new toy to the P vs. NP problem. And I solved it.

I can't explain the shock to a layman. Working on P vs. NP is like alchemy in the middle ages. We mathematicians guard our formulae greedily, because whoever finds a provable solution would have the world at their feet. And it was easy. It took me an hour.

Oh, the actual transformation into Rigolo space was very complex indeed – taking the numbers through that labyrinth of equations – but once I was there, I could turn them this way and that, and demonstrate that every problem a computer could readily verify, it could also solve.

I didn't believe it. I checked my maths, and then again and I still didn't believe it. Then I called over Jayne Shen from Cornell and swore her to secrecy. It took her all night to understand, but that was just to grasp the transformation. Once she understood where I had sent the numbers, the P vs. NP proof itself was child's play.

And once she knew, I had to go to the faculty and make the announcement because Jayne wouldn't be able to keep silent about something *that* big forever.

This started my two weeks of fame. For those two weeks I was the most celebrated individual in the academic world.

Because the Rigolo Transformation was the magic key to every door. I could prove Yang-Mills theory too, and I was suddenly closer to filling in all the holes in the Navier-Stokes equations than anybody had ever been. Rigolo space was a mathematical wonderland, where insuperably complex problems broke down and yielded up their secrets at the merest push. All you had to do was work through my dauntingly complex steps to get there. That alone lost most of my peers. Only a few ever managed to work through the Transformation themselves, and inelegantly. It was an art of which I alone was master, and it could do anything.

For those two weeks, just about every pure mathematician in the world was praising me in public and damning me in private because I'd put them out of work. Reuben Tolly, the faculty dean, was especially effusive. I was going to be the figurehead of his new expanded maths department. I was his new golden girl, who would bring in the money and the students and the prizes.

Tolly was never a man for numbers, aside from accounts. And for those two weeks everyone else was too dazed with trying to understand the transformation to discover the one shortcoming with my work. I didn't see it myself. I was too busy believing in my own genius.

Then Han Lin at the Beijing University of Aeronautics sent me a polite email. He had been working on the P vs. NP problem longer than I'd been alive and was a noted speaker about the real world effects of a solution. While everyone else had been wrestling with the transformation, Han had quietly gone about attempting to actually *use* my results.

I was a pure mathematician. I had never thought to try and apply those maths to the world, That was someone else's job.

Doctor Han discovered the one key problem with the Rigolo Transformation. It wasn't reversible. Once the numbers had been shunted into Rigolo space, you could do with them what you wished; they were endlessly compliant. Except, in order to use my golden solutions in the real world, those Rigolo numbers needed to be transformed back into regular numbers. And when you did, as Doctor Han found out, they made no sense. They arrived back through the hedge of my equations stripped of all meaning. None of my proofs carried over.

For a week after that, a blazing argument raged in the polite and restrained way of international mathematicians. And I was so convinced that Han was wrong and I was right. Because, for all the others found it so impenetrably complex, the Rigolo Transformation was beautiful, irresistibly elegant. I couldn't believe it was not also true.

But there came a night when I set to repeating Doctor Han's calculations, if only to prove him wrong. I couldn't prove him wrong. What went in as rational numbers, and was transformed to mathematical gold, came out as gibberish.

And I went further. I had already applied the Rigolo

Transformation to the great mathematical questions of the age. Now I applied it to wilder matters, ludicrous problems with no solutions. I found that, in Rigolo space, I could prove anything. The numbers became infinitely malleable. I could prove without a doubt that two was two. I could prove with equal ease that two was three.

The Rigolo Transformation, for all its perfection, was meaningless. Nothing of it survived into the real world. I had, with great and global fanfare, discovered a minor mathematical curiosity. The big questions remained unsolved, because my solutions to them meant nothing.

The next morning I gave an official statement accepting the Beijing position. Immediately after, I went to Tolly and offered my resignation.

Even after I gave up, a few of my supporters would not let go. They were seduced by the hollow beauty of Rigolo space and claimed it for more than just a mathematical magic mirror, showing you whatever you wanted. They became more of an embarrassment to me even than my own brash foolishness.

That was when I first heard from Doctor Albrecht Schochtauer and became aware of his own far-from-spotless reputation. Just then he was one of many whose continued support was a reminder of something I was trying to get away from.

Tolly was properly condescending as he refused to accept my resignation. My colleagues behaved similarly. In my two weeks of fame I had not been humble about my discovery. Women in my position too often kill their careers by being so humble that others get all the credit. Personally, I have never known where the line is drawn: too reserved, too brash, too proud, too well dressed, too pretty, too plain. The one thing most of my colleagues, superiors and students never cared about was whether my work was good, and that was the only arena I have ever felt equipped to fight in.

So, being a female academic who had displayed, I was told,

more than a little untoward arrogance, of course my career fell into a spiral. Not dismissed, no, but overlooked, talked about, made the butt of all those little jokes, the way people do. Not so different to the way things were before, to be honest, but now they had ammunition. And the Rigolo Transformation, that goldmine of useless equations, sat idle and gathered metaphorical dust.

One by one my crackpot supporters fell away, leaving me on my much-preferred own. I got on with my life, with my lessened prospects and straitened resources. What happened next was Schochtauer.

I had not had an email from him in four months. I had forgotten to delete them on sight. And when he contacted me again, it was with something different. He sent me a problem. I looked at it briefly – the numbers alone had earned the right to my time. It was nonsense, so unbalanced and off it looked like a first-year student's work. I deleted the mail and moved on. Next week he re-sent the problem with the line "Show me the R Transformation".

Perhaps I felt flattered that anyone still remembered. The mathematical world had moved on, after all, even if the name Anne Rigolo was still a byword for levity in certain academic fields.

And so I indulged Albrecht Shochtauer. Even after a few months the equations remained second nature to me, like a tune I'd heard long before, but could always bring to mind. I sent Shochtauer's numbers into Rigolo space and solved his equation, and I sent him the answer both ways: the perfect solution in my notation, and the nonsense it became when you returned it to the realm of numbers we knew.

The next week he sent me another, and another, as though I was playing some one-sided game of postal chess. I solved them for him. In truth, the simple act of manipulating the numbers gave me pleasure, just as I imagine a pianist must feel, playing a complex piece with skill.

He called me within hours of the third solution. He had my mobile number, which I give out to almost nobody. His voice was rough with smoking, still with a little touch of Austrian to it. He told me he represented interests who were impressed with my work. They wanted to meet me. They would fly me to their offices at their expense.

I wondered what misrepresentations he could have made to his employers. "You've seen the work of Doctor Han…"

"My employers aren't interested in Doctor Han," came Shochtauer's voice. "They are interested in you." There was travel laid on. There was compensation for my time. Everything was very neat. I didn't believe it; it might be some final prank by the world of mathematics, to put down the woman who had dared to overstep the line. In the absence of adequate data I had a hundred unwelcome scenarios.

But by then I knew Albrecht Schochtauer, by vicarious reputation. He was not well regarded in mainstream mathematics. He would not be serving as the front man for a practical joke played by the orthodoxy. I had read about him not in peer-reviewed journals but in sensationalist rags that dealt in ancient astronauts and theories about the antiquity of the pyramids. Schochtauer's field had been to take the proportions and the measurements of ancient wonders, or the numbers and patterns found in old folk tales, and spin that straw into mathematical equations. While respectable mathematicians discovered the real secrets of the universe, Schochtauer prostituted his poor numbers in the name of some elder secret maths "known by many names to the people of antiquity". His name still found its way into mathematical journals, but only as a greater joke than even I had aspired to.

So I told him no. Of course I did. I had a career to rebuild, and being associated with a man like Schochtauer would do me no favours.

The next morning a fresh email was awaiting me. It contained seventeen scanned pages, equations in Schochtauer's execrable handwriting. They set out a sub-transformation in Rigolo space, a small but elegant expansion of my useless theory. The numbers were beautiful. I guessed even then that they were not his, but that wasn't the point.

When he called later that day, I was already packed.

*

Schochtauer's employers spared no expense. A helicopter picked me up from Providence and flew me north. Schochtauer himself was the pilot. He was a paunchy, balding man with a black spade of a beard and he welcomed me with a degree of bonhomie I felt quite misplaced. Our destination was a building in the hills beyond Montpelier, Vermont. The lights of the city were visible from the helipad when we landed, but this place – some corporate retreat, I guessed – was set well away from any other structure. Once the blades had stopped and the engine noise had fallen into a disappointed whine and died, the night air was surprisingly quiet. I could hear only a distant whisper of traffic from Montpelier itself, and the dark, wooded slopes around us were deathly silent.

On the pad, Schochtauer continued with his over-familiar manner, trying to take my arm, which I wouldn't give to him, and then making a grab for my hand, which I kept out of reach. At last, with a reinforcement of his smile, he resorted to broad gestures towards the interior of the building.

"Why two helipads?" I asked him, for as well as the roof-space we had landed on, there was a higher platform, a tower at least another two stories up, and unlit. Shochtauer made some comment about their being busy sometimes, with comings and goings. There was no stair, no rungs that would allow access to that height from where we were. It was just a dark square cut from the stars.

We descended into a windowless realm of sterile-looking office rooms and corridors. Everything was very white and surgically clean, and un-peopled. It was night, and perhaps the staff were not simply in their beds, and the company policy tended towards the Spartan. Still, the utter abandonment of the place began to weigh on me, despite my normal heedlessness. Our footsteps sounded hollowly, the echoes rolling away until they merged with a faint and omnipresent background hum. Mazes of cubicles lay vacant, cable-ends showing where terminals had never been installed. Even the security desk we had passed when we entered had been unstaffed, the screens showing view after view of empty spaces. This was valuable corporate real estate, but it seemed to be all for outside show, as if Schochtauer's employers had bought the place but were yet to find a use for the interior beyond bringing Providence mathematicians in to interview.

I was taken to a boardroom with a big screen on one wall, and mirrors on another. There was no other human being present, but I guessed those mirrors would look like windows from the other side. More cloak and dagger, but I knew that big companies could be very secretive when money was involved. I was assuming they had found some way of monetising the Rigolo Transformation, or why would they want me?

Schochtauer explained that I was going to be tested on the applications of my transformation. He relentlessly called me "Miss Rigolo", and I just as relentlessly corrected him to "Doctor". I also explained that Rigolo space had no applications.

"My employers beg to differ." Schochtauer's smile was very wide and white.

I found that I was profoundly uncomfortable. Partly it was just his over-familiarity and condescension, although that was hardly a novel experience when dealing with a male colleague. The room was not small, but without windows it was claustrophobic, and there was a curious vibration that I ascribed to the air conditioning. It seemed to resonate at an uncomfortable frequency within me, producing an emotional response that was entirely reasonless, but also entirely negative: a dread which bypassed the rational centres of the mind entirely. I had difficulty concentrating.

But then Schochtauer began his tests, throwing up equations on the screen and asking me how I would go about this business or that in Rigolo space. They were not questions of his invention, I could tell, and I was far from sure at first that he actually understood the answers himself. I acquitted myself admirably, dealing swiftly with each problem. My very terseness seemed to become a challenge to Schochtauer, whose attitude devolved into the adversarial. He began challenging my answers, requiring that I showed how I arrived at each. He came very close to hinting that the entire business of Rigolo space was a fraud. I pointed out that I was no longer claiming anything more for it.

Then the other voice broke in.

It came from the screen, which had bloomed into grey static. It was not a woman's voice, though I was intended to think of it in that way. It reminded me of nothing so much as that voice they gave to mobile phones: those calm, assured and artificial tones. Schochtauer's corporate overlords were being extremely cautious with me. They did not even want me to hear them speak.

"Doctor Rigolo," the screen addressed me. "Forgive Doctor Schochtauer. He is having difficulty following your reasoning."

Schochtauer bristled, but I was far more interested in his employer just then.

"We, however, understand," the voice informed me. There was a backing of static that rose and fell behind the words, not matching their smooth cadence but following a weird rhythm all of its own, a buzzing interference. Its pulse rose and fell against the background drone of the air conditioning, and I felt that the interaction of the two was not random, but guided by some subtle arithmetical pattern. Numbers, it all came down to numbers.

"In your proof of the P vs. NP within your mathematical space," that pleasant machine voice said, "can you elaborate on the effects of incremental reductions of the quantity r?"

I could and did, at some length, discovering that the proof could be salvaged by adjustment of several other factors. They followed up with three similar questions, each pushing the capabilities of Rigolo space further. Shochtauer shuffled and fidgeted, but of my unseen interlocutor I sensed only an abiding patience. I realised I was grinning, because I was learning more about my own theory through their questions.

"Examine these equations," the voice told me. "How would you determine e?"

The new display showed me something that felt like real world physics already transformed into Rigolo notation. By then I was back in love with my numbers and my own cleverness, and I did not stop to think that none of my peers had really been able to implement the transformation quite as elegantly as this – which is to say as elegantly as I. And the world of international mathematics is not so very large. I knew all the minds on a level with mine. So who was the wizard behind the curtain?

I worked swiftly through their calculations, turning the numbers this way and that. The problem was an order of magnitude greater than my previous outings in Rigolo space, but that was just meat and drink to me. I had their solution, and in reaching it I had a sudden flash of what the original equation might represent. The abstract quanta that I had been working with could be descriptions of time and space, distance and speed ... travel at a speed incalculable in ordinary mathematics or quotidian physics.

I presented my solution to them, deciding it was not my place to ask questions. Besides, it didn't matter. Even if I had reached a theoretical solution for travel beyond the speed of light, that carriage would turn back into a pumpkin as soon as the numbers underwent the reverse transformation.

The voice did not sound impressed, of course, but it told me I had done well. Shochtauer broke in, then, saying, that was enough of the test, and I should hurry to get back to the helipad for my return journey. Noyes would show me the way.

I opened my mouth to ask what he meant and started as I saw another man in the doorway, the first in all the time we had been here. This Noyes was a tall, lean man, seeming around my own age and younger than Schochtauer, but he carried himself gingerly, as though he was ill at ease with his own body or far, far older than he looked. A sense of years was about his eyes, too. They stared at me and through me, like a veteran whose experiences had half-severed him from the world. He wore a brown suit of oddly antique cut, or possibly it was just some recent retro fashion I was unaware of.

I had the impression that Noyes and Schochtauer didn't like each other, but the newcomer showed me a quaintly old-fashioned courtesy. His voice, when he spoke, was hoarse and rough, as though he hadn't used it much in a while. I could sympathise. I could work for days without feeling the need to exchange a word with another human being.

"You're very lucky, Doctor Rigolo," he told me. "They don't show this kind of interest in just anything. When they make you an offer, you should know it'll be like nothing you've ever known."

I was going to make a sarcastic remark to the effect that probably every corporation felt that way about its benefits package, but the words seemed trite. Instead, I tried a very frank question. "Dr Noyes, have I been speaking with an artificial intelligence of some kind?"

"It's just Mr Noyes," he corrected me mildly, with a wry smile that suggested he had been privy to Schochtauer's dropping of my own title. "And no, Doctor. Intelligence, yes, but nothing artificial about it." Only later did I consider just how unsurprising he had found the question.

We arrived at the security desk, still with its empty chair, and Noyes went up to ensure the helicopter was ready for takeoff. I stared at the screens as they showed office after vacant office, and then abruptly I saw Shochtauer, back in the boardroom I had come from. The curious thing was that he was engaged in a discussion – an argument even – but with nobody. He was not looking at the dark screen nor the false mirrors, and he was … oddly placed, pushed almost into a corner, as though his antagonist was face to face with him and dominating the room. At one point he even threw up his hands as though anticipating a blow, and yet the camera saw only him.

I examined the desk's controls and found how to bring up the volume so that sound joined image. Schochtauer was saying, "Her transformation made her the mockery of the academic world. She's a joke. You're wasting your time with her."

It hurt to hear it said so bluntly, even though I knew it already. I reached out to kill the sound, and the other voice broke in and froze me.

It was not the polite Siri-like voice that had tested me, but simply all that background noise, that droning murmur of static and buzz, twisted in some way to form words. It was not an artificial intelligence, because any mind made by man would have a voice like ours, if it had a voice at all. What I heard was a mash of audible vibrations in some awful conspiracy to form intelligible language.

It said: *You do not grasp her work. She does not grasp what her work truly describes. For too long we have made do with those who have only a partial grasp of Sothic space. We have had to dress our instructions in the language of ritual and religion, invocation and spell, because that was the only doorway to the true universe that you could understand. But she —*

And then Noyes was clattering back down from the helipad and, spasmodically, I shut off the volume and smiled at him, and went meekly back to the helicopter with a hundred questions. The pilot who took me home made no attempt at conversation.

And then I went back to work. I would like to say that the whole Montpelier episode was behind me, but instead I was waiting for a call. I had, I thought, impressed Shochtauer's secretive employers. Perhaps they were military; perhaps there was some billionaire eccentric behind the screen. Whoever it was, they had an appreciation of numbers that spoke to me – more than the daily derision of my colleagues, more than Schochtauer's blustering. For the first few days I practically waited by the phone for them to contact me. And yet no call came. I know why, now, but at the time I felt only bitter. Perhaps it had all been an elaborate joke after all.

Two weeks after my trip I dreamt of that buzzing, droning voice, the weird tones that had rebuked Shochtauer over the security desk speaker. It told me that all the world and space and numbers I knew were contained within Rigolo space, and that the failure of my notation to translate to the real was not a fault of my mathematics, but merely showed the crippling limitations of regular matter and the few dimensions that were allowed to me. In my dream I saw the great coils of String Theory like a worm burrowing through the fabric of the universe; I saw the worlds that exist within the kernels of black holes and the radiance that awaits on the far side of the light barrier. I woke in the small hours, realising that the buzzing voice was just the vibration of my phone at my bedside.

That calmly artificial voice was there, when I answered.

"Doctor Rigolo," it said, "would you like to travel?"

I made some sound in reply.

"Doctor Rigolo, we have a proposal for you." I could hear the wax and wane of that buzzing static behind the urbane tones. "We value your affinity with numbers. In all the world there is no other who can manipulate what you call Rigolo space with your facility. For this, we invite you to join us."

"In Montpelier?" I asked, still half asleep.

"At first. Doctor Rigolo, what is important to you?"

"Numbers," I said immediately.

"What of your work? Your colleagues? Your home?" The buzzing swelled suddenly, as though I was hearing alien thoughts behind the human words. "What would you leave behind to pursue the truth of your numbers?"

I was confused. "Are you offering me a job? Then I'll need to…"

"This is not a job," that calm voice said. "We are offering you the chance to travel. We are offering you the chance to realise your dreams."

And I was desperately afraid, because those dreams were real and vibrant in my mind still, just as had been the dream that brought the Rigolo Transformation to me. Right then, I would have believed that the voice knew exactly where my sleeping mind had been.

"No," I whispered. I am ashamed now, but fear got the better of reason, for just that moment.

But then the voice said, "We will show you how to make your transformations real."

Why did I believe the voice? Because it fit with everything else. It was the only explanation for why they were so interested in a mathematical curio the rest of the world had written off long before – and yet that remained a stone about my neck. I would always be the woman who had become the laughing stock of the world for my phony theory. Unless it wasn't. Unless the Rigolo Transformation really was the key to the gates of the universe.

*

Again, there was a helicopter piloted by Schochtauer. The chief difference here was that the man's avuncular friendliness was gone, which I felt an improvement. He barely looked at me when I embarked, and maintained a tense silence throughout most of the flight. I am not sure what he would have done, had I been of a more talkative nature. As it was, a journey in utter silence was entirely agreeable to me.

But he was a man fond of his own voice and opinions. As the lights of Montpelier were visible, his reserve broke and he said, "It's not what you think, what they've promised you." He sounded very bitter.

I made some noncommittal sound.

"You don't know what they mean for you to leave behind," he told me. And then, so incongruously that I laughed, "They only want you for your mind."

His expression was not amused, though, and he said, "I've served them for a decade now." *Served them* not *worked for*. "They said it would be me, that I would get to go … and then you come along with your nonsense maths and…" and I just about tuned him out, from there, because there has been nothing in my professional life I have achieved that has not come with a chorus of people like Schochtauer complaining that I have somehow usurped an honour earmarked for their own kind.

"I'm saving you, really," he said then, and I realised we had diverted from our previous course, because Montpelier was over to our left, and he was flying out across dark farmland, dropping low enough that we were in danger of clipping trees and rooftops.

I demanded to know what he was doing, but he was concentrating now, finding a place to land, jockeying with the controls to bring the helicopter down on the flat expanse of a meadow.

"Get out," he told me, the moment the vehicle came to rest.

I opened my mouth again, but I saw that he had produced a pistol from inside his jacket, which rendered most of my objections void. At his repeated command I clambered out of the helicopter. I had it in mind to run, but I had got only a few steps before he was out himself and ordering me to halt.

"I really am saving you, you know," he told me. Why do such men always feel the need to justify their actions to themselves? "Did they offer you the chance to *travel*? Believe me, it's a mode of travel you'd need to sacrifice all of yourself for." The gun's aim shakily described a course from my head to my toe.

"And yet you would take it?" Because keeping him talking right then seemed wise.

"Yes! Because I have spent a decades researching them and their places, their ways. I have *earned* my place with them. And I'll get it, too, when you're gone. When they think you've turned away from them. They'll turn to me next."

I laughed, which was probably not wise. I couldn't help it, though. "They'll turn to Doctor Han in Beijing, or even to Jayne Shen from Cornell. They at least understand. You never have."

He scowled and jabbed the gun at me, and I thought of how I had never known when to speak and when to be silent. My lack of tact was about to kill me, it seemed. Except that Shochtauer was still in love with the sound of his voice. He wanted to make me *agree* with him before he killed me.

"I'm twice the mind you'll ever be," he hissed. "I've spent my life piecing together the words of ancient rituals, the invocations and rites that open the gates of Yogg-Sothoth and allow travel to the furthest reaches. The ways the ancients did it, the ways our ancestors reached out into the universe. There are entities to be appeased, you idiot woman. There are sacrifices and prices to be paid! And you think you can accomplish that with nothing but *numbers?*"

All this had taken place in the pool of yellow radiance shed by the helicopter's lights. Other than the orange glow on the horizon that was Montpelier, and the silent stars above, the rest of the world was dark. And I had reason to be glad of that, because now I saw there was something atop the helicopter, crouched around the hub of the blades.

"Yes," I told Schochtauer. "I think that you can do anything with numbers."

It must have come down silently from the sky, just a shadow against the greater blackness. It had landed there with barely a sound, covered by Schochtauer's brash boasting. I could see nothing of it but a shape that owed nothing to the human. There were great outspread wings and many limbs.

As I watched, whilst trying to show Schochtauer that my attention was on him, it shifted forwards, swaying like a chameleon does as it readies its strike. One limb shifted forwards and I saw something like a crab's pincer emerge into the light and take hold of a spar. It was half the size of the helicopter, in silhouette, but it seemed to weigh nothing at all as though it was made of some substance that simply did not interact with the world as normal matter might.

Schochtauer was still howling that there were traditions and old ways that must be followed, and then he actually began some bizarre chant, "Ia! Ia!" and similar unfamiliar sounds, so that he slobbered and spat about the awkward syllables. The gun was waving wildly.

I ran. In that moment it was not the man, not the gun, but an overwhelming dread of what the helicopter lamps were about to reveal. His chant broke off in a bark of fury, and he shouted my name, and "I'll shoot! I'll shoot!" as if he had some other purpose all this time to train a gun on me.

But I looked back. The urgency of his voice dragged at me despite my common sense, when I should just have kept running. I looked back, and saw *it* in the moment that it fell on Schochtauer. Just one moment I saw it, before I tripped and fell. I saw the great bronze sweep of its wings and the segmented, curved body busy with limbs. I saw the bristling lump it had for a head, which threw back the light in new and unknown colours.

I saw it in that instant, and then the ground drove the breath and senses from me. My last recollection is of gunshots and screaming.

*

When I awoke, I was in the building, propped in the security desk chair, and for a moment I wondered if it had all been a deranged dream. Was Noyes about to come and take me to the helicopter after all? Was Schochtauer still back in the boardroom arguing with his unseen employers?

And then I saw Schochtauer on the screens. He was indeed in the boardroom, laid out on the table there, quite naked. There were no marks at all on his sagging, pallid flesh, but his face—!

There was such a look on his face, of terror in the face of the unknown. As I watched, he twitched slightly, and I thought he must still live, but his face remained locked in that horrible goggling stare. When the twitch repeated it was not the motion of something moving, but of something being moved.

I thought of matter that is not like our matter, heedless of our gravity and our light. I thought of what wings might serve, to soar the vastnesses of Rigolo space.

Then there was a polite cough, and Noyes was there.

My return to the building, I learned, had been no less mundane than Noyes himself driving to get me, on his employer's instructions. "They cannot carry us as we are," his croaky voice affirmed, and I thought of Schochtauer saying, *You'd need to sacrifice all of yourself*, and *They only want you for your mind*.

And that perfect artificial voice over the phone, *Would you like to travel?* and *We can show you how to make your transformations real*.

"There was an offer," I told Noyes, and he nodded sagely.

"Are you here to accept?" he asked me, and I had the sense of others listening, all around and yet unseen.

"I'm ready for my transformation," I confirmed.

New Build

Adam Gauntlett

"Hi, I'm Maidah," she said, and held her hand out. She hoped she didn't seem nervous. This was her first solo; she wanted everything to go smoothly. "You are?"

He shook her hand. "Call me Mike."

"Okay. Is that your name, Mike?"

He shrugged. "It's what people call me," he replied, and any possible offence drifted away with a dazzling smile.

Handsome, she added to her mental checklist. *But not for me.*

"Have you visited the site before?" She started walking. The quicker they got there, the sooner they could get on with the job.

He fell in beside her. "Haven't been inside yet, but yeah, I was by last week to get a look at the place. It looks … well, I suppose you can guess what it looks like." He gestured expansively at the street and shops they were walking past.

"This is the new Hoxton." She laughed. "Or so they tell me."

"Looks more like the old Hoxton to me."

"You didn't park your car near here, did you?" Maidah's brow furrowed.

"No fear. I left it a couple streets back. I figured that was better than trying to find a space near the site, you know?"

"Yeah. The senior partner got a look at the place the first time a few days ago, and when he walked out again he didn't have his brand new mid-life-crisis mobile. I think it ended up a cinder. I can't complain, though, since I'm betting the reason I have this project is because he didn't want it after that.

Speaking of, I think that's our baby across the road."

It was. Built in 1880-something-or-other, it had all the late Victorian marks of excess, apparently complete with third floor ballroom, transformed in the 1970s to a second bar. To Maidah it was like seeing a distant relative for the first time; the brief, which she'd read again and again, was pretty extensive.

"Five quid says there's asbestos."

"You're on. We had the place surveyed; they didn't find any."

"I still say there's some lurking in here somewhere. Hang on, I've got the keys ... there we go. Careful as you go in."

The cavernous interior hadn't been touched in decades. Dim, uncertain shafts of light snuck in from outside through cracks in the layers of wood and posters over the window. To most it would have seemed a dump, but Maidah saw opportunity. Saloon and public bar, with snugs, and was that original frosted glass? It might just be, and if so, she blessed whichever unsung saint had let it survive the '70s holocaust. The carpet underfoot was beyond unsalvageable, but the floorboards might not be. The air lay heavy on them, thick enough to see. Mike's face twitched comically, and he clapped his hand over nose and mouth.

"Breathe it in," she told him. "That's the smell of money."

"If money died a week or so back, yeah."

More ticks on the spreadsheet: coal fire, two of. That might be the source of the smell. It wouldn't be the first time some bird had gone to dust in a chimney. The extension at the back was a shame, but it was the only way to get a kitchen in, and food service was a big seller. It would have to be redone of course, and they needed seating, which might mean further extension. At least there was space for it. By London standards, it was almost indecent how much room for expansion they had.

"Damp problems?" She was pleased to see Mike professionally assess the job in front of him.

"The gutters have been buggered for years, so yeah, but it's not as bad as it could have been, according to the report."

"I read that report. He left a lot out, didn't he?"

"Well, that's the risk you take. 'A survey report is not a guarantee that all defects that are present, or which may occur in the future, are covered by this limited inspection,'" she quoted. "But they were pretty optimistic. That reminds me. There was a space downstairs that the surveyor couldn't inspect; something about lack of access. Shall we?"

Both of them had torches, and the stair access was in reasonable shape. Whoever had tarted the place up, back when The Sweeny went around thumping toerags, hadn't bothered to touch anything the customers were never going to see. Maidah was pleasantly surprised not to detect the tell-tale smell of rat; the air was almost clean, compared to the bar above.

The door in question probably led to a storeroom, but over the years bits of rubbish had been added to the pile, such that the door was barely visible behind a mountain of aged and ragged tat. Judging by the expression on his face, Mike half expected Maidah to back out at this point, but she put her gloves and mask on, and when he saw that, so did he. It was a messy job, but not troublesome. She wondered why the surveyor hadn't gotten off his duff and tried to do the same.

The door was a little unusual, in that it wasn't a recent import, but judging by appearance was original to the building, which made it more than a century old. Thick, sturdy wood, and a lever lock that hadn't been touched in God alone knew how long.

"Don't suppose you've got the key?"

"I've got half a dozen, but none of them long barrel. I don't think anyone's had the key to this, not for a long time."

"How much do you love this door?"

"I hate it."

"Give me a little room to work, then."

It took some bashing. Just when Mike worried he'd bust the thing for good to no purpose, it sprang open.

The room was small and stuffy. It had been bare brick, once upon a time, but someone had plastered over every least thing, even to the extent of sealing the one window permanently off. It was as if the unknown meddler had tried to turn the place into the inside of an egg, smooth-walled, and not even damp and the passage of years had thwarted that intention. The plaster was as featureless as a baby's dream. It made Mike think of the Tate Modern, some surrealist art exhibit where you had to inhabit the artist's mind.

"Someone's been drawing on this," he pointed out. Symbols adorned the walls. "Looks like algebra, or something like it."

Maidah was more interested in the piles of clothing on the floor. Despite the passage of what probably had been a very long time, they were still more or less intact. Monk's robes, or more likely some kind of modern religious; they almost seemed Egyptian. Gold thread aplenty, and colour, with silver headbands, and what seemed a staff, with a pine cone at its top. She was thinking furiously, and making a very quick decision.

"Right. We didn't see this."

Mike's jaw sagged. "You what?"

"Didn't see it, didn't find it, don't know nuffing and never did. You'd better take this stuff away," she prodded the costumes with her foot, "and burn it. Make sure nobody sees you do it, okay? And when you bring some blokes back to clear the place out, make sure they smash up that plaster and cart away the rubble."

Mike wasn't at all sure about this, and it showed.

She sighed. "Look at it this way. Nothing will kill a job quicker than bad publicity, right? And this stuff, to me, it just screams bad press. We'll have the conspiracy nuts in here, the ghost hunters, Christ alone knows what. Then it'll be the council, and if we don't have people breaking in with their bloody cameras to get a closer look, I'll be amazed. The whole job will turn into a circus, and we don't need the bother, all right? Just get rid of it, all of it, and don't tell anyone where you got it from."

*

CAD was a sod.

Maidah had never really been comfortable with it, even in college. Ratchet wasn't much better, but she was happier with it. The senior partners were not, and so when drawing architectural plans Maidah was stuck with good old CAD, several updates behind the current version. But even pure hatred wasn't enough to get her through this one, so, she hoped, stubbornness would have to do.

At least the project was going well. Mike and his crew were getting on with the clearance. Everything that was not to be harmed in any way had been carefully pointed out, especially those lovely snugs and their lovely, lovely frosted glass. The council was even obliging and quick to respond, a condition unheard of in Maidah's admittedly limited experience. With a bit of luck the last permits they needed to start the rebuild would be done by the end of the week. Then it was off to the races; or, more accurately, off to the *quants gnomes*, who would add up their sums one last time before the job went out to tender.

After that, of course, several months of sheer bliss. Mike had already sent one picture through on her phone. It was a lumpy bit of yellowish nothing, hidden up in the roof void. The tagline simply read, 'asbestos?' with a smiley face attached. It was going to be a busy week.

"Senior wonk at six o'clock," hissed her bench-mate, giving Maidah enough time to put on a professional smile. It was Malcolm Hughes, one of the leading, indeed founding, partners.

Hughes was one of those people you didn't trust. She knew that much from the office Christmas party – lecherous old sod

– but it was more than that. He had the knack of coming out of nasty situations smelling like a rose, which, she knew, invariably meant that someone else was covered in shit.

"Hello Maidah," he said. "Hard at work on the Angell Street project, I see. Any updates?"

There hadn't been anything too dramatic since the Monday meeting, but she filled him in on the progress since. She had the impression his mind wasn't on what she was saying. Oddly enough, it didn't seem to be on her chest, either.

"Good, good. You had the inspection, yes?"

"We did. I met with the clearance firm's rep, and we went over the details. Everything's on target."

"That's fine. You didn't find anything unusual on site?"

She straightened in her chair. "Like what?"

"Oh." He gave her his very best not-trying-to-screw-you, honest, smile. "Anything, really. Nothing to report?"

"No. It was pretty much as you'd expect. In fact, it was in better condition than I'd have given it credit for, no surprises at all. Barring accidents, I think this is going to be a good contract for us."

"Brilliant. Keep up the good work."

Then he was gone, leaving a very puzzled junior in his wake.

She phoned Mike.

"Before you start, no, it is not asbestos," she told him, "And anyway, I'm not calling about that. I need to know something. You dealt with that room, yes?"

"Sure did."

"Bashed up all the plaster? Carted it off-site? Burnt the gear?"

"Yes, yes, and what the hell, yes. Anything the matter?"

She ignored the worry pulling at her brain. "No. It's all good."

*

Mike wondered whether he ought to tell Maidah what had

really happened to the clothes they'd found.

He knew what he ought to have done. But he loved a mystery, had done ever since he was a kid watching cartoons, when all you had to do was fix up a cunning trap and pull the rubber mask off the villain after they got caught. Plus, the costumes were in decent nick, all things considered. Someone had gone to a lot of trouble over them. Only something well made, out of good materials, would hold up as well as those robes had.

Then there was the wand. Or was it a staff? He didn't know; he supposed it could be either, but as soon as he saw it he knew he wanted to find out what it was.

So instead of burning it all, he'd taken it home with him. A few minutes on Google would tell him what they were, or so he thought. If they turned out to be valuable, well, lucky day. He could just see himself on the *Antiques Roadshow*, modest in his victory. "Found them in a skip, during a house clearance. Good job I pulled them out, eh? How much did you say they're worth?"

But Google was not being kind to him. He hadn't the least idea what the things were.

"Hey, Mike?" It was the main gaffer, the one who could speak a little Polish. Not that the clearance team couldn't understand English, goodness gracious no, perish the thought. After all, if they couldn't understand English then they couldn't understand the health and safety lecture they'd been given, and that would never do.

"Please tell me you haven't bust that frosted fucking glass."

"No, Mike. You want to come take a look?"

It was the exterior that had him worried. Mike took one look and swore.

"We've got our own little Banksy, have we?"

It was graffiti, quite well executed, Mike had to admit. The froth on the attack dog's lips and teeth, the glaring eyes, the whip-thin body, all indicated an art school graduate who, in his spare time, was a bit of a cunt. The dog leapt from the corner of the main entrance, away from the door and across the wall.

"When did the little bastard have the time to do it, that's what I want to know. I mean, it wasn't here when we set up this morning, was it?"

"No."

"That's what I bloody thought. So whoever the cheeky fucker is, he had to do it while we were in the building. In fact, he had to do it while your crew was working in the saloon bar, which means if they'd just looked up, they'd probably have seen him. Bastard! Okay, clean it off, would you? I don't want the PM team to find out about this. We've got a decent chance of getting the rebuild as well as the clearance, and I don't want them thinking we can't even keep one lousy tagger off the site."

*

The train rocked, sending its sardine-packed commuters swaying. Not that Maidah would have noticed if a bomb went off. Her attention was fixed on her Metro, the free paper.

Police have no suspects in Angell Street killing, she read.

The body was discovered after police and paramedics were called to Angell Street, following reports of a woman's collapse. Despite the best efforts of the Ambulance Service, the woman could not be revived. The area around the building site where she was found has been sealed off, pending a forensic examination…

"Oh shit."

Dare she check her mobile? There was bound to be a dozen calls at least, not counting anything the police might be sending her. No, better to call first; Mike might have news.

"Did you see…"

"I was there when the cops showed up," he interrupted. "Yeah, it's a bloody nightmare."

"There when the cops showed? What were you doing that late at night?"

"Checking up on a couple things. Listen, I'll send you the gory details over email, okay? But don't get too worked up, it's not as bad as it looks. The cops say they'll need the site for a couple days, that's all. We were nearly done anyway, so this won't put a huge dent in our schedule. You should be able to go ahead with the tender on time. It's just a bad break."

"Who was she?"

"Dunno. Just some kid. Looks like someone gave her a good bashing then dragged her off where it's quiet, you know? I'll send you the deets later, okay?"

Mike rang off. Maidah stared out of the window, collecting her thoughts.

The passing landscape had become her familiar routine. When she first arrived in London she made a game of spotting the changes, the new graffiti, building works going up. Now it was soothing white noise, flowing past.

The massive coiled hound, its red eyes gleaming, was new to her. It lurked near the tunnel entrance, posed in such a way that it seemed to be staring at the train as it went by. Real artistry, she thought. Pity it was wasted on something so bloody trivial.

The train passed through the tunnel, and the hound vanished out of sight.

*

Mike was glad Maidah hadn't tried to pry, else he'd have difficulty explaining why he'd been poking around after hours. Truth to tell, he'd been trying to confirm a suspicion. He'd come armed with a bunch of photos, hoping to match them to the reality on site.

The inspiration, ironically, had come from Maidah. "We'll have the conspiracy nuts in here, the ghost hunters, Christ alone knows what." That's what she'd said, and he'd let it pass, forgetting it, until he started banging his head against the Google wall trying to find out more about the costumes. Then it occurred to him to wonder why she was worried about ghost hunters, and before long he was poking around in the wilder recesses of Google, where the nutters gathered.

That took him to Ghostquester.co.uk, and from there he was in.

Back in the 1900s, he discovered, there'd been a split between one bunch of occult nerds from another, and the other bunch followed a bloke named Crowley. They set up what they called temples all over the place, and more often than not they closed down again soon after because they couldn't be buggered to pay the rent. But the one set up at Angell Street had been different, because that had been backed by a fellow named Nuttall, and Nuttall had money, as well as being one of Crowley's best buddies. So they were able to fix the place up just as they liked it, and what was more, they left a record. Ghostquester had all the pictures on its site, showing the pub – known back then as The Hound, though Nuttall and his mates called it The Shuck, he wasn't sure why, and Ghostquester didn't say – in all its former glory. Including, incidentally, those famous frosted glass panes, not that he was about to tell Maidah that. If he did, he'd have to explain how he knew, and he suspected that would lead to some unpleasant complications.

If only because the same picture that proved the glass' history also had Nuttall, Crowley and all in their very best priestly robes, with Crowley holding the staff-thing. It was a Thyrsus, according to his research. Something to do with fertility, apparently. Or more accurately, something to do with big dicks, since that seemed to be what Crowley, and more especially Nuttall, was into.

Maidah must have known something about this, or she wouldn't have made the connection. No wonder she hadn't wanted it advertised. Occult nerds, gay or not, and high-end gastropubs did not mix, even in this tatty bit of London town.

Coffee in hand, he went to check the site. His team couldn't do much, but at least he could show willing. He had to avoid the police tape, but the bloke in charge knew who he was so he didn't have much difficulty getting past.

He stopped before he got to the door. The gaffer had done as he asked. The tag had been completely removed. In fact, more completely than Mike would have expected; he'd worried that there'd be some damage to the brickwork, but it came up without a trace left behind.

But now there was a new one, and it was right next to where the forensics blokes were working.

The black hound's gaping jaws seemed to be laughing at him. Cobalt, acidic liquid dripped from its mouth, little smoking stains carefully painted in at ground level, just about where the girl's body had been found.

"Bollocks," he said to himself. The tagger had come back.

Was it worth mentioning to the coppers? Mike hesitated. He still didn't want Maidah to know too much about what had been going on, but if he told the cops then it was bound to come out about the other tag. It was the one thing he hadn't taken a photo of; he'd recorded everything else he'd found, including the plaster room before it had been given the bash, on his smartphone, but the graffiti hadn't seemed worth the bother.

No, he decided. Better to keep shtum.

*

Maidah had been in some peculiar meetings but, when she reeled out after four hours, she acknowledged that one took the prize. It was in fact the Gold Standard, against which all future peculiar meetings should be compared.

Hughes had been on top form, oiling his way through it all. It was clear he was edging into the Angell Street project, though it had never been his to begin with and he had a workload that would kill a horse, so why so eager? But eager he undoubtedly was.

It wasn't even as if it was a top priority. Sure, it had been lean times, but not for the last twelve months. If anything the firm was running at capacity, and had half a dozen other jobs with much more profile, and profit, than the Angell Street refurb. But no, it was all about having an experienced hand at the helm, very important client, couldn't afford to muck it up.

The other seniors sat there like stones. One of them, Angelo, was as pale as a ghost, and he was the one who usually weighed in when Hughes was talking crap. It was like someone had shot him before the meeting, and he was sitting there bleeding out, too polite to say anything about it.

So now the job was Hughes'.

"No hard feelings, Maidah," he said after the meeting. "I'll keep you on as my junior. It won't be the same as running the job yourself, but you'll get good exposure."

Which was short for *you'll get all the donkeywork I don't want to deal with, and you'll deal with the council too, because those fuckers bore the pants off me.*

Maidah sat in her chair, head whirling. She had to put all her files on the server for Hughes, and she did, one after the other.

Her bench-mate was on a smoke break. His monitor showed some kind of YouTube crap. Very bad idea: if the seniors saw it he'd be due for a wigging. It was on loop, but the sound was off.

She glanced it out of the corner of her eye. Attention caught, she studied it. No, not YouTube but some other site, she wasn't sure what. The hound drawn on the screen seemed familiar, but she couldn't place it. Long, and lean, and hungry, with eyes as crazy as a full moon, and behind it, something … something large.

The screen went blank.

"The hell?"

But it stayed blank, no matter what she did, and when her bench-mate came back it was time to call the IT blokes, because his box had completely fried. The fuss that followed drove the hound out of her mind.

*

Second death at Angell Street, dangerous animal to blame?

Police are asking people to be on the lookout for a dangerous animal, possibly an escaped dog, after a second death at Angell Street. The body of Laura Taylor, 17, was discovered Monday at a building site. The police have since confirmed that a second victim was found unresponsive, not far from the first scene, just before midnight yesterday. A spokesman for the force said that a detailed forensic examination of the second scene is taking place…

*

"Christ, mate, you look like death."

Mike didn't respond. Not even coffee was going to save him.

He hardly ever dreamed. The only time he remembered dreaming was just before he went travelling; he never liked flying, so the night before his mind kept itself busy showing him all the wonderful ways the plane might crash. Other than that, though, he slept like a log, and didn't remember anything about it the next day.

Not this time.

He'd been walking down Angell Street, only it wasn't the Angell Street he knew. It was more crowded, for a start, and there weren't any cars. In fact, at one point he saw a rag and bone man with an actual horse and cart, something he hadn't seen in thirty years living in London.

The people didn't look at him, and he didn't look at them. He was afraid of what he might see in their faces.

There was no sound in his dream. Not at first.

As he got closer and closer to the Shuck, he could hear it baying.

It was a hungry sound, an angry sound, and it got closer and closer with each step. He tried to stop walking towards it, only to discover that no matter what he wanted his legs had different ideas. Each step was a step closer to destruction, and he knew it, but he couldn't stop.

The baying was at its loudest when he woke up.

"You ever have one of those nights?"

The gaffer nodded. "Every Saturday morning. Coppers been to see you yet?"

"Yeah, they got me this morning. You ever see a dog round here?"

"Naw, not unless it's the fucker's dog. Speaking of, he left another one."

"Shit."

"I would get the blokes in, but..." The gaffer's embarrassment was written on his face.

"What?"

"Well, they won't do it, Mike."

"What do you mean, won't do it? They won't clean it off? Why not?"

He shrugged. "Dunno, mate. I thought it was money, so I put some cash out, but it was no doings. They don't want to touch it."

Mike sighed. It was all they needed. Maidah was due for a site visit this morning.

"Is it somewhere visible?"

"Back entrance."

"Fine. I'll make sure the PM people don't see it, and you make sure you get some blokes in who don't go girly when the big, mean tagger puts his mark on our building, okay?"

After that build-up he had to see it, so while the gaffer returned to his business Mike went to the back entrance to get a look.

It had an oily, smirking look to it, as though it were sneaking home after a night's debauch, pissing on the garbage bins and shagging all the ladies. That face, though, it would never win friends. Those jaws, with their jagged teeth, that azure tongue lolling. It would always be hungry. It would never stop.

Mike shivered.

"Goose over my grave."

*

"I had to see it for myself," said Maidah, as she poked her head inside the hidden room.

Mike and his team had been thorough. Every least bit of plaster had been smashed and removed. The little window, for so long sealed away, threw a small amount of light into what was otherwise a featureless brick storage room.

Maidah's nose wrinkled. "Was that smell here before?"

Mike didn't answer. He wasn't at all happy about the smell. When they'd started the job, it hadn't been there, he'd swear to it. If anything, the rooms below stairs had been positively fresh, compared to the fug up top. Now there was an acrid, unpleasant something hanging in the air, and each day it grew stronger. At first he'd thought it was something to do with the forensics blokes, who'd been working just outside that small window. Maybe some chemical or other, but it had been days since the forensics blokes had packed up and, if anything, the smell was stronger.

"Anyway, glad to see everything's progressing. You'll probably need to speak to Malcolm Hughes at some point; he likes to poke his nose in after the hard work's done, but I wouldn't worry about him. All he'll want is to be reassured everything's going well." She looked at him. "It is, right?"

He couldn't hide it.

"Bollocks. What's the problem?"

Which led to an unhappy Mike taking Maidah back upstairs, but just as he thought he was about to make the Big Reveal he was stunned to discover that the graffiti had vanished.

"Okay. So what am I not seeing?"

Mike touched the wall – and snatched his hand away. It had to be his imagination, couldn't be anything else, but it was as if the bricks had stung his fingers, somehow.

"Look, I don't pretend to understand…"

Mike interrupted her. "What do you know about a bloke named Nuttall?"

That caught her out, and he knew it. "So you do know something. What is it?"

"I don't know if I should be telling tales…"

She saw the look on his face. "Right. But this goes nowhere else, you understand? I don't know a lot about Nuttall, but I do know he was an architect, and he had a bit of a reputation. Lots of big-money jobs, more than you'd expect even if he was any good, and I don't know that he was all that clever, really. But he still collected one hell of a payday while he was living, and when he died a rival firm bought up all his papers, notebooks, the lot. That rival firm was taken over in its turn, and after a while, we obtained the Nuttall stuff when we bought out the practice that bought out, and so on.

"I've never seen any of those papers. I don't even know why we keep them, the stuff's massively out of date, and I don't think even ten buildings Nuttall worked on still stand. Even if they did, it's not as if he was Sir George Gilbert Scott, you know? Nobody remembers Nuttall's work these days, except us."

"And the blokes on Ghostquester?"

"I don't know what that is – but yes, Nuttall had a reputation. That's why I didn't want anyone to know this was one of his jobs. We'd have loonies crawling out from under every rock in London."

"Can you get me into that collection?" asked Mike.

"No bloody way." He despaired, and she unbent a little. "There's no chance I can get you in to see those papers, but I can have a look, if you like. After all, it might be important." She wondered what Hughes would say if she came out with something critical, something that added big bucks to the project. She had no idea what that might be but for the sake of an hour or two looking around in the archives, why not? Couldn't hurt, and might help. "So what am I searching for?"

"Anything to do with dogs. Or the Hound. Or maybe the Shuck."

"Okay … you sure? Right, then. I'll have a nosey and call you later on tonight. That good?"

"I'll be waiting."

*

Nerves didn't begin to describe it.

Mike couldn't sit still, couldn't sleep, couldn't even drink. He'd tried a beer to take the edge off, but it turned to sewer water in his mouth, and he had to spit it out. It was the same with food. The curry he'd bought from the place on the corner sat, uneaten, on his Ikea table. He'd tried one mouthful but couldn't swallow it. He didn't have the energy to throw it in the bin, either.

There was nothing but rubbish on telly, so he went to his tablet and brought up the Ghostquester site again. He'd already poked through pretty much everything it had to offer, but by this point it wasn't about what he hoped he'd find any more. It was about shutting up that little voice hiding behind his eyes, the one that wouldn't stop screaming.

The videos on the site were a laugh, at least. Ghost hunters chasing through abandoned houses, some of them in pretty decent nick, all things considered. While they were poncing around for the camera, he was looking for signs of damp or other decay.

"You can't trust your eyes," the bloke in the video was saying for the umpteenth time, as he navigated some post-war bungalow. "The things that live inside the fourth dimension, inside time, they can't be seen, and they usually can't see us. But if someone creates a weakness, then they can see us, and they won't stop, they won't ever stop…"

Mike shivered, and in shivering realised he'd been napping. The spasm woke him up.

His tablet was silent. The room was cold, very cold, and he rose to turn the heating on. He had to pass the window as he did so – and glimpsed it.

The Hound splayed across the wall opposite, caught in mid-leap, its eyes firmly fixed on something above it.

Firmly fixed on his apartment. On him.

*

No Hound, no Shuck, but Nuttall's archive was a very strange artefact indeed.

It would have puzzled the hell out of his peers, Maidah was certain. The Victorians liked their Neo Greco, their Renaissance Revival, their Romanesque, their Queen Anne. Anything that looked old and could be added on to make it look even more impressive, that was meat and drink to a late Victorian, early Edwardian designer. But they wouldn't have known what to do with a Gherkin, a Walkie-Talkie, or a Strata Tower, spiky, angular, proud winner of the Carbuncle Cup and excoriated by architects all over the country.

Nuttall would. The designs in his notes, though clearly of their time, embraced concepts she found difficult to believe he could conceive. The materials alone would have been beyond him, never mind the style. Yet there it was, in elaborate detail.

Though "Hound" never once appeared in Nuttall's notes, another word did, and that often: Tindalos. She had no idea what it meant – but it obviously meant a great deal to Nuttall since it recurred on every third or fourth document, and often with that strange stretch of algebra or whatever it may have been that she remembered seeing on the egg-smooth walls in the pub's store room.

"Found what you were looking for?"

Maidah nearly jumped out of her skin. "Ma— Mister Hughes?"

That gentle, shit-eating grin.

"I'm afraid the more important papers are in my office. I wanted to make sure nobody saw them but me. I was reasonably certain no one else cared about poor old Nuttall and his experiments, but I never saw sense in leaving too much up to chance."

Maidah's phone began to ring.

Hughes waited while she checked the number. "Perhaps you ought to take that."

*

Mike frantically scrolled through the pictures he'd transferred to his tablet. The pictures he'd taken of that strange mathematical formula. Perhaps it would save him; whoever built that room must have thought it was important. It was a slender thread but at that moment he'd have put crosses on all the walls and hung garlic from every window if he thought it would do the slightest good.

He looked out the window.

The Hound wasn't on the wall any more.

It had moved on.

*

"They inhabit time," said Hughes. "That's a poor way of putting it, but language doesn't really help when describing this kind of phenomena. Ordinarily we don't notice them and they don't notice us, but under certain conditions those of us in this humble reality can force a breach. To my knowledge they have been observed at least three times since Nuttall's experiment, and those are only the examples I'm aware of. It's likely there have been other breaches. I sometimes wonder, if we can force a weakness on our side, can they force one on theirs? Are they more aware of us than we would like to think?

"Of course, we can't really see them. Our minds make sense of it by interpreting the image in a way we can understand. That's when they're some distance away. When they come closer, you see them for what they really are. Or at least, so I've always believed. Nobody has ever been able to report back after the event.

"But the inspiration! The designs! That's what Nuttall was after, why he went digging around in the past, with his drugs and incantations. Or what he thought was the past, anyway.

That sort of thing appealed to his Victorian mind, you see. He thought he would discover, and steal, the ideas of fellows like that old Roman Vitruvius, and the other classics. He wasn't expecting to find what he did: a strange, alien existence, with impossible, beautiful angles, designs beyond anything he could comprehend...

"Of course, it's different for us. The things he couldn't build, we can, and they'll laud us to the skies for it. Tindalosian inspired, utterly unique designs. Do you want to be the next Foster? The next Hadid?"

Maidah accepted the call.

Coming out of the wall... Mike's voice was tinny and far away. *The angles in the wall!*

"Of course," said Hughes, "I know how to keep it at bay, at least for a while. In time it may lose your scent, or get bored. Or not. My understanding of their psychology is limited. But you can't save him. Why not save yourself?"

*

Third death linked to Angell Street animal.

The death of a local contractor has been linked to the recent Angell Street killings, according to a statement from a police spokesman. The man was found unresponsive in a King Street apartment, early this morning. It has been confirmed that his injuries are congruent with those found on the bodies of the two Angell Street victims. The spokesman confirmed that a detailed forensic examination of this scene is taking place...

*

The wall was freshly plastered. Smooth as an eggshell, the store room in the basement of The Hound had been restored to its former condition.

"How long will I have to stay here?"

Maidah was shivering, but not from cold. The things Hughes had made her do ... no, she'd agreed to it, to all of it, but still ... and there would be more, she knew that. She knew that smile. She saw it in her dreams.

"Impossible to say, my dear. But I would estimate two to three weeks, to be on the safe side. So long as this room is kept intact, the breach point is sealed, which means it can't break through here. It can stalk around, make a fuss, but it almost certainly can't get back through this point. Of course, if it is aware of other weaknesses nearby it may try there and then attempt to return here, so it's best you stay put for a while."

His gaze lingered.

"No clothes, of course. Might form an angle, you see, and then what would happen?"

She hid herself behind her hands, knowing it wouldn't do much good.

"Not to worry. I'll bring food and supplies. Time will go by quicker than you think. After that, of course, we'll have to discuss your future within the firm." He smiled. "I've always liked the idea of having an apprentice."

Somewhere far in the distance, a dog wailed its hatred at the unfeeling stars.

The Branch Line Repairman

Adrian Tchaikovsky

The Labourer's Tale

It amazes me how swiftly people have come to trust the London Underground after the incident, but then the beating heart of City commerce has an urgency to it that not even the inexplicable can slow. I myself will never venture down there again, not with what I know and what I saw.

And of course nobody goes on the Circle Line, and they have sealed every access way with concrete, and they think that is an end to it.

But I have gone in the small hours to Edgware Road Station, and I have put my ear to the new and hastily-painted wall, and heard the rush and shunt of constant motion. I have heard the voices of all those who never escaped, crying out forever.

*

My name is Patrick Chillet and I was a historian. The focus of my study was always the London Underground, its construction, its socio-economic context, all the footling minutiae of its expansions that form the carcase on which we specialist academics feast. It is not a trade I can, with all conscience, still espouse. I know the deeper history that makes a mockery of everything I ever wrote.

There were always rumours of irregularities concerning the construction of the Underground, but none that could not be accounted for by embezzlement, rivalries and incompetence. The root cause of the Underground was plainly the influx of commuters who choked the roads in their grim desperation to reach their places of employ each morning, and equal desperation to flee them every evening. As early as 1830 the first plans were laid, though the Metropolitan line would not open for another three decades. We will never know just how the project was suborned. Somehow I think they simply dug too deep. They found, beneath the bustle of London, a strange quiet like the sound between stars, and they were lost. I have stood down there, and heard that sound.

Maintaining the Underground has always been a constant battle. In particular, there always seem to be major works around and beneath Paddington Station. It is a fact I had given little significance to until I was contacted by one Raymond "Teddy" Leary.

Leary was employed by Unigraft Labour, which had been brought on site as additional labourers in an attempt to bring the works back on schedule. You might recall the considerable discontent and media coverage about the frequent delays this work caused. What nobody raised at the time was the actual purpose of the works. Nobody appears to have asked, and I myself did not wonder. Living in London, such inconveniences are so engrained that we accept them, as if they were the judgment of an arbitrary deity.

Mr Leary was not a Londoner. He had come to the capital seeking his fortune from Boston, Lincolnshire, and perhaps was simply less accustomed to take the ways of the City in his stride. He was also a man with a history of drink and psychological instability and, by the time he came to see me, Unigraft had dispensed with his services. No doubt it was at least partially for an opportunity to air his grievances that he sought out someone – as he felt – "in authority". I do not know why a specialist historian fulfilled this criterion for him, nor how many other "authority figures" he tried before someone directed him to me.

As it was, I was regretting agreeing to see him within minutes. I had to endure a great deal of acrimony concerning his employers and his working conditions, none of which was of any relevance to my studies, so that eventually I suggested he seek out some firm of solicitors, or else the Citizen's Advice Bureau, who might better be able to assist.

He had, it transpired, already exhausted these options. They would not take him seriously, he explained with a confidential air. There were things he had seen, down in the works, that nobody was talking about.

He then began to complain about the workforce employed by the main contractors, who had been on the job from the start. They were a stand-offish, clannish lot, by his estimation. They worked in silence, never sharing a joke or a cigarette, never going to the pub after hours.

"There was this one bloke," he told me. "We were digging deep, all sorts of pipes and cables, nobody knew what for – he just went down, keeled over. Thought he'd had a stroke or something, I did. Didn't make a sound with it. They took him away smartish, all his mates, and none of them saying anything. Only…"

I waited, but I had to prompt him. The sight had plainly upset him.

"Only, when they picked him up, it was like there wasn't a joint nor bone in his body. It was like he was a sack of lard." He shuddered, and needed a strong cup of tea and a cigarette before he was ready to go on.

"Had the man been electrocuted?" I asked.

"I've seen that, and it weren't that," Leary assured me. "When he went down it were like he was tired, just … run out of steam. But he never got back up."

There was more. Leary said the works had broken into older tunnels beneath Paddington Station – his description placed their architecture squarely in the mid to late nineteenth century. Except he claimed they were, "Big, big so you could've driven a truck through 'em. They led from down there up towards the main line – you could feel the shake when the trains went by." He recalled the cold of those elder tunnels clearly, and other peculiarities, that had finally led him to call in sick and not come back. "There was a breeze," he told me. "All the time, but it was blowing *in*, deeper down, where we didn't go. And there was this, like writing on the wall – like, marks."

"Graffiti?"

He shrugged. "Real old. Like that blind stuff, Braille; like someone had got a jackhammer and pounded all these dents in patterns in the wall. And stars."

"Stars?"

He fidgeted with his cigarette packet. "Drawings like stars, or maybe starfish, they were, in with the dots."

That, then, was the testimony of Mr Leary. It is to be recalled that he had a history of alcohol abuse, and had when young been in and out of institutions, correctional and medical, but there was an undoubted conviction in his words. It was enough for me to write to Transport for London asking if a historian might have access to the Paddington works to see these carvings he spoke of. I received no reply.

I have since attempted to locate Mr Leary, but he expressed an intention to return back north, having acquired a peculiar horror of London in general, and what lay beneath it in particular. Thus far my enquiries have found no trace of him.

The Carnot Expedition

Mr Leary did leave me one souvenir of his visit. From his phone, he mailed over to me a graphics file showing the peculiar graffiti he had uncovered beneath Paddington Station. The lighting was poor and the resolution low, but I could make out curiously grouped clumps of impressions, indeed like some system of Braille. There was one star-like imprint as well, which appeared to contain an almost leaf-like pattern of veins and branches. It reminded me of nothing so much as the test of a fossil echinoderm. I wondered if the Victorians had planned some odd, abstract mural.

With my curiosity engaged, I took the photograph to some of my colleagues to see if any of them had seen anything of the like before. In truth, I was anticipating something fairly mundane – if not merely decorative then some notation of Nineteenth Century architects perhaps. I copied the file and sent it to various institutions with an interest in the civil engineering of the period, and later events suggest that my curiosity was noted in other places beyond the circle of my immediate enquiries.

I ended up travelling to the London Transport Museum in Covent Garden to meet a young American scholar named Emma-May Watts, out of Chicago. Miss Watts was ostensibly working on a new biography of Charles Yerkes, the speculator and financier whose efforts had made large sections of the London Underground a reality. However, as she happily confessed, she had become side-tracked within days of arriving in London, and had been pursuing her own tangential studies ever since.

She had sent me a very brief email to say that she did indeed recognise Leary's inscriptions, and when I met her she was as good as her word. With a slight smile, she presented me with photocopies of what appeared to be rubbings of very similar designs.

"Where did you get these?" I demanded.

"What would you say if I told you they appear in the passageways beneath the Pyramids, and in the stone-lined tombs of the Orkney islands?"

I goggled at her, aghast, and she fairly collapsed in laughter. "Oh Doctor, your *face!*" And that was my first real introduction to the somewhat mercurial nature of Emma-May Watts.

When she had gotten over her mirth at my gullibility, she went on, "It's good that you at least entertained it for a moment though, because if you want to learn about *this*," and she waved the photocopy, "then it's a wild ride, believe me."

"But what are they, then?"

"Carnot's Dots," she explained, or evidently she felt it an explanation.

After a blank moment, though, I did feel a faint tugging in my memory. "Do you mean Carn*ot*?" spoken to rhyme with Poe.

She shrugged. "Well, I only saw it written down and I liked the rhyme. You've heard of Gideon Carnot then?"

I had, but little more than that. The name surfaced as a footnote in transport history, principally because of his eccentric fate. After the Metropolitan Line had been opened in the 1860s and proved such a profitable success, work had begun on the District, and the two together would eventually pave the way for the Circle Line that would link all the major rail terminals in inner London. Carnot had been a secretary of the Board of the District Line, and his personal story had been almost totally lost in the shadow of that organisation's considerable pecuniary woes.

"Didn't he…" I racked my brains "…end up in an asylum?"

"He did indeed." Watts grinned wolfishly. "I'm going to have to swear you to secrecy, Doctor Chillet, because – well, I don't know whether I'll ever finish the book on Yerkes, but Yerkes has been written about so much there's scarcely room for another commentator anyway. But Carnot, Carn*ot*," mimicking my pronunciation, "is another matter, and I have some primary sources that *nobody*'s ever had access to before."

The publicly-known facts in the matter of Gideon Carnot are that he was deputised by the District board of directors to investigate certain irregularities in works going on under the control of its sister-line, the Metropolitan. The two corporations were at the time negotiating the future of the Circle line, and the nexus of the two lines was, of course, Paddington Station. Officially, Carnot then disappeared until he was pulled from the rubble of a collapsed tunnel beneath that station seven days later, injured and not in his wits. He retired to the family home where he remained out of sight for many years, the stigma of a mental breakdown ensuring that polite society – and the board of the District – did their best to pretend he had never existed. In 1884 the house was sold to pay debts and Carnot ended up in Berkshire Asylum, where he ended his days soon after.

By dint of determined investigation Watts had unearthed considerable further evidence concerning Carnot's exploits and fate. As prologue, she had a handwritten memo to Carnot from three directors of the Board directing him to *secure yourself several men of capability and enter covertly into the works beneath the station in order to ensure that the excavations there situate do not pose a further financial risk to the extension of the District Line.*

"'several men of capability,'" I mused. "Sounds a little racy for our field."

"Doesn't it just," Watts agreed with one of her irreverent grins. "Look, here," and she had a handful of photocopies that appeared to detail expenses. "Always follow the money when you can," she explained. "These were in a box in the storeroom right here in the Transport Museum, if you can believe it."

I looked over them. Individuals called Cooper and Ashworth had charged for lamps, fuel, rope and other equipment suitable for spelunking. More alarmingly, someone with a wild hand and an illegible signature had put in a claim for ammunition of three separate calibres and some mining explosives.

"Theodore Grant-Souborne, based on other samples of his writing," Watts explained. "He was something of an adventurer, went all over the Empire oppressing the natives, like you Brits are good at. A bit of a celebrity even, except he vanishes from sight around this time. But that's not the craziest part." And she showed me a list of necessaries apparently purchased by someone named Amelia Cecil, whose small, neat letters listed opium and cocaine in quantities that would have the modern-day vice squad scrabbling for their handcuffs.

"She was a psychic and ghost hunter," Watts explained. She had a photo of a young, intense-looking woman in a high-collared gown. "Again, nobody mentions her after the Carnot expedition."

"Expedition?"

"Well, isn't it? What else would you call this?" Her grin was back. "Fighter, mage, couple of rogues. Only thing they were missing was a cleric."

"I have no idea what you're talking about," I said stuffily.

"Well, another thing nobody has any idea about is what actually happened. They set out on November 4th, according to this. Carnot turned up alone on the 11th, babbling like a loon and with both legs broken. That's a long time to be lost under Paddington Station."

"So where did your rubbings come from?"

Her grin widened to truly Cheshire Cat proportions. "I found them among Carnot's papers, when I went to the old family home. It's some training retreat for your Civil Service now, but one thing the Civil Service is really bad at is throwing stuff away. Had to put my charm into overdrive, but they let me into the attic, where I found this little lot."

Her treasure trove was a box of loose papers, yellowed with age and in a very poor condition. Some were stained or torn, still more were actually singed.

"Someone's tried to burn them."

"Someone's succeeded in burning quite a lot of them. I've ordered them as best I can. There are big gaps. I..." She shrugged. "I can't prove anything but I wonder if Carnot didn't try to destroy them when he had to leave the house for the asylum."

"Well, he was unbalanced," I admitted.

"Or else it was the only sane impulse he had left," Watts murmured with what I thought was unnecessary drama.

We pored over the papers in instalments over the next few months. They were handwritten in the shaky hand of the inmate and much that was legible remained disjoined, non sequitur after non sequitur tumbling out as Carnot's recollections churned.

There was a fair chunk of the earliest writing which was relatively coherent, and it appeared that the writer had begun the account in an attempt to exorcise the demons which were plaguing him. He refers to his companions – the same names as in those expenses claims – and specifically notes that only he was fully briefed as to what they were to find. Of that purpose, no complete picture existed in the fragments we retained. Certainly there had been some alarm bells ringing at the District Line regarding the works below Paddington, but Carnot's concerns do not seem to be solely financial or even structural – as evidenced by his choice of companions.

There was a passage that caught my attention because it recalled the words of Mr Leary. Carnot goes into some detail as to the labourers employed at the deep works by the Metropolitan Line. He says:

As reported they make a very curious, even unnerving spectacle. They are sullen and say nothing but, perhaps, single words relating to their tasks, instructions to one another, or confirmations of readiness. The uniformity of their work dress seems almost to have bled into their faces. Each has an identically stoic expression that scarcely changes, and indeed the features bearing those expressions have little variation as though all these slab-faced, slope-shouldered mechanicals were hired from the same remote and inbred village. Cooper kept watch from our hide last night and witnessed an accident where a sling of iron scaffolding came down on two men. He reported, in a shaken voice, that no warning was called by the others, though they must have seen what was to occur, nor did the killed men make any cry or sound as the weight descended on them, nor anyone apparently lament their passing. The remaining workers simply cleared away the wreckage, both organic and inorganic, and resumed work. No word was sent for police or doctors. The one advantage in this strangeness is that these men seem so focused and unobservant that slipping by them shall be easily accomplished.

I showed Watts notes of my conversation with Leary, which echoed this. True to form, she just laughed. "I read this as Carnot the high-falutin' twit being stuffy about the working class."

"We were right to be concerned," Carnot wrote, in one of the last segments where his script is easily legible.

Of the days he spent out of sight of the sun, little has survived; it is here his most ardent attempts at destruction were focused. What remained showed a hand growing increasingly disordered, sentences collapsing into occult notation. Watts had already collected surviving fragments, copied them and arranged them as best she could, with her own guesses as to what might be missing. Amanda Cecil features frequently, and there is the suggestion that she was in some way guiding them through whatever underworld they had uncovered. We also retained scraps of his speculation about the spaces they were exploring: that some were plainly recently dug but that there were lower chambers, occasionally glimpsed, which they were trying to access. At some point all mention of Ashworth and Grant-Sourborne simply ceases, with no surviving clue as to their fate.

As well as the Braille-like rubbings, two were three sketches preserved, each with a brittle brownish edge to show how close they had come to the fire. One seemed to show some manner of duct-work or piping, or perhaps bizarre Heath Robinsonesque machinery. The other was a sketch of some chamber, the floor and ceiling ribbed and veined with what looked almost like vines. A central column rising floor to ceiling, widest in its midsection, made Watts comment, "TARDIS control console, what do you think?"

I confessed I had never seen the popular television programme in question.

There was no immediate context for these images. Instead Carnot devotes his writing to some bizarre speculations by

Cecil concerning the workforce. She refers to servants able to carry great burdens, who knew no voices save their masters' – which, I suppose, is what all masters want of their servants. There is also talk about such servants being un-biddable, and these unnamed masters settling on lesser workers, imperfect and inadequate for the task. I speculated that this referred to the rise of socialism amongst the lower classes in the mid-nineteenth century. Watts was not convinced.

Cecil was also apparently a fan of the Symmes' Hollow Earth hypothesis. Carnot felt it important to record her ramblings about a connection to some kind of polar lost world, and talk of some growing horror at the South Pole inexplicably related to the works they were exploring. I wondered how much of her illicit expedition supplies Cecil had consumed by then.

The pride of Watts' restoration was a single complete page, maniacally scrawled, that must have come within the midst of the destroyed section. I imagined the deranged Carnot clawing up great handfuls of sheets towards the fire, and this one leaf falling free, unremarked. As best as we could decipher it, it read:

...says that when the masters first built their great house they gave their time to the upkeep and raising of servants who should do most anything for them and never answer them back save in their own voices. But the servants overthrew their masters and sit in their house and multiply and grow clever and call to the stars in their master's tones. She says the masters heard them long ago and knew they must stem them before their servants found the keys that might unlock all their masters' doors. But the masters could not call on such servants, for they were all in arms, and so...

It seemed curious that Carnot's concerns were for such a domestic matter.

The final section of the papers that Watts had ordered relates to an encounter Carnot claimed to have had with one of the subterranean labourers of the Metropolitan Line. By this time he is apparently alone, Cooper and Cecil lost or abandoned, and has been trying to find his way out of the tunnels. He speaks about finding his way back from "that sunless place" and also "the unlit city", which I nervously ascribed to London at night. He refers to finding some manner of hatch or opening leading back up – or that is my interpretation of his choice of the word – "portal." He writes: "The others had to take their chances," and that is the last reference we hear to any of his companions.

Then, as far as we could piece the narrative together, Carnot was heading for the surface when he ran into some of the Metropolitan workmen. What may have happened, precisely, is unclear. He refers to them in terms of abject horror, certainly, and then, in the next coherent section, he refers to the roof coming down on them all, Watts speculated about Grant-Souborne's explosives, but in truth we had no evidence either way.

This tunnel collapse was what crushed Carnot's legs and, if he is to be believed, killed several of the labourers. He was then left in the dark, in incredible pain, for an unknown period of time before the rescuers dug down to him.

According to Carnot's account, he was not alone down there. There is – almost – nothing in the rescuers' accounts to support this contention. Certainly Carnot's was the only body drawn from the collapse, living or dead.

However, Carnot – meaning the madman thinking back to a time when he must have been doubly mad with pain – writes that he was trapped down there with a labourer, one of those men he had so unkindly described at the outset. The man had plainly also been injured – though Carnot uses the word "damaged." When Carnot regained consciousness, he reports that his fellow casualty's condition had apparently made the man loquacious.

He plainly devoted considerable time to reproducing the feverish babbling of the trapped workman, although only four charred fragments survived, and I reproduce them here in full:

Spoke of needing to repair the line. Gathering mass at the pole. Feedback beyond safe parameters.

Repair before feedback floods the system. Asked what then. The end rushing down the branch line to the station until all their lines and termini were undone.

Left too long unmaintained. Can't get the staff, they say. The servants rose up, they say. What was made can't be unmade. Too much pressure. Can't repair the line until it's tapped.

And, the final fragment: *He has gone. He has finished speaking and gone back to what he came from. The servants only ever had the words of others, he said. The elder servants had the words of elder masters. The inferior servants have our own to speak back at us. He has no more words. He has gone back to what he came from. I lit my lamp and saw. God help me, I wish I had not. In the lamplight I saw him flowing.*

That is all we have of the final account of Gideon Carnot. Watts and I agreed that it must represent the ramblings of a fevered and pain-deranged mind, that the words originated in Carnot's own disordered brain, and that he had imagined his supposed companion. After reading through his harrowing ravings, that was a comforting enough conclusion, save for one thing. There is an account in the newspapers, a statement made by one of the rescuers. It quotes, *"Further efforts to find Mr Carnot's alleged companion uncovered only a workman's ruined and soiled clothing."*

The Descent

It was with Miss Watts that Lewis Yon first made contact.

For a few months my investigations had been curtailed by other professional duties. However, the peculiarities of the Paddington Station works were never that far from my mind. Of course Carnot had been deranged when he had written – and then partially erased – his account. He had been trapped, in agony and in darkness, for a long time. His companions – the existence of whom was amply evidenced – had not returned, perhaps claimed by some kindred collapse unreported in the newspapers. Such an experience is likely to impact on the most stable of psyches. Reading too much into such things is the province of an over-active imagination.

Of course, Watts was well furnished with such an imagination, and she and I remained in contact after our exhaustive perusal of the Carnot papers. I was aware that she continued to collect material for her book on the man, though it never seemed to near completion. At the same time the Yerkes book, which actually bore the expectations of a major US publisher, languished entirely untouched.

In that time she occasionally sent me details of incidents which seemed to echo Carnot. A lunatic had killed a workman on the Metropolitan line in 1893, crying for the deaths of "the servants" and expressing an ardent opinion that they must be kept down or they would rise up to destroy everyone. The culprit was a scion of an elevated family escaped from private care and so an understandable interpretation was put on his words.

In 1922, a well-known eccentric and a score of his followers had attempted to enter the Circle Line tunnel on foot claiming it contained a hidden underground route to the South Pole, and had to be forcibly prevented. In 1947, a shell-shocked soldier returned from the war was killed on the tracks at Paddington, going under a train as he wrestled with some manner of hatch between the rails. His last words had been "Release the pressure!"

"There surely can't be something about Paddington Station that drives people mad," I complained to Watts.

"Perhaps there's something about being mentally unbalanced that opens people up to Paddington Station?" she suggested.

Two days later she called me in some excitement and said

that she needed to meet with me. She had been contacted by one of the workmen – not some subcontractor, but one of the core workforce maintained by the shadowy main contractor. In short, one of the very men than Mr Leary had so complained of. This was Lewis Yon.

I'm not sure what I expected, going to meet him. My head was full of Carnot's report of slab-faced, taciturn brutes who could watch their colleagues get killed without shedding a tear. Yon was a big man, certainly: over six feet and broad shouldered. His eyes were a little skewed, the left wandering sometimes as though conducting a patrolling surveillance not shared by the right. He had a long face, the mouth downturned, the eyes melancholy. I was braced for some sense of the unnatural, perhaps, but the chief impression was that he was tired. He looked to be around fifty, his short-cut hair shot with grey and his large frame starting to hollow out. He smoked every moment he was outside and drank cup after cup of strong tea – at our expense – during our meeting, both habits like an addict who has built up a resistance to the drugs that once fuelled him.

"Heard of you two, asking questions," he told us. His tone wasn't friendly, and I wondered if Watts had brought me along as a security measure. If so, I reckoned Yon could break the two of us in half without us being able to do much about it. Thankfully, we were meeting publicly in a café – a greasy spoon of a place three streets away from Paddington.

"Heard from whom?" Watts asked him.

Yon shrugged. "People." He stared at us. "You were asking about the marks, before."

"That was me," I confirmed. "The dots and stars. You've seen them."

He nodded slowly. "Oh, seen them, all right. Whole walls of them, down below."

Watts and I exchanged wide-eyed glances. "Can you … show us them?" she asked.

"Gone now." The thought seemed to exhaust him still further. "Knocked down for the works."

I suspect Watts and I both knew the instant agony of the scholar, discovering that some piece of history is gone forever.

"Didn't need 'em any more," Yon added obscurely. "Been asking other questions, though, eh?" He glowered at Watts. "All sorts that's gone on, on the Line."

Watts nodded cautiously. We were both expecting a threat.

"Ain't right." Yon stared into his teacup and got the café owner to refill it. "Something ain't right with it."

"Could you be more specific?" I enquired.

He glared at me with one eye. "None of it makes sense. Pipes and wires and crawlspaces all shot through everywhere under the station. None of it connects. And sometimes when you go to dig, it's dug out for you, like they came and did it years back and covered it over and forgot. And you do forget. Day in, day out: go to the works and can't think what you did yesterday. There's only today's work. Nothing connects up."

We both bent closer to hear for his voice seemed to be drying up to a parched whisper, no matter how much tea he doused it with.

"What about the other contractors, the outside men?" I pressed him, thinking of Leary.

"Don't do the hard work. Do the above work, the stuff the public'll see. Not grubbing in the dirt like us, digging up who knows what, finding … finding spaces where there shouldn't be spaces. Don't get…"

"Don't get what?" Watts asked.

Yon turned haunted eyes on us. "We get sick," said his ghost of a voice. "Something wears you out, down there. Seen men just … give up. Don't care, the bosses. They're breaking us."

"The work's that hard?" she queried.

"Not the work, the *place*," Yon insisted. "Place is doing it to us."

"Well then I don't understand why you keep at it," Watts told him, baffled.

The look he gave us was sickly incredulous. "Can't *stop* the work," he hissed, as though confronted with some kind of blue collar sacrilege. "It's almost done."

"They told you that?"

"Must be almost done because *we're* almost done. Men I worked with for … for a time, a long time. Getting sick and you don't see 'em again, but no more coming in to replace them. They're wearing us out, all of us." As if for emphasis he hacked out a cough that sent a fat line of phlegm across the tabletop, veined with dark lines. "Won't be long now," he got out. "Can't be. S'why I came to you."

Watts and I exchanged another glance. "Why?" she asked.

"Because I want to see," Yon told us fiercely. "Know it's down there, and I'm going to find it, the heart of it, what it's all about. And I'll take you. Don't know how long I've got. Not feeling good these days, not since … time. Since a time ago. But someone should know what they've done to us. If you'll go."

*

We went; of course we went. Lewis Yon met us outside the station and guided us in. Paddington was still busy even at that hour, and we could hear the works over the traffic. He had hi-vis jackets and helmets for us, and a clipboard, to pose as some nebulous form of inspector. We tried for a brisk, assured stride as we followed after Yon into the station and then down into the construction site, and nobody glanced at us twice. We passed the bright livery of various subcontractors, and had brief glimpses of men working on the public-facing areas of the station, talking and swearing and laughing on occasion. None of this was what we had come to see, and Yon kept leading us downwards. Soon the sound of human voices was muffled, and only the clatter and clang of the inanimate could be heard from before us. The dimming of reassuring sounds put me uncomfortably in mind of being buried alive.

Then, turning a corner and clattering down a flight of scaffolding stairs, we were amongst Yon's fellows. There were a dozen of them in view, crammed into a space too small for them and each of them working diligently, laying wires or connecting ducting.

They all had a similarity with Yon, as though they all shared some uncertain ethnicity or distant family connection. It was not as marked as Carnot had written of, but certainly there was *something* about them. More, they all shared Yon's general impression of exhaustion. They regarded us with stony expressions on their long faces. Yon nodded, and they nodded back, and eyes flicked to us but nobody asked any questions.

"Where's Dave," Yon asked. For a long time they just stared at him, then one shook his head, and the rest did, too, as though silent negation was somehow contagious.

"Dave," Yon said, not forcefully, just in his hoarse used-up voice. "Said he would meet me. Was here when we did the … the work on … the other day."

More head shaking, and it became apparent that whatever malady was attacking these men had prevented this Dave from turning up for work.

Neither Watts nor I had thought about protection from whatever it was that was attacking Yon and the rest. Right then, seeing these worn-out, grey-faced men I thought of viruses and radioactivity and who knew what buried horrors they could have broken into. Tiredness, loss of memory, illness – there are plenty of perfectly mundane hazards capable of causing these symptoms.

But we were there. We wanted to see.

Before Yon led us further, one of the men took up a walkie-talkie from where it was clipped to his chest. I thought he was going to report us, but instead he just listened. What issued from it sounded to me like audio feedback, just a weird, ear-tweaking whistling and keening. I assumed there were words lost within it, for they had all got back to work the moment the transmission ended, sparing Watts and I the occasional forlorn glance.

Yon coughed at length, hacking up what seemed like a lung-full of discoloured mucus. At last he straightened up, wheezing, and beckoned us to follow him.

We were heading down again. He opened up a circular hatch like a manhole and just let himself drop through it, turning on his torch below. Watts and I joined him in its wan radiance.

The torch showed us a broad circular tunnel, far larger than I would have expected and set at a slant. This was what Leary had spoken of and, if he were to be believed, it must access the regular underground train network up above.

"This is for … repairs? So they can divert trains off the track?" I hazarded. I knew that London's subterranean rail lines suffer from only having single tracks, rather than having two, where one can be maintained while the other runs. "Mr Yon, what is this?"

We could only see the pale ghost of Yon's face in the darkness. "What they told us to build. What the instructions said."

And then he was heading off downslope and taking our only light with him, leaving us hurrying to keep up.

"Do you hear something?" Watts whispered. "Sort of … pipes, wind?"

Her ears were keener than mine. What I had noted was the breeze, though. Just as Leary had observed, there was a constant, gentle movement of the air, and it was washing past us – not out towards the open but deeper in. The temperature was dropping as well. The torchlight showed Watts' and my breaths pluming like silver mist whenever Yon stopped to let us catch up.

Soon after, we were out of the big tunnel, through a side hatch so flush I would never have seen it on my own. That led to a concrete-lined pipe set vertically in the earth, with corroded iron rungs as handholds. Yon slung his torch around his neck for the descent, and we followed him down with some trepidation. I tried to guess at our depth, but I reckoned we were already deeper than any tube works were supposed to be.

As we crept down, hand over hand, a grumbling murmur reached me: Yon, muttering to himself.

"Running out of time," he mumbled. "Not up to the job. Have to do our best, but so tired." And then, grotesquely, a scrap of song. "Show me the way to go home. I'm tired and I want to go to bed…"

"Did you go down here before, Mr Yon?" Watts called.

The ghoulish singing stopped, and then he grunted back, "No. Not in the plans." A thunderous bout of coughing rang along the pipe. "Know it's down there, though. Know that's where it's coming from, what wears us out. Want to see it just once. And you…"

"We'll see, and we'll get back," Watts promised, somewhat optimistically.

Then the light was abruptly fading, as Yon reached the bottom and stepped beyond the edge of the pipe. Soon enough we were all standing down there, in a tunnel low enough that I had to duck and Yon had to stoop low.

"Look," Watts hissed. On the ceiling were marks – Carnot's dots, as she had called them. There had obviously been quite a panel of them, but the intrusion of the pipe had obliterated much. "Barbarous," she tutted. "I don't understand how they just destroyed all of this."

"Didn't need them," Yon said. "Carried 'em out already."

"I say, what?" I asked him. "Carried out what?"

"Instructions." And then he was loping off down the tunnel, almost bent double. The walls around us were a mishmash of stone, concrete, tiling and close-packed rubble. None of it looked safe, and much of it looked as though the original builders had just taken whatever they had found lying around above, and thrown it together. We were constantly tripping and stumbling over the uneven floor, always falling behind Yon and his light. I had faint glimpses of more of the imprints, but no time or chance to study them.

Then Yon stopped. He had found a point where the dots and starfish had been overlaid with something else. It was a bas relief covering one side of the tunnel for a good twenty feet, too grand in scale for us to be able to see it properly, bounded as we were by the cramped walls.

"What is this doing down here? I thought we were below anywhere the public could go?" Watts asked, but Yon just stared.

It told a story in sequence, this relief, and I thought of the only people who had ever been down here, those slab-faced, plodding workers. The style was simple, powerful, almost Brutalist, although it must have predated the movement by decades. It showed men of two stripes engaged in a sequence of interactions: workers and managers; servants and masters. The servants were solid, broad-shouldered, iconic and identifiable in caps and overalls; the others were barrel-bodied, looking like the Fat Controller in tails and top hats. It was a Victorian conceit of class warfare. In the beginning the workers were tiny, spilling from the hands of their masters or crushed underfoot. They were everywhere, working in a city of bizarre perspective but familiar landmarks, a London designed by M.C. Escher. As the panels went on the labourers grew larger until at last they loomed over their employers, who were shown in attitudes of fear and distress. In the penultimate panel they workers had their bosses by the throat in a display of proletariat might and were casting them down. The last panel was the most affecting, because of the way it played with space and composition. The city was filled with the massive bodies of the workers, tessellated together in weird, uncomfortable positions as they strained against the very boundary of the bas relief.

Down here, men had worked silently and obediently since

the middle of the Nineteenth Century, sullen and silent and hard. But at some point some of them had broken from their labours to make this remarkable, hidden record.

"They were complaining about their lot," I mused.

But Watts was shaking her head, and her voice shook, too, when she said, "'But the servants overthrew their masters and sit in their house and multiply', remember? I think it's … a history. As best they could record it."

We pressed on, and soon afterwards Yon stopped again, his light this time unequal to the task of illuminating what he had stumbled into.

We had seen it before. I knew from her gasp that Watts must recognise it just as much as I. It was the cave from Carnot's drawing, with the swollen column at its heart. Carnot had been a poor artist, though. He had not done that outlandish central feature justice, and besides, there were other aspects of that chamber that no pen and paper could record. Even I had a bizarre sense of vertigo, stepping out past Yon into that toroid space beneath the earth. In truth it was perhaps twenty yards across, wall to wall, and no more than ten feet high, but I had the sense of a far greater distance hidden somewhere within it, a gulf that might reach out and swallow me. Watts saw more, God help her. Her mind was more open to that place than mine.

What I do remember was the quiet. That cave should have cast our voices back and forth in a cacophony of echoes, but instead the sound just receded away, as though there were distances in that place which the eye could not account for.

Lewis Yon was waiting by the entrance, his torch directed out like a weapon. His hand shook with it, and when the light touched his face, his skin glittered with sweat despite the icy chill that suffused the chamber. I called him over to examine the column, which I saw was ornately worked, but with the details lost in the interplay of shadows and the unsteady beam. He took three steps into the chamber and then halted, and I could hear him whisper to himself again, some fearful abjuration.

I thought we must be in some place very old indeed, some Stone-age temple buried beneath London for thousands of years. I took the column for an idol.

Its centre, the broadest part of it, was like a ridged barrel, with whorled and knotted mounds at regular spaces around its midsection, like coiled bunches of vines. At its base it spread out into a five-pointed pedestal, the ridges of which ran along the floor for more than the length of a man before ending in broad pads. At the column's top there was a similar, stubbier, pentadactyl arrangement, lumpy and uneven, and each finger of it ending in some reddish stone that gleamed where the light touched it. I had never seen anything about it: coming close I saw ice crusting its edges and angles. Then Watts' voice grabbed my attention.

"Chillet!" she exclaimed. "The spaces!" She was standing at the edge of the torchlight, reeling back from … nothing I could see. "There are doors here," she choked. "Doors to … to everywhere. Can you feel them?" She stumbled forwards, arms outstretched like someone playing blind man's buff.

"There's nothing!" I told her, but then Yon's voice came to me, thick with phlegm. "It's happening."

"What? What is?" I turned back to him.

His face had finally lost its stony quality. The torchlight surprised real expression there: bitter, grieving. "Been working this job for … time, a long time. Was there ever anything else than the work? Had a family, didn't I? Was a home, wasn't there? So why can't I remember them? Only the instructions and the work." The tears running down his face were dark and oily.

"Chillet!" Watts called again, and I looked round and saw her vanish. Before my eyes she just ceased to be there, stepping through an invisible gap into somewhere else entirely. Even as I cried out her name she was back again, staggering, her clothing stiff with frost. I ran over and dragged her back to the column, feeling her shiver uncontrollably. Her skin was blotchy with broken blood vessels and the whites of her eyes were red. I thought of Carnot and his portals. "The others will have to take their chances," he had written, and I wondered just what awful distance from home they had all found themselves, for him to pen those words.

"What happened?" I asked her, because I couldn't make myself say, *Where did you go?*

"The city…" she said, shuddering. "The stars…" She jumped up suddenly, then had to lean on me or fall. "The breeze, Chillet. I've seen where it's going to."

"Workers," slurred out Yon's voice. "All we were." He took another step towards the column, which had become the focus of his world. "The old lot went wrong, so they need us to fix it all, and then what?" His shout echoed about the chamber, and abruptly the breeze was strengthening, the air beginning to rush past us and tug at our clothes. My wide eyes raked the room but still there was nowhere that sucking wind could be *going*. Nowhere except that unseen nowhere which Watts had briefly vanished into. My ears were filled with the howling of the air through miles of passageways as it was ripped past us and into oblivion. I held onto Watts, and then we both clung to the column, the only fixed point we had.

"Listen!" she shouted. "Do you hear it now?"

And I did. Or it was the wind keening through ducts and vents and funnelling down to us there, but it seemed like flutes and pipes in complex interplay. It seemed like language.

"Repairmen?" Yon demanded of the carven column, or of us, or the universe. "That's all we are? What about when the repairs are done? When we've fixed the damage the others did? What about *us*?"

Watts put her mouth to my ear and quoted, "The servants overthrew their masters and sit in their house."

And multiply and grow clever, I completed Carnot's words in my head. "But what master? And Yon…"

Under my touch, the frost-crusted surface of the column shifted, caked dust and ice cracking and sloughing from it. I looked up from where we crouched, and saw one of the carved clutches of vines convulse and then reach out, branching and branching fractally, flaking away and crumbling even as it did so. That fluting sound – that *voice* – was clear now, shrieking over the wind.

"You bastard!" Yon choked out. "You're all the same!" His torch dropped to the ground and then skittered rapidly away from him on its way to infinity. Watts lunged for it and snagged its strap with a fingertip, just enough to haul it in and leave us its light. A moment later the ground shook, and I felt one of the column's pedestal ridges ripple beneath me, throwing us both off.

Watts turned the torch on Yon. He was staring at the column as it flexed and shuddered into animation after who knew how many aeons of slow contemplation and design. His expression was not one of fear or wonder but of the aggrieved working man exploited by his boss. His face was discoloured and flaccid; inky fluid ran from his nose and eyes and trailed in strings from the corners of his mouth. As we watched, some horrible dissolution took place within his chest so that the right half of him slumped and sagged without involving the left. His hands fumbled stickily, the fingers bending and squashing as he tried to light a final cigarette.

With a gargle of grief and betrayal, Lewis Yon began to come apart. *I saw him flowing*, Carnot had written, and we saw the same: the piecemeal autolysis of the human form into a thick black ichor. His expression lasted longer than it had any right to, even when the component pieces of it were floating like froth on the bulging, oozing effluent into which he was breaking down.

The column shifted and moved, the five toes of its base twisting and knotting at the floor for purchase, the lumpy head breaking free of the ceiling. The torchlight caught those gleaming red stones and they stared back at us from an unthinkable distance of space and time and species. One of the writhing dendritic clumps of tendrils that ringed its midsection reached out – not to us, but towards the collapsing thing that had been Yon.

"Their old servants rose up," Watts said. "So their new ones had a best before date." Her eyes were wild; she almost seemed to be laughing. Perhaps she was mad but, if so, it was the right place for madness.

The chamber around us fell away. The walls were still there, but the doors that Watts had felt were gaping wide. I could not see them. They spoke to a sense I had never known before, and one I would have plucked out if I could. I felt we were falling into the abyss even as we crouched there, feeble vertebrates with our bellies to the stone. Above us, the branching whips of the *thing* waved, beckoning, adjusting, controlling … *what?*

"It's coming!" Watts cried out.

In that instant, I felt it too. One of the yawning gulfs that had opened sightlessly around us was not empty – was full, overfull even. Now it had been opened, something was rushing towards us. The wind, which had been rushing through the chamber towards nowhere, was suddenly being pushed back at us, stinking and hideous, forced out just like the air rushes from a tunnel before the train arrives.

"The … workers…" Horribly, the gurgling, sloshing voice was still recognisable as Yon's.

The *thing* that we had taken for a column had gone still, not dead but waiting. Some of its tentacular limbs had broken away, and I could see thick flakes of its leathery integument peeling away from its barrel of a body. There was nothing in its stance that could be read by the human eye, but when it reached out and touched the spreading pool that had been Yon, I told myself I saw a kindred weariness, magnified over a time and a distance I could not conceive. Where were the mighty masters who had set all this in motion? What if this vegetable *thing* they had left to guide their endeavours was no more than a labourer itself, a lonely repairman that had waited forever and done terrible things, and in the end just for a job that needed doing.

We both heard the thunderous rush of something weighty and monstrous coming towards us with the speed and force of a locomotive, hurling itself down suddenly open passageways from where it had been pent up. Was there a city where it came from, a worker's paradise? Not in any way we poor apes could comprehend. We heard its cry as it came close: a weird echo of that whistling, fluting call. *They had no voices save their masters'*.

We braced ourselves in the shadow of the branch-limbed thing as the room shook around us, and I had a blurred glimpse of something that was at once fluid and shaped into many forms. It foamed and seethed, but somehow trapped *within* the walls of the cave, pushing and prying just beneath the surface and driven by its own pressure to surge onwards. We felt it pass, shaking the chamber so that the walls cracked and dust sheeted down on us in a whirling blizzard. A great gate had been opened to that place where the servants had grown and swelled until they filled it, and now the pressure was tapped – tapped into the tunnels leading up into the Circle Line.

I found myself giggling hysterically and could not stop. "The train now arriving at Paddington Station!" I cried out. There would be homeward bound partiers, night-shift workers, late travellers trying to get across London. They would be lining the platform, inching past the yellow stripe as they felt the vibration of something coming from the tunnel. They would feel the air ghost into motion, but what the darkness vomited forth would not be what they sought. The thought was so horrible, such an innocuous combination of images, that I laughed and laughed until I shook.

Watts dragged me out of there. Watts got me along the

tunnels even as the cracks crazed their way along the walls, obliterating Carnot's dots, shattering the mural of the workers' uprising. They who carved that tableau had made the revolting servants like themselves. They had not realised it was the other way around: that their claim to humanity was no more than a thin skin over a well of darkness, and that in their last moments they would return to the same substance that those elder servants knew.

What happened to the vegetal *thing*, the repairman, I cannot say. Perhaps it was crushed in the collapse; perhaps it fled through one of those unseen portals that Watts could sense and I could not. Perhaps it is still down there, as betrayed by its masters as its servants were betrayed in turn. I don't know – I will never now – whether in its buried sojourn it detected our scratchings and pickings at the earth, and found a way to weave its own plans into ours, or whether we were its tools from the start, and all the lines of the underground were just tendrils of its grander design. I don't know if everything I ever professed to be an expert in has been a lie.

But whatever it wrought, it wrought well, for the surging tide of corrosive, malleable life that vomited out into the Circle Line did not burst its bounds, but simply surged and surged, chasing its own tail and howling out in its second-hand voices. And nobody understood what had happened, but people talked about terrorists and weapons of mass destruction, and they concreted over every access point to the Circle Line. And only Watts and I know, and we do not speak of these things, not yet, not now, perhaps never. Carnot was right to burn his notes.

But I *do* know and, although I have given up my study and my profession, I cannot sever myself from the knowledge. So sometimes I go down to Edgware Road, one stop off Paddington, and I put my ear to the concrete and listen. And I can hear them above the rumble of constant heavy motion, all those late night travellers. I can hear their cries and screams, their last words, their suddenly interrupted phone calls. Because the servants have no words but those that are given to them, and where once they had their masters' fluting calls, now they have ours.

Devo Nodenti

Keris McDonald

Peggy awakes, as usual, with Eustace squatting on her chest. For a moment the panic of her tangled dreams – Laurel had tried to phone but she hadn't picked up in time; she was trying to ring back but she kept getting the telephone number wrong, her fingers stabbing the keys over and over, back to the start, do it again, seven *eight* zero – for a moment that panic stays with her. She can't breathe. She looks up into Eustace's non-face, looming down over hers as if he's trying to kiss her, and she can't raise her hands to fend him off or even draw breath enough to scream.

No. No! Relax! Just give it a second! Hands first!

Her fingers, which have been pinned to the sheets by paralysis until now, wake at last and twitch. They're always the first. Then a heave of her ribcage. She sucks in breath.

Eustace tilts his head, black horns silhouetted against the pale bedroom ceiling. One might, if one chooses, read disappointment into that motion. His faceless face withdraws.

"Get off me," Peggy whispers.

Deferential as ever, he flips backward off her torso and hangs upside down in the corner of the room like a gigantic bat, his long boneless fingers and toes clutching the plaster cornice. He's much lighter than his black and rubbery bulk might suggest, as she knows only too well. He never crushes her chest when he sits on her, after all, though she does ache all over now as she sits up. Just like she aches every morning.

The bed sheets are soaked with sweat. She sleeps naked despite her respectable age, just because she hates the feeling of a clammy nightie clinging to her. Peggy gets up slowly, finds her slippers and dressing gown, then pulls all the bedding back to give it a chance to air. Eustace flicks out his long, wickedly barbed tail, and begins to trace the tip along the many grooves and lines in his skin. She'd call it preening, if he were a bird. His oil-black form looks like it's been skinned to reveal the intricate musculature, or maybe built from chopped up car tyres. Yes, she saw an exhibition of tyre-art once, and it made her nod sourly with recognition.

"I expect you had a good night?" Peggy mutters as she tries to straighten her back. "Ate well, I'm guessing? Well, I'm glad at least one of us enjoyed it."

Eustace doesn't answer, of course. He has no mouth to speak with. No facial features at all.

Peggy decided years ago that what he sustains himself on is delta waves. That's why she never gets any proper sleep – the deep dreamless healing sleep she craves. All she's known for decades is the riotous circus of REM. Frustration dreams, confused memories, nightmares, circular OCD repetitions. She almost always wakes feeling completely worn out. Right now her eyes are as dry as if she's spent the night staring into the darkness.

Moving stiffly to the window – she's still too young to hobble, damn it – she pulls back the curtains and lets light spill into the bedroom. Outside, the September morning is bright and sunny. Yellow leaves splotch her tiny patch of front lawn. She'll rake them up today, she tells herself, if the arthritis in her hands is co-operative.

When she turns back into the room there's no sign of Eustace. He's never seen in direct daylight, and for many years Peggy thought that sunlight drove him away. Now though, she's come to suspect that he's still there, always there … just not visible.

He is, after all, more in her head than anywhere else.

As she stands in the shower, with her eyes closed against

the flow and the prick of shampoo, Peggy can see Eustace quite clearly in her mind's eye, lying couchant on the pink bathroom mat. He – well, *it*; he has sex organs no more than he has a face, but Peggy has given him a name and with the name has come some sort of spurious gender – even resembles a great dog sometimes, if he tilts his head back to disguise the curve of his horns against his bulk, and he moves on all fours as is his preference. His body is so dark and gnarled and cartilaginous that it's hard to make out his true outline. Only when he unfurls his wings do you realise that what you'd taken for a muscular hunched back was nothing but membranous skin, and see for the first time how skeletal he is, how barbed and demonic.

She'd had some vague idea that a name might help make him less horrible, or at least more bearable. Is that so weird? Some people give their tumours names, she's heard.

It's easier if she thinks of him as dog. A big silent dog that follows her around from room to room. Faithful, in his way.

Cave canem, she thinks, remembering the black-and-white photograph of the little statuette of the hound on the cover of the paper she'd held out, fifty years ago, to Rory DeAngelo.

*

"What the hell is this?" she asked.

"Oh, you've got a copy?" He smiled as he glanced at the title under the University's coat of arms: Report on the Second Excavation of the Prehistoric, Roman and Post-Roman site in Lydney Park, Gloucestershire. *That title was a direct nod to the original Wheeler excavation report of 1932; a little archaeological joke. "It looks splendid, doesn't it? The Society of Antiquaries are printing a précis next month."*

"It looks splendid for you*, Rory. Where the hell's my name in it? I've read every damn word, and I don't get a mention."*

He cocked an eyebrow, bemused. "Well, I did write the paper. Of course I'm the one credited." His silver hair managed to be perfectly coiffed, even in the midst of a wet dig on a hill overlooking the River Severn.

"Huh? I was the one who sat up at night and typed up every note!"

"Yes, you put in a great deal of the leg-work. I'm very grateful."

"I was the one who found the votive statue." She flicked the photograph with nails that had dark rinds of dirt engrained so deep under them that no amount of hand-washing under the cold tap of the community hall would ever get it out. "I was the one who first suggested to you that we were looking at a bloody temple abaton." She was trying to keep the rage out of her voice, but it wasn't working. "Why don't I get credit?"

"Peggy, darling, you will." He looked pained by what was clearly a childish display of temper – he'd never liked displays of emotion, after all. "All in good time. You're only twenty-one, and I'm sure you have a splendid career ahead of you, but let's face facts. Who's going to take any notice of a girl postgrad trying to suggest the existence of a hitherto-unsuspected cultic practice here in Britain? You need my name. My experience. My gravitas."

"I need the credit, for my work and my ideas!"

"Don't worry. I'll put in an excellent word for you for your next position. I'm on your side, Peggy, and you need that in this field."

"You…" Her mouth flapped.

"I think you forget how competitive archaeology is as a study, and how important word of mouth is in establishing your reputation. There are so many bright-eyed young girl-archaeologists out there, just desperate for the chances you've been offered. The recommendation of your Professor is gold-dust at this stage, Peggy." He smiled benignly. "Now let's not quarrel over trivial matters. There's so much work that's still to be done. We only have a week left on this dig, remember."

Brushing a little dust off his knee, he rose and strolled out of the hut. Somehow he always looked immaculate, even when wearing overalls. Even when everyone around him was covered in mud. Peggy, hardly remembering to breathe, watched him stroll across to the principal trench in the central shrine, where the undergrads were on their knees scraping the mud with trowels. The watery sunlight turned his silver hair to a halo.

She watched Alice, a first-year student, look up as Professor DeAngelo paused to squat at the lip of the trench and talk to her. She held up a tray of her finds – Peggy knew exactly what sort of thing was being found here: Romano-British pottery and coins, bronze pins, maybe a little lead petition scroll begging the aid of the local god Nodens – and the look of pleasure on Alice's young and eager face as she gazed up at the handsome older man was visible even from here.

*

In the shower, Peggy opens her eyes.

Damn him. That creepy cradle-snatching bastard. That thieving son of a bitch.

No, she hasn't forgiven. Not even after all these years.

If she forgives him, she'll have to accept the guilt that she's held off at arm's length for five decades.

Wrapping herself in a towel, she sits upon the toilet lid to comb out her wet hair and muster her strength. Everything takes so long these days, even getting dressed. Between her arthritis and her exhaustion, each step in the process is a hurdle to be clambered. What she really wants to do is make a cup of tea and go back to bed for the day, but she can't let herself off that easily. Nigel is due to visit later on with wife and children in tow, so she has to be ready. She enjoys seeing her only grandson, though she can't find quite the same enthusiasm for the three children, each of whom takes it in turn to be variously sulky, hyperactive, and riddled with germs. At her age, the prospect of catching even a cold is daunting.

Searching for her vitamin C tablets, Peggy pauses with the bathroom cabinet open, looking at the bottles of pills within – stock-piled from decades when Valium and sleeping tablets were handed out like sweeties. Not that they've ever brought her the true unconsciousness and rest she craves, just longer nights of seething frantic visions.

She picks up a brown glass bottle and shakes it gently, listening to the rattle within. *Easy*, she thinks. *It would be so easy.* "But in that sleep of death, what dreams may come?" she quotes out loud. "Aye, there's the rub. Isn't that right, Eustace?"

At the corner of her vision, Eustace twists his boneless neck quizzically to invert his head altogether. He's companionship of a sort, she tells herself, and isn't that something? At least he responds to her voice, and sometimes she can convince herself that he understands the words. Plenty of people her age are all on their own, with only memories for company.

*

Too wound up to sleep that night, fifty years ago, she wandered out among the low walls of the Lydney Park excavation while everyone else went back to their ex-army cots in the village hall. The stars were muted behind high and hazy cloud, but the moon was full enough to cast black shadows from the trench walls. All was silent. In the valley below the bluff, the broad slick of the Severn was a pale wedge driven like a spearhead into Britain's guts.

Back in the fourth century, she brooded, when the stone temple was built over the old mines to replace whatever rustic fane had served the native Britons, this must have been a magical place. The uncanny wave of the Severn Bore had processed up the face of the river twice a day. The earth had yielded iron ore, an extraordinary treasure wrestled out of those dangerous low tunnels. The old gods had still lurked in the woods, and joined with the new Roman deities to create strange hybrids.

Nodens, now, he was amongst the strangest. Archaeologists couldn't agree, even now, what he'd been a god of. The Romans identified him with Mars, with Neptune, with Silvanus, with Mercury – which suggested everything from warfare to sailing, forestry to the afterlife. Nineteenth century scholars had glossed his name as Lord of the Deeps, *or* Lord of the Abyss. *A young Professor Tolkien – yes, that one – had analysed it and suggested he was cognate with the later Irish god-hero Nuada of the Silver Hand and the Welsh Nudd, and that it meant* snarer, catcher *or* hunter. *The hard archaeological evidence hinted at an oceanic nature – but also at a strong connection with dogs, which might mean hunting or might mean healing, given the symbolism of the time. A curse tablet* found here in the 1880s had aimed at bringing back and avenging a stolen gold ring. And that long row of little cells right there, at the back of the main temple – that was the building Peggy had identified with the famous Abaton of the medicine god Asclepius. A place for patients or petitioners to be put into a drugged sleep – enkoimesis – for the purpose of incubating a visionary encounter with their god.

Peggy wished bitterly then that she could have a dream that would lay out the solution to all her problems.

"Bastard," she said under her breath, sitting down on a low wall and leaning back against a stone. It felt cold through her canvas trousers but she didn't care. She'd had a pint of Guinness at the pub – all she could stomach of both the fluid and the company of her fellow diggers – and now she felt heavy-legged and queasy. Tears burned the backs of her eyes. Her anger was a hot stone buried under her ribs. If she'd had a sheet of lead – and any faith at all in dead gods – she could have quite happily cursed DeAngelo.

"Devo Nodenti Silvianus anilum perdedit demediam partem donavit Nodenti. Inter quibus nomen Seniciani nollis petmittas sanitatem donec perferat usque templum Nodentis," she rattled off under her breath. She knew the inscription by heart. Looking up at the blurred stars, she mulled over the incontrovertible truth that neither Silvianus' loss nor hers mattered a jot to them.

*

Sitting in her kitchen with a slice of buttered toast and the mug of tea she's been longing for since waking, Peggy catches herself wondering why these memories are coming back to her today. It must be something she dreamt about last night, she thinks. Something about the dig, so that all the old scab is picked off and the raw memories exposed to the air again. It's not as if they are ever far from her consciousness – Eustace is an ever-present reminder of that night in 1965 and all it led to – but she does try not to brood. What good does it do, after all? She made her bargain and she's paid the price ever since.

As if hearing his name spoken, Eustace drops down from the central light-fitting he's been clinging to and crawls across the floor to settle in the shadows under the kitchen table. If she moves her foot slightly she could touch him, she realises, and she wonders what that would feel like. She feels his weight on her chest nightly, but has never voluntarily touched that skin. It's slightly sheened, as if oily, and she imagines he'll feel cold. He's a creature of the underworld, after all. He even smells like a damp coal bunker.

*

She looked up suddenly among the ruins of Lydney Temple, as if startled – though she'd seen nothing, heard nothing – and there in front of her, set in the grass, was a door. There had never been any question that she was still awake. Obviously she was dreaming; she recognised the door. It belonged in the street next to her parents' end-terrace house in Newcastle-upon-Tyne.

Every other house in that steep street had a back yard with a coal bunker next to the outside toilet, both built of brick. Theirs however had a hatch in the street, covered by heavy wooden doors, that allowed the coalman to drop the coal straight down into their cellar. Her Da thought that maybe their place had once been a pub, and probably this was the delivery entrance for beer barrels. If so it had come down in the world, because they kept their coal down there now and no beer. Peggy had always been nervous of that cellar as a child – a filthy place her Ma hated her brothers and her playing in – and positively scared of the hatch, which she always felt might give way under her feet and drop her into the darkness. Of course, that meant she had to try standing on it every day after school.

Now that hatch – she recognised the vestiges of faded green paint – stood there hundreds of miles from home in a Roman ruin on a hilltop in the West Country, one leaf open and leaning back. A faint glow shone up from within. It looked like an invitation.

Rising, she approached the drop. Not a coal-hole, as she'd anticipated. No, the open door revealed a spiral staircase of polished wood descending vertically into the earth. The walls of the shaft were covered in shelves full of books, and on the first step sat a lamp, an old-style miner's lamp like her Da used to use when she was little. That was the main source of the illumination, though there was faint shine on the shelf edges that suggested a glow from far below.

Picking up the lamp, Peggy began her descent. The staircase coiled round, lapping itself, her footfalls clunking on the wooden treads. She glanced at the books, thinking that they seemed familiar; she saw bright modern paperbacks, the kind she liked to read on the train, and bound copies of archaeological journals such as she consulted in the university department. Then a set of worn Dickens hardbacks like her Ma kept in the front parlour – no, not like, identical to, *even down to the torn cloth spine on* A Christmas Carol *that was her fault – although she couldn't actually read the faded lettering on the spines; it seemed all mixed up somehow. A Margaret Murray she recalled borrowing from the local library. Yes, lots of library books with inked shelf-numbers. And now, further down, fifty steps down, children's books she had long forgotten but which now stood out like the faces of old friends in a crowd. She recognised the pictures on the covers even though the letters danced out of focus.* Alice in Wonderland *– of course. What could be more appropriate? Enid Blyton;* The Princess and the Goblin; *a rare, treasured golden-era* Perrault's Fairy Tales *that her Ma had read to her at night.*

Peggy pulled this last one out of its shelf and tried to flick through, but although the colour plates were there just as she remembered, the text was blurred beyond legibility. Of course, *she told herself.* You can't ever read in dreams.

She replaced it carefully in its slot, because the blackness at the back of the shelf – and the cold draught blowing out of that hole – was oddly unnerving.

Then she took the last turn of the stairs, and that warm glow that had been growing all through her descent, rendering the lamp more and more unnecessary, made her blink.

Seventy, *she said to herself, not even sure why she'd been counting. She was standing in a broad cavern with walls of rough-hewn rock and a floor of marble so highly polished that for a moment she thought it was glass. In the centre of the floor was well-head from which a column of flame rose, twisting like a tornado. The fire flickered from red to yellow to violet as it burned, and it took a few seconds for her eyes to adjust.*

From either side behind the flame stepped two tall men. They were dressed in tunics of white linen, with broad pectoral collars of blue beads. Both sported long stiff beards dyed blue, both had their heads shaved bald and their eyes heavily outlined in kohl. Peggy had never seen men wearing eyeliner before, at least not outside a historical illustration, and she found either their makeup or something else about them deeply disconcerting.

Egyptian, *she guessed.* Or Roman. *She couldn't tell.* Romano-Egyptian priests. What is this?

"Peggy Anne Connings," said the first man, looking her up and down as he frowned.

"What are you doing here, child?" asked the second.

"I … er … I don't know," she muttered. She'd spotted what it was about them that she didn't like. The column of flame threw their shadows up the walls of the cavern, making them dance and loom. But the heads of those shadows did not match the heads that cast them. They weren't shaven. They weren't even human.

"What did you come here for?"

She bit her lip, trying not to stare at the shadows. His black eyes bored into hers and he was so close now that she could see herself reflected in them; that silly little backstreet girl with her grammar-school education and her scholarship grant and her fake aspirational accent. The girl who'd let herself be charmed and used and then dropped like an empty chip paper. The girl who'd reached out for the ladder up and found it snatched from her reach.

"Justice," she said, licking her dry lips. "I came here for justice."

*

"Just us!" Nigel cries merrily as he opens the front door. "Hello Gran!"

Peggy happily accepts their greetings, as the kids push into the house and run round checking out the dusty collection of weird stuff – Malaysian masks, Burmese puppets, anthropomorphic Peruvian pots – that makes visiting the old lady bearable. Nigel looks jolly and Andrea looks mildly harassed, as ever. For years Peggy thought he'd never marry – it wasn't good for a boy to be brought up by his grandmother no matter how hard she tried, she'd berated herself – but he's somehow pulled it off at the final moment. He seems to thrive on fatherhood, she is relieved to see.

She has no worries about anyone spotting Eustace. He's only a figment of her imagination, after all, so they never notice him. As they all settle down for a drink and a chat, he drapes himself across the top of the big dresser as if watching with his non-eyes. His long and wickedly spined tail hangs down like a cat's, twitching gently.

After a cup of tea, Nigel loads Peggy and the children into the car and takes them out to the shops, while Andrea stays behind to give the house a bit of a clean – an arrangement that suits everyone. Gaps in the buildings give them glimpses as they drive of the Clifton Suspension Bridge over the Avon gorge, and the brick towers and graceful Victorian span catch the children's attention.

"What's that? What's that?"

"Can we drive over it, Dad?"

"No," says Nigel firmly, casting Peggy a worried look.

"She told me she could fly, in her dreams," Peggy murmurs.

They spend an hour looking at home furnishings and toys in the big warehouse store, where Peggy buys birthday cards and a new washing-up bowl. Then they eat lunch in a burger bar chosen by the children, much to Nigel's embarrassment.

"It's fine, Nigel dear. Don't worry," Peggy reassures him for at least the third time. "I don't mind where we eat." It isn't like she has much appetite these days, anyway.

She steals a glance around the café, wondering if Eustace has come out with them. It's much harder to see him outside the familiar confines of home, she's discovered, but he's still there.

"I drawed you a picture, Granny," announces Bo, the youngest great-grandchild, hard at work with the free kids' meal crayons.

"That's lovely." She holds the paper at arm's length,

squinting at the stick figure next to the black scribble. "Who is that?"

"That's you," he says, "and that's your doggy."

"Gran doesn't have a dog," Nigel says when she doesn't answer.

"I dreamed she had one."

"You know," says Peggy, "there's a theory that we are all dreaming, all the time. The mind is in a constant state of visualisation, even when awake, but the brain overrides these hallucinations and doesn't let the consciousness register them. Unless you take LSD or are totally exhausted or something, of course." She blinks and then realises that everyone is staring at her, confused.

*

The first priest lifted his painted brows and stepped back as if this was no longer his responsibility. The second spread his hands.

"Choose a door then."

There were two tall doors on the right-hand side of the cavern. Set into the rough rock, they were themselves exquisite works of pointed Gothic art, carved and traced with abstract designs. Peggy, a little warily, walked closer. One door was made of pure white ivory, its swirling inlay all of gold. The other door was more ominous, a yellow-brown with even darker mottled patches, and its filigree inlay looked like wrought iron.

I know these. Virgil, isn't it? *The Aeneid*? The Gate of Horn, through which true dreams pass, and the Gate of Ivory, which sends out deceptive ones.

There was another gate, on the far side of the cavern, but that had no door and she could see that it was another stairway, leading downward. She didn't like the look of that one at all.

"This," she said, laying her hand on the door of horn. It swung open without resistance.

She was standing on a cliff edge. Whether she was still underground it was hard to tell, but the cavern roof – if it existed – was lost in a pale grey haze in which black birds flocked and wheeled.

The cliff dropped away in a tangle of jagged black rocks, and washing against those rocks, far below her feet, was a great sea of clouds. She watched the waves of vapour roll in and explode against the cliff-face, sending up showers of spray that splashed against her face with no sensation of wet at all, but dry as rice. There was a faint pattering as the spume fell back and drained from the inky stone.

All around her feet the rocks were patched with silvery grit. Pearls, she realised – seed pearls flung up from the deeps by the cumulonimbus surf. Mixed among them were paler specks that turned out, when she scooped them in her hand, to be babies' teeth.

Of course, she told herself. Nodens was no god of the ocean or the forest, not even of death, though all those things were metaphors for his domain. The Great Abyss was the wilderness inside our heads – the unknown and unknowable depths of the subconscious. The land of dreams and terrors and lost memories. He was god of something that had no material existence, god of nothing at all. Yet that no-thing shaped us and made us and drove us. It was the place all our gods and our selves came from. He was a tiny insignificant god, and at exactly the same time he was Deo Maximus.

After all, the things that truly mattered were those that existed only inside our heads. Love and loss and pain. Everything in the real world was just the shuffling of atoms.

Another wave spat foam high, and the birds circling overhead caught her attention on the upward glance. They weren't rooks after all, though they were just as black. Bats, perhaps? Their dusky wings looked translucent. There were thousands of them, and they were flying closer now.

No, not bats. Legs too long, and tails like whips. Demons, like in some Italian fresco depiction of the falling angels.

Shuddering, Peggy spun round – and there louring behind her waited Nodens.

Grey was her first impression. Grey and awful. Its long hair was grey, exactly the same colour as its draping robes, and covered its face so fully that she could only guess the shape of the head beneath, and imagine the hollows of the eyes watching her.

At its feet lay the carcass of a dolphin, gutted to expose its pink entrails and the silver spill of the fish that had formed its last meal. Crabs were feasting on both.

"What do you want, Peggy?" Nodens' voice was a whisper, a trickle of shale fragments on a barren scree slope.

Then she realised that the hair, just like the silks, was nothing more than cobweb, layer upon layer of the stuff, thickly coated in dust. Those drapes were neither hair nor robes, and the true form of that hunched and shrouded figure was something she suddenly did not want to descry.

For a moment she wavered, wondering whether she could flee past it back to the safety of the gate. But she couldn't see the portal from this side, just a towering cliff-face reaching up to the maybe-sky. And she could feel the watching demons overhead; her scalp crawled at the thought.

"Professor DeAngelo," she said, clearing her throat. "He's a thief and a liar and he picks on young girls who don't know any better." She felt that the words were coming out wrong, but she had to explain.

"What do you come to ask of me?"

"He hurt me. So I want him hurt." She sucked her dry lips. "He has to be stopped, or he'll just go on and do it again."

Nodens tilted its head. There was something weird about her vision, she thought – she could not tell if the figure was human-sized and close, or further away and unspeakably vast. It seemed to change every time she tried to focus.

"I will do that. If you are willing to pay the price."

"What's the price?"

"Peace of mind." That desiccated voice fluttered and sank, as if spoken down a tube miles off. "You will always remember what you did, and you will never sleep easy."

"I can live with that," she answered, drawing herself up.

"You will have to, for many years. Now go home."

*

"We should go home now," says Nigel, gathering up Bo's crayons. "I promised to fix that porch light today, didn't I?"

They drive back, and Nigel fixes the back porch light while

the kids run round the overgrown garden – "This is really too much for you now Gran, you should hire someone to take those shrubs out and put in a nice patio" – and Andrea hangs the laundry out. They've brought along a DVD of some cartoon show Peggy doesn't recognise, which keeps the kids quiet for an hour while Nigel replaces the batteries in the remotes and does a second load of laundry, and Andrea pops out with the car to do a supermarket shop and stock up all the cupboards.

Peggy is grateful for their kindness, but exhausted. She finds herself wanting to sit in her armchair in front of an old movie, with just Eustace crouched on the rug or hanging in the corner of the room for company. The noises of life and youth are too much these days. Shrieking and squabbling voices make her head spin.

Had she misheard Nodens, she sometimes wonders wryly. Had he said *peace of mind* or *a piece of your mind*?

"I've got something to show you, Gran," Nigel tells her with a smile. He's holding out his laptop computer like a silver tray. "Take a look at this."

Peggy has never bothered with owning a computer, though she does have a smartphone which she'd been bought for Christmas and barely uses. She sits with Nigel at the kitchen table and watches with what she hopes is proper enthusiasm as he opens up browser windows.

"This is Wikipedia," he tells her. "Do you know what that is?"

She shakes her head.

"It's an online encyclopaedia. There are literally millions of articles on every subject you can imagine here, in hundreds of languages. Anyone can access it, and anyone can contribute to it... Well, sort of. You have to prove you know your stuff, and cite sources and back up your arguments. But it means there's not just a handful of people telling us what we should think about a subject. There are millions of people all over the world sharing their knowledge. The *Encyclopaedia Britannica's* dead in the water, Gran – this is the future of information sharing. Now, look at this."

He clicks on a star. A new page opens, headed *Lydney Park Excavations*. It's divided into several subsections – the Mortimer Wheeler dig in the 1920s, the Casey et al excavation in 1980-81 – and between them, to Peggy's alarm, a couple of paragraphs on the DeAngelo digs in 1963-5.

She doesn't want to look.

"Is the text big enough for you, Gran?" Nigel asks, doing something that makes the screen zoom in. She has no excuse. She scans the first few sentences and then comes across one that makes her heart cram into her mouth:

DeAngelo's postgraduate assistant, Peggy Connings, was the first to identify the range of buildings behind the temple as an incubation *(Greek:* abaton*), a place for guests seeking divinatory or healing dreams.*

"Oh," she says. She can feel her pulse racing. "Really?"

"Yep. Everyone can see it now, Gran. Everyone in the world."

"That's…" She passes her hand over her face. "My goodness. That's wonderful."

"About time, eh?" He looks so pleased with himself.

Peggy's gaze slips back to the text. She reads everything twice, including the last lines:

The excavation concluded in tragedy in September 1965 with the discovery of Professor DeAngelo's body in the nearby River Severn. A verdict of suicide was recorded.

*

She woke quite suddenly, without having to retrace her steps up from her dream. An owl was hooting in the trees. Feeling foolish – as well as damp and stiff and chilled – Peggy returned down the moonlit track to the park gate and then the village hall. The remnant of her dream clung to her like a cobweb on her face; no matter how much she tried to brush it away she could still feel it.

Professor DeAngelo was leaning on the fence outside the hall, smoking the pipe he affected to go with his silver hair and his tweed jacket. "Peggy," he greeted her affably. "Had a nice walk?"

She was opening her mouth to tell him to get stuffed – or maybe to acquiesce noncommittally, she could never afterwards be sure – when a shadow dropped from the night sky. Bat-winged, black as coal-holes and murder, it fell without sound to wrap lithe arms about DeAngelo's chest and throat. He yelled once in pure shock, and by the light of the porch bulb Peggy saw a snaky tail whip up and jab him lightly under the ribs, over and over again. God, she knew how horrible it was to be poked there. It might not actually harm but it was an assault that tore the breath away. DeAngelo jerked with each stab and tried to scream, but he couldn't draw air into his lungs. Flailing spasmodically, he completely failed to fight off the four clutching limbs that gripped him tight. In a second his thrashing carcass was hauled clear of the ground. In another he was dangling over Peggy's head. Soon professor and abductor were nothing but a single dark shape occluding the stars.

And then he was gone.

Peggy clutched the wooden railing for dear life, frozen in disbelief. It was all over so fast – and so violently. She had no words for the midnight gargoyle she'd glimpsed only in outline. She couldn't name or explain what she'd just witnessed, even to herself.

The front door opened and Alice the undergrad stuck her head out. She looked surprised to see Peggy. "Is Rory out there?" she asked.

"He, uh…" Stunned, Peggy pointed toward the park. Her voice sounded like it belonged to a stranger. "He went off that way."

"What on earth for?" Wrapped in her candlewick dressing-gown, her arms tightly folded, Alice edged out onto the porch. "He just came out to check the weather. We were talking about fourth century architecture. Where's he going?"

"I haven't," said Peggy, "the faintest idea."

*

"Gran," Nigel breaks the long silence humbly, dropping his voice so as not to disturb the kids in the next room. "I hope you don't mind me asking: was Professor DeAngelo my grandfather?"

For a long time Peggy does not answer. She moves only to blink. Then at last she nods. "Yes." *And I knew. I carried Laurel with me down those steps into the cave. I took her into the Presence.* "He was a real piece of work, that man. Very charming – but unscrupulous."

Nigel lets out a long breath that sounds like a sigh.

Conscience pricks Peggy. "Your mother was nothing like that, of course. Don't think that, dear. She was…" She shakes her head in wonder. "She was quite extraordinary. Such an imagination."

"Not like me, hey?"

No, Nigel is quite the opposite to his mother. Staunchly prosaic. He never even reads novels, only non-fiction.

"Gifted, that's what the doctors called her. Even as a small child, she would tell the most incredible stories… Oh, sailing on a river boat through a city with golden towers, and riding her elephant to jungle palaces made of ivory and chalcedony. I don't know where she even got that word from. It's not like she could have read it anywhere." She can feel a wobble in her throat as she speaks. "She'd talk about sunsets, Nigel, and the way the moonlight made a path across the bay to the mountains beyond – though she'd never seen the moon, or the sun. She must have heard it on the radio I suppose – she never had any use of her sight, the doctors assured me."

Nigel puts his hand over hers and squeezes. "It's alright, Gran. Don't get upset."

"I don't want you thinking Laurel did what she did because she was a bad person, or because she didn't love you. You aren't to think that. She was a beautiful, loving girl."

"I know. Post-natal depression is just a thing. A terrible random thing."

"She said she couldn't sleep any more. I think that was what broke her. I tried my best to help…"

"It's not your fault, Gran."

Isn't it? She swallows, and sniffs back the tears. "She was too good for this world. She wasn't meant for it. That's what they say, isn't it – that only the good die young?"

He pats her hand, straining for jocularity, "Well I hope that's not true, because you must have been terribly wicked in your day, then."

She tries to smile, but has to turn her face away so he can't see the look in her eyes.

*

When the family depart at long last, she swallows two aspirin for her headache and takes herself off to bed with a warm cup of Ovaltine – a lifelong ritual that borders on addiction. Eustace slithers out from beneath the wardrobe and hops up to squat like a gargoyle on the counterpane. His face is an inscrutable darkness.

"*The first to identify the range of buildings behind the temple as an incubation,*" she muses out loud. It's all up there on the Internet, for the world to see. Millions and millions of people. Smiling, she twists the cap off the little brown glass bottle, ignoring the twinges of arthritic pain, and spills the pills out into her palm. "I think I'm ready now, Eustace."

After swallowing all the sleeping pills one by one, with sips of the milky malty drink to wash them down, she lies back against her pillows. Eustace looms forward over her supine form, not quite touching her, his horned head blocking out the evening light. She reaches up and touches him, for the first time. His skin is oily beneath her fingers, and it flicks at her touch almost as if he's shocked. He feels neither warm nor cold. *All in my head*, she reminds herself, closing her weary eyes.

"Good boy," she whispers, letting her hand fall back to rest upon her ribs.

He waits, patient as ever, as she drifts off into a doze.

At the end she feels his hands slide round her, lifting her from the mattress.

Maybe, she thinks, like Laurel, she'll be able to fly.

Season of Sacrifice and Resurrection

Adrian Tchaikovsky

The absence of a quiet man: Kevin's loss is felt in many small ways. The labs cleared poorly, jars and samples never quite back in place with the millimetre-accuracy that they once were. Late hours of silence without that tacit presence near midnight, for the new man knocks off at ten. Most of all it is the department's museum, its T-shape of narrow galleries, which misses Kevin. He had been its tender and its master. Now he is gone the exhibits grow untidy, the displays lack the precision of his touch, mislabelled, out of place, a garden growing wild

I never loved another human being as I do the ancient dead. The more ancient the better: fifty million years is a bit fresh, for me. In other walks of life this would be the doorway to psychosis, but a doctorate in palaeontology has reworked me into a productive member of society. I have been at the department here at the university for over a year now, nominally teaching – though it is debatable whether my students learn anything from me – but hired on mostly because I was and am a ferocious publisher for the greater glory of the department, churning out papers every few months on such world-shaking matters as the precise function of trilobite morphology, or an overview of our current state of knowledge on the Tommotian shelly fauna.

One would think that this would qualify me to become part of the team, but in truth my academic colleagues have fuller lives than I: pub, telly, amours, divorces, talk of which is as dry and dull to me as I always suspect my lectures are to my students. Home holds no amenities for me beyond my bed, which is never jealous of the time I spent working late. I can find in the microscopic intricacies of a fossilised mollusc an infinite fascination that the rigors of human contact deny me. Working late was how I got to know Kevin, in as much as anyone ever did.

His real name was something like Cieven Slovornik, but he was introduced to me as Kevin, and it was Kevin that stuck. He was from somewhere in Eastern Europe, I guessed, or else the Balkans, or somewhere, his speech accented and queerly stressed. He spoke little to anyone, little enough to me even after I struck up our acquaintance. His job description was lab technician, and he had been there four years before I joined the department. In the manner of many quiet, formidably efficient and skilled men, he made his job look effortless, and was consequently underappreciated by everyone. He tidied and filed, categorised and dusted. He cleared up the labs after the students had been in, and he helped classify new finds that came into the department, leaving them with whoever was the best specialist without being asked to, every decision impeccable, invisible. By the time I came along the entire department was running on a frictionless substrate of Kevin's attentions without anyone ever quite realising.

I didn't know what his qualifications might have been, over in Belarus, or even if he had any at all, but his understanding of the field was broad and detailed, more than many men with letters to their name. Night by night, the two of us the only living souls in the place, I discovered that he would confidently take on tasks I would not trust to my most senior students, performing them swiftly and to the minutest detail: preparing slides, cleaning and uncovering fossils with picks and acids. Most of all he tended the museum, that odd appendix to the department that was mostly ignored by staff and students except for sudden bursts of activity ahead of open days or summer schools, when members of the wider public might be enticed by it. Without Kevin the place would have been an embarrassment, but he spent many painstaking, nocturnal hours turning displays into dioramas, matching predators and prey, creating miniature wonders of juxtaposition and revelation. He was the Balkan Michelangelo of the display case. I have no idea whether the work was actually in his job description or not.

On one occasion I had landed a contract for a children's book about dinosaurs, a task that failed entirely to mesh with my usual technical writing style, and only Kevin saved me from ignominy. In his halting, Slavic speech, he sat by me for three nights, retelling the story of the Cretaceous period in a way that I had never envisaged, slowly gaining in confidence as a raconteur while I scribbled down every word. The sounds! The smells! The bellowing clashes of the armoured reptiles, the sudden quiets, water rippling to the silent coursing of leviathan. I, who had lived for things long dead for decades, discovered them again in Kevin's passionate retelling. The book was, if I say so myself, a modest success, but I have Kevin to thank for it.

"You make them live," I told him when we were done.

"But they do live," he insisted. "They are there, in the Then, alive, all of them. They leap and stride and crawl." He, who normally said nothing, was now in the full flow of his eloquence. "Put your hand here," touching a chain of vertebrae from a plesiosaur, "and in the Then it is moving, swimming those seas, swift and hungry." I had never before come across a man who so shared – and exceeded! – my passion for the subject. It was the beginning of the closest thing to a friendship that either of us really owned to.

He was a fugitive, and that explained a great deal of his reticence. From where, precisely, nobody was sure. He never named a country, but there were plenty of places east and south of central Europe where having the wrong ancestors could abruptly become hazardous to your health, fossil feuds from generations back springing to life and howling for the blood of the living. He had come to England fleeing persecution, that much was known, his people under threat from some ancestral enemy. Years later, he still lived in the shadow of it. His daily routine was an exercise in getting in nobody's way and attracting the least attention possible, his diligence, I assumed, born from memories of a land where any excuse might suffice to move him on or worse. Even at his most relaxed, as we talked over the latest articles in *New Scientist* past midnight, sitting in the museum and surrounded by his handiwork, I always felt that he was looking over his shoulder, an edge of nervousness never far from him.

Then there was his religion, another topic he never addressed directly. I soon learned from colleagues that Kevin was a member of some odd little sect, some import from his unmapped homeland. Certainly he had sporadic days off for some observance or other. Doctor Rillental, the department head, whose doctorate was apparently in inter-departmental politics, was far too aware of the number of minority boxes Kevin ticked, and never demurred.

So the days went on, smoothing seamlessly into months, and then close to a year of our odd camaraderie, a friendship sutured together around an interest in the dead stone relics of forgotten times, which were more real and immediate to both of us than any of our fellow staff members. I settled down to the job, bored my students, published my papers with a frequency and regularity that became the envy of the department, and assumed that the pattern of my life had been set for the next decade or so.

It was not to be.

One night in mid-March, it was, that Kevin came to me. I had not seen him that evening at all, but this was not unusual. A defining feature of our friendship was a lack of obligation, and he would drift by as and when he had the time and the inclination. At one in the morning, however, just as I was typing up notes on ammonite shell perforations and the probable causes thereof, he was there at my shoulder, strangely reticent, some new nervousness to his manner.

We exchanged a few words and it was clear that he was ill at ease, but I did not press him. Eventually in his own time he came out with, "I have a request, a favour from you."

I think that, discounting immediate family who have a claim on one's loyalties regardless of actual *like*, nobody else had ever said this to me, nor been in such a position of intimacy from which to venture the plea. Faced with that realisation and self-knowledge, I nodded for him to continue without hesitation.

"I need you not to be here one night next week, on March 20th," he explained, a little awkwardly. "It is a very important favour."

"What's this about?" My mind was completely blank. I could not imagine.

"I need to … use the museum." He was not looking at me, staring fiercely at the desk.

"You need to?"

"We – some of my – my people."

Something was nagging at me, the desk calendar catching the corner of my eye. The date he gave was marked there: vernal equinox.

"Kevin, is this to do with your … religion?" I asked carefully.

For a moment he was not going to admit it, but then he nodded, once, sharply.

I frowned. "Your religion needs the *museum*." I was being rude, I knew, but the thought baffled me. I knew Kevin to be a man of broad scientific knowledge, and in my experience religion and science seldom touched hands. Certainly, Kevin had made the museum a very temple to rationality, every detail intricately researched. I could not think what any religion might find to exalt in there.

"We are very greatly interested in the things of the past," he said slowly, picking his way through the English words with more hesitation than I had ever know. "They are of much importance to us. Each year since I came here, there has been a ... ceremony in the museum. Before you came there was never anyone else, at such an hour, to object. Now ... this year, this is very important to me. To me, more than any other. This year is my ceremony." His eyes met mine at last. "You must tell nobody. I have trusted you with this."

"Nobody," I echoed, and the thought of mentioning it – to Doctor Rillental or anyone else – never crossed my mind. "Kevin ... this is that important, to you."

Again that curt nod.

And then the point that I took a step too far, presumed too much, forgot myself. The question that should never be asked. "Could I watch?" because I was intrigued, as no human activity had ever caught my imagination before. A religious ceremony (or was the word *ritual?*) in a museum, some strange sect that revered the past. I felt as excited as if I was describing a new species of bivalve.

The silence stretched itself out, until even I, social inadequate, felt moved to fill it with "I mean, I'd be interested to see..." and "if it isn't..." but the pause I had taken for offence was instead Kevin thinking patiently over the request I had made of him, weighing pros and cons, considering the chance of a betrayal if I refused, and other variables inconceivable to me.

If the reasons for my asking had surprised me, the reasons for his agreement were a closed book. In retrospect, though, I can only think that, whilst our odd friendship had led me to greatly overestimate the ways in which we were alike, his own assessment of my similarity to him had been so much wider of the mark. And in the end, I think that he valued my companionship on a level that I could not appreciate. He was, after all, very far from home, and I think that he was lonely.

"You must promise not to interfere," was all he said. I wasn't sure why I might be moved to interfere, at the time, and – again in retrospect – I should have thought more about it.

*

"It is a matter of practicality," Kevin explained to me, on the chosen night. "We value rationality above all other things. You know that the calendar on your desk, it is a recent thing, yes? In truth, in logic, without sentiment, that point when the days are starting to grow longer than the nights is the start of the year."

We were waiting for his co-celebrants, approaching midnight, March 20th. Kevin could not keep still, and he spoke in halting rushes, more words than I normally got from him in a week.

"But there is sentiment, even for us. Your people have always known that the turn of year is a special time: for death of the old, birth of something new. You have your own celebration, yes."

"Well, Easter's not for a month, yet but…"

He shrugged, casting off all the complex ecclesiastical negotiations that had placed Easter where it was in the year. "Death and renewal," he insisted doggedly. "The year, your saviour's sacrifice, is all from the same thoughts."

I wondered then, and not for the first time, just what brand of religion Kevin espoused. I had always assumed some splinter of the Orthodox Church, some offshoot of Slavic Christianity with its own proud and almost extinct traditions. His words suggested otherwise. "So what is it that you celebrate now?" I asked him. In truth I had never seen anyone less celebratory.

"It is to do with the land we have left, and the land we will go to," he told me, quite seriously, leaving me quite at sea, wondering, *Is he Jewish, then? This promised land business? Or does he mean an afterlife?* He watched me try to assimilate this, and touched my arm slightly, more human contact than either of us had initiated during the year. "You are aware we have enemies, and that we are fleeing them."

Have, or had? Fleeing or fled? But all I did was nod, and he seemed satisfied.

His compatriots arrived then, and all at once, a little band coated and scarfed against the chill of the early year. Kevin let them in without comment, without introduction. They did not seem surprised to find me there, although their gazes were narrow and suspicious. There were half a dozen of them, and they had heavy duffel bags and rucksacks, bulging awkwardly with rigid contents. Their manner, entering, was less celebrants and more tradesmen here to perform some task with the minimum of fuss. With their coats off – and meticulously hung up – they were a strange spectrum of humanity, none of them seeming to have much ancestry in common with Kevin or each other. A broad-waisted man wore overalls, a woman in a skirt suit, a dark man in shirtsleeves, an elderly lady in woollens, a broad-shouldered man with a gym-toned body. One was a young man with a strange caste to his face who had the most striking snake-eye contact lenses I had ever seen, or at least I hoped that was the case. There seemed nothing to connect them, save that they moved with a uniform efficiency and determination, exchanging barely a word as they followed Kevin into the museum, with me trailing behind.

Our museum was fitted around other rooms, a meagre T of galleries with an open space in the centre that was the only place that a group of any size could possibly gather. One gallery of the T's long crosspiece was currently devoted to a time-ordered display of fossils from the Cambrian to the Cretaceous, while its opposite hall had a presentation on continental drift, climate change and sea levels. The spur of the T had been given over to Pliocene and Pleistocene exhibits, mostly early hominids, and a little set of stone tools. All Kevin's work, of course, and now I began to wonder whether there was some deeper significance to it all, invisible to the uninitiated.

"What now — ?" I whispered but, even as I began to speak, they were in motion, setting down their bags, pulling zips, releasing ties, revealing a variety of pieces, fragments – components might have been nearer the mark. Each neatly-packed container held rods and wheels and clips, and dozens of pieces of metal and glass that I could not even comfortably categorise.

They set to work with the careful speed of professionals – professional what, I could not say, but still there was nothing of the sacred in what they did, merely a complex practical task that they were plainly all very familiar with. As they assembled their shrine or idol, whatever it was, they spoke to each other, not conversation nor catechism, but something that was plainly technical instruction and interplay. None of it was in English, but neither was it anything that would have fit Kevin's accent or the Eastern Europe that I had assumed for him. This was when I started wondering about the wisdom of staying on at the department that night, but by then it was too late to back out.

The language they spoke was comprised of strings of hard monosyllables interspersed with slurred sibilants, a weird agglutinative speech that made me think of old Sumerian, that proto-language from the dawn of human civilisation which seemed to spring into and out of history with neither heir nor ancestor. Aside from a tentative reconstruction of that ancient tongue I had never heard anything like the language those men and women used between themselves. It was as distant from me as the speech of stars, of bees.

Occasionally one of them directed a brief string of sounds at Kevin, who replied effortlessly in the same manner, with none of the awkwardness he showed with English.

I had thought they were constructing some art deco altar or reliquary at first, but then as their quick work progressed I guessed that it was some sort of three-dimensional model representing some religious truth, for the internal construction was complex but ordered, and yet not merely symmetrical. That there was a functional plan was plain, what that plan was eluded me.

"You don't…" I gestured at the work, voice hushed.

"Last year, other years, I did," he told me. "Tonight is … my night. Tonight it is my turn. I am spared this." His body language had not changed, nor his voice, but something beyond these overt tells communicated to me that he was sad, and perhaps a little frightened.

"Kevin, tell me what this is about," I hissed.

"It is about our people," he replied, plainly including everyone in that room except me. "Where we were, our enemy, whom we once cast down, rises up. Our stay there comes to an end. We move on to where we will be. Each year, at the year's turn, we must … the phrase 'test the waters' is good." I thought at the time that stress was bringing the worst of his grammar to the fore, his tenses hopelessly muddled.

"You believe in a promised land?" I pressed.

"There is such, and that is where we will go, where we have gone," he told me, sincere and baffling in equal quantities.

The construction was nearing its close, the end result a far smaller assemblage than I would have dreamed possible from all the parts – a loosely cuboid structure of glass and metal rods dominated by a great curved lens.

"It looks like the time machine," I said wonderingly, and then stopped, for the complete and combined attention of all of them there, motionless and silent, unnerved me more than I could tell. "Like in the film, or the Wells book," I managed, my voice abruptly hoarse with the perception of some hidden danger, and a little tension leaked out of the air, and then went back to work.

By then, though, I knew I had hit on at least something – it was a machine. I could see no moving parts, nothing that would hint at any technology I ever saw, but everything about it, every line and piece, insisted on function and functionality.

Were they some sort of spiritualists? I remember thinking. *Are they going to try and speak to the dead?*

Up until that point I was still clinging to the idea that, any moment, they would begin some service or invocation, or gather around and join hands. Even fits and speaking in tongues would have fallen within the bounds of my expectations. Then one of them turned the machine on.

I thought all the lights had gone out, at first, although I could still see. The bulbs in the ceiling were still glowing like embers, but they illuminated nothing but themselves, nor did the machine appear to shed any radiance. Instead there was simply a brooding, undersea light that had no origin at all, but hung in the air and touched everything with an unhealthy pallor.

At the same time, something happened to the ends of the three museum galleries. From being some twenty feet distant at most, their ends receded abruptly and then were gone, lost in a kind of creeping mist that seemed less an obstruction in the air than a limit to my meagre human perception. There were shapes, though, backlit by a silvery light and only dimly perceived in the fog. I had been looking down the fossil gallery when the machine came on, and what I saw finally convinced me that there were more things in heaven and earth, as the man wrote, than are covered in my philosophy.

The shapes themselves did not stir overmuch alarm. I saw structures, or what I thought were structures at first: great conical forms with nebulous, shifting caps – or then I thought they must be plants, for there seemed to be some manner of branches growing from their narrow points. They were still, though, wreathed in the unnatural mist, mere silhouettes against the deadening white glimmer. The movement that claimed my attention was not theirs, but resided in the exhibits of our museum for, where the mist touched, I saw flickers and shapes, and then more than that, clear glimpses of our little relics of stone coated over with flesh: a trilobite waving its whip-like antennae, an ammonite shell buoyed up in an invisible medium, tentacles emerging tentatively from within. When the mist touched the partial plesiosaur skeleton that Kevin had mounted on the wall, I saw the marine behemoth twist and writhe, the reconstructed head rolling its yellow eyes and baring needle teeth.

I backed up, mind devoid of anything so substantial as a thought, and ran into Kevin, who steadied me with a firm hand. His expression was fiercely engaged, as I had never seen it, and I remembered his words of months before: *They are there, in the Then, alive, all of them.*

"That is the Then," he told me, as if reading my mind. "My people are in the Then, under threat from the resurgence of our great enemy." And he gestured towards the far gallery, where climate change and global warming had been consumed by mist that was enlivened by a thousand scuttling, shelled things so that I could only parrot, in my mind, *an inordinate fondness for beetles.* "That is the Yet to Come, when our enemy, though they are the child of three hundred million years, have ceased to be."

My asinine words recurred to me. *Time machine.* "Will they come...?" I waved towards the great conical shapes, the moment-to-moment animation of the fossils, imagining some stream of refugees like Kevin, stepping out onto our museum floor en route to some unguessable refuge.

"All that is flesh, there, shall perish," Kevin said. There was fear and mourning in his voice. "Only our minds, the most gifted of our minds, can leave the Then and escape that ending. Only those few minds shall find new homes in the Yet to Come."

"And...?" I could only point down the spur of the T, where the hand-axes and ancient human detritus had been swallowed by a limitless dark abyss, where a fickle, reddish light touched on great tumbled stones of black basalt. Not for one moment did I doubt him, or think him mad or misled. He spoke the words as they were unshakeable fact. Any scepticism in me died before that certainty.

"That is the Now," Kevin explained gently. "That is the Now, in the last places of our enemies, their deep strongholds at the edge of their time." He looked at me searchingly, seeking that kinship we had pieced together over the year, and he must have felt that he found it, because he was moved to try some few more words to enlighten me. "We are not safe in the Now, my people. Only we few conduct our experiments at the turn of each year. A time for resurrection that predates any reason your people might assign to it. Resurrection and sacrifice."

"Your experiments?" Each answer had only spawned more questions. I could not stretch my mind far enough to understand him. I expected more of the same, every word a cipher, but this time his response was such that even I could comprehend him.

"Each year we must test to see if our great enemy has succumbed to time. Each year one of us must journey to their haunts in the Now."

He had taken a few steps away to me, towards that dark, far place, where the ancient, vast stones lay, and I remembered him saying, *This is … my night.*

Although the half-life of the fossils, the Then of Kevin's people, was at my back; although that dreadful, beetle-haunted Yet to Come chattered and thronged at the far end, it was that offshoot, that sideways glimpse into the Now that truly chilled me. Those stones had been worked, no natural formations, and yet the scale and the aesthetic were something inimicable to me, far beyond anything else that I had seen that night.

"You have to go…?" My hands made inconclusive gestures at it. "But what if these … *enemies* are still there." I knew beyond doubt that the nemesis he spoke of was not simply some other tribe or religion of man; far more than ethnic differences lay behind the enmity.

"They are," he told me softly. "They are not gone yet, nor for many of these years to come. They are tenacious of life, while they wait for our return. In the Yet to Come, we know to the year when their last scion shall fade and decay."

I did not understand, as with so much else. "But if you know, then why go now? Why not just wait?"

His face creased, and I saw there his fondness for me, shining from an expression that there were no human names for. I saw also that he was very afraid of those black stones and what lay behind them, far more than I. As loathsome as I found them, my ignorance was yet my shield.

"How else will we come to know the extent of their time, unless we experiment? Without our ritual of the years, where would our minds in the Yet to Come find the knowledge that they have? We do what must be done. We do what we know we did. The turn of the year demands it: for resurrection, there must yet be sacrifice."

He was past the machine now, standing at the mouth of that spur gallery, the stalk of the T, and I saw a wind start up, amongst the black stones, swirling the dust into unwholesome patterns.

"You're going to die?" It was a fool's question to ask anyone, save someone whose life, and the ending of it, was apparently already written in the histories of the far future.

"Something will die," he replied calmly. "But I shall live on." The thought seemed to sadden him, but then he gathered his resolve, and was walking away into darkness. Now I could hear the moaning of the wind out there in the lightless reaches, hungry, strung with wordless sounds that yet promised meaning, for anyone mad enough to listen for it. I started after him, just one step, feeling the tensing of the machine-builders as I did so. *You must promise not to interfere*, he had said. In truth, it was my own fear that stopped me, more than obedience to his wishes.

His walk seemed to take far longer than was possible, passing down and down into that place, far beyond the museum's walls, until the true size of those great basalt blocks became apparent, and he was just a tiny form moving amongst them, as the wind whipped at his clothes, growing stronger and stronger, its unseen voices raging and fluting.

He turned about one block, lost to sight on the instant, and a moment later I heard the scream that has stayed with me ever since, and lurked in every dream I have had. It did not seem, to me, like a sound Kevin would ever have made, but it was human, without doubt, lost and alone and in dreadful fear, and then gone, cut off and silenced by some invisible stroke.

The machine-builders showed no discernible emotion, simple scientists whose experiment has demonstrated some unfortunate but undeniable conclusion. They looked towards the Yet to Come, as if confirming that whatever lurked there, amidst the hints of mandible and carapace, had made its own record of the result, and then they looked back to the Then, and I did too.

One of the cone-shapes, those hazy-edged silhouettes, had moved, come closer until it seemed almost within the confines of the museum. Seeing it, I saw something living, but of no classification of animal or plant that Linnaeus had ever known. Even so, some part of my mind was instantly casting my thoughts to odd, strange fossils I had seen, unnamed and indecipherable, curious relics that seemed to match no known phylum, incomplete fragments that might, yet, had once belonged to this: a great cone-shaped thing, with four snaking limbs sprouting from its top, one of which terminated in a nightmare bundle of tendrils and eyes, for without doubt it was looking at me.

I saw something, then, that I have tried to deny to myself ever since, but the sense of it was so strong that even now I cannot dissuade myself from it. Staring into that alien gaze I touched a spark of something I recognised. No expression, no stance, nothing of the man I knew could have shown itself in that huge, unthinkable form, and yet I knew instinctively that what I looked on had last spoken to me with Kevin's voice.

Only our minds, he had said, and if they could send them forth, why not drag them back as easily, to mount another expedition at some later date, *to* some later date. What limits could a race know, for whom time was a road they could travel at will?

Then Kevin's compatriots did something to the machine, and the world I had known sprang back, leaving me blinking in the electric light as they dismantled what they had built. None of them had anything to say to me, and I knew that, Kevin gone, they would find some other suitable place for their tasks next year. My mayfly part in their aeons-long story had come and gone.

And now Kevin is gone, too, and the department decays in a hundred subtle ways without his constant attention, and despite everything I saw that night, despite everything that I *know*, about him, about the world, I would welcome him back, if I saw him again.

And I have faith, atheist as I am, that I will see him again.

Some days, when visitors come, or when I must travel amongst strangers, I find myself watching their faces, looking for that spark of kinship that was enduring enough to cross the boundaries of species and ages to make itself clear to me. He is out there, in the Then, living amongst the living, breathing exemplars of the fossils I have loved all my life. He fights his peoples' enemies and plans their exodus, and one day, I am sure, he will find the Now again. Any man, any woman, no restrictions on colour or creed or country. Sacrifice and resurrection: Kevin is gone, but Kevin may yet return.

Prospero and Caliban

Adam Gauntlett

Professor Extraordinarius Paulinus Sigurdsun, whose ears were badly burnt by the sun, searched the deserted pleasure yacht hoping to find a replacement for his hat, now lost somewhere in the weed. The yacht, the *Agamemnon,* late of New York, had been adrift in the green for a little under a year, Sigurdsun judged, and though her decks were beginning to feel unfirm, and her superstructure was pregnant with mould, she was still in good shape. A testament to her builder, not that whoever it may have been would care to see her now. A fine example of Victoriana was the *Agamemnon.* Sigurdsun looked forward, past the smut-spreading smokestacks, for her master cabins, and was not disappointed.

He ignored the suggestive brown stains – there was no sign of a body – and eventually his search was rewarded. A new hat, straw weave, and it fit him well. Pleased with his find, he paused in front of a spotted mirror for a moment, to admire it.

He did not recognise the face that looked back at him.

He collapsed, not caring where he landed, or how. He was close to weeping, but there were no tears left, just an aching that would not ease. How long had it been? Was it really as long as that? Was that old man with grey streaked though his hair and beard, that starved tramp, that dull burnt-brown face, was that really him?

He searched frantically for his diary. He'd kept track of the days as best he could, but after a while it became impossible. He'd wake in the morning, go about his business, only to think later in the day, did I make my mark this morning? Or did I forget? Then lack of paper became a problem – he made copious notes at first, not thinking for a moment that he'd ever have difficulty finding more to write on – so he started keeping a tally stick instead, carving his mark on it. Except he lost his stick – and had to start another. But how long had it been? What was the latest mark?

He left the *Agamemnon*'s faded finery, heading back up on deck to stare across the vastness of the weed.

It, at least, had not changed. Infinite and impersonal, it stretched as far as he could see, and there were times, moments of utter despair, when he thought it stretched further than he could imagine. The larger drifts concealed other ships, or aircraft, or perhaps some other floating thing. Since becoming trapped in this vast Sargasso, he had stood on the deck of a trireme as seaworthy as any in Pericles' fleet, navigated the rotten and perilous decks of a tramp steamer some hundred years or so trapped in the weed, and encountered many other strange craft. He had no idea where his own ship, the research vessel *Boreas*, was now. He wasn't certain he could pinpoint, among his many marks, the day he had abandoned it for good.

The human voice, when he heard it, startled him so profoundly that he hid, shivering, without a moment's thought or hesitation.

"Now," it said, clear and bright, "does my project gather to a head! My charms crack not; my spirits obey, and time goes upright with his carriage!"

Sigurdsun did not recognise the voice. He reasoned, when he overcame his terror, that it could not be one of *them*, for they did not speak. *They* grunted, yelled, or gibbered. The speaker wasn't English, or at least, he did not have an Englishman's glottal, guttural voice. He might be American.

Sigurdsun risked a look over the *Agamemnon*'s rail.

The stranger wasn't trying to hide. Sigurdsun, who had made a religion of caution, and with reason, marvelled. The newcomer walked about – the weed was dense enough, in places, if you were careful – as though there was no danger. He was young, probably in his twenties, though his lined face made him look older. His clothes were a little old-fashioned, but not by that much; Sigurdsun's father might have worn a workingman's jacket like that.

"Say, my spirit, how fares the king and's followers?"

"Ahoy there!"

How cracked and reedy my voice is, Sigurdsun thought; I am my grandfather, now.

The stranger, hearing him, swung about so quickly that the weed nearly lost its grip, and he half-tumbled into it.

"Hag-seed!" he screeched. "Hence!"

Sigurdsun stood, hands outstretched, palms up. "I mean..." What was the word, the word, oh let me not stumble now, he thought. "...harm not. I mean no harm, that is. I will not hurt you. Please, I am ... my name is Paulinus Sigurdsun. I am alone. I will not ... oh please, do not go!"

For he was backing away, this American dropped from Heaven, though his speed was not so very great; he could not afford to be too swift, or he'd fall through altogether and then probably sink into the ocean depths.

"Please! Oh, please! I promise! I promise no harm!"

It was no good. The American scrambled up into a larger patch of weed, and vanished. Sigurdsun, almost sobbing, pleaded for another minute or two, hoping that tone of voice would do what his ragged appearance clearly could not. When he realised that his hopes were vain, he sank back on the deck, chest heaving.

It was a long time before he thought to see if the trail the American left behind could be followed.

*

It was a newer ship than Sigurdsun was accustomed to. Some of the things he had found in the Sargasso had been there months, years, in one case perhaps two centuries or more – more a rotten shadow of a thing than the thing itself. But this small craft had been adrift here only a week or so. It was heavily damaged, and not from a storm; Sigurdsun, no navy man, had spent his war service in muddy fields and shell holes, and he knew what high explosive could do. This tidy grey warship had been near cut in half. Most of the stern was gone, and had it not been for the weed Sigurdsun suspected it would have sunk some time ago.

It was so fresh, in fact, that there were still corpses aboard. Usually by the time Sigurdsun found a ship there was little left, perhaps a suggestive pile of ash and some gnawed bone, but this one was untouched.

The American's trail ended here. Sigurdsun stepped as cautiously as he dared, trying not to startle him. The crew cabins were forward; that was where the American probably was. Sigurdsun stopped to briefly admire what seemed to be a machine gun, though more sophisticated than the ones he'd used over a decade ago. He wondered briefly if he could get it off of its pintle mount, then dismissed the idea. Even if he could, it was unwieldy and he had no ammunition for it. Better if he found a pistol.

He stood at the entrance to the crew cabins. "Sir? Mister American, are you there?"

Something certainly was. He could hear it shifting weight. He hoped to God it wasn't one of the others.

"For this, be sure," the voice floated up from the darkness, "tonight thou shalt have cramps!"

Sigurdsun both knew and did not know the words. They were familiar to him, and given time and thought he could probably put a name to them. But time he did not have, and his thoughts ran now like wet paint spilled over a floor; he could no more remember the thing than he could fly like a bird.

"Please, Mister American. Please come out. I will not hurt you, I swear it! You don't understand, you don't … it has been so long. Please. Have mercy!"

"Side-stitches,,," and he gloated over them "…that shall pen thy breath up; urchins shall, for that vast of night that they may work, all exercise on thee!

"Give me a look!" It was the work of desperation. "Give me a face, that makes simplicity a grace!"

Sigurdsun had no idea what the words meant. He remembered them from his time in England, in the camps, when earnest young people tried, with some success, to teach them English. He'd no need of their lessons, having already a good grasp of the language, but he remembered some of the poetry, a few snatches here and there, mice wandering in an empty storeroom.

It was so very quiet.

"So glad of this," came the voice, at last, "as they, I cannot be, who are surprised withal."

"May I enter?"

The American made no reply, but was not hostile either. Taking that as the best kind of permission he was likely to get, Sigurdsun crept cautiously down the stairwell.

It was a cramped space. Not long out from port, either, since there were still bags of food – Sigurdsun eyed a sausage hungrily – hanging from the ceiling. He remembered his cousin, a submariner, telling him how the crew would bring extra supplies along, eating them quickly while still fresh. The American was tearing busily at a hunk of bread. Sigurdsun reached out for the sausage. Landjäger! The American made no move to stop him. Sigurdsun ripped into it.

"I had never thought," he said, "a man could be hungry, in a dream. But this!"

The American nodded. "Spirits, which by mine art I have from their confines call'd to enact my present fancies."

"But see! Paper! I am always in need, and these poor fellows need nothing any more. And again, the dream! Look at that!"

The American, puzzled, shook his head.

"But see! Ach, you do not. It is the National Socialist symbol. *Nationalsozialistische Deutsche Arbeiterpartei.* Stupid! Every man knows that little monkey is under the thumb of the industrialists and the Junkers, and in any case, we have signed treaties. We shall never have a military again. Phantoms, all of it! And yet, so detailed. I have seen little *portunus sayi* – crabs – playing in the *Sargassum natans*. And there is no question that it is Sargasso, though I have never seen the stuff first hand before now. It resembles exactly that which I have seen drawn in books. You, yourself, must be someone I have met before, for in a dream everything comes from within, is it not so? But I do not remember you. I am sorry, I talk too much. It has been so long. So long."

The American had finished his bread, and begun poking around. His hand closed on something that turned Sigurdsun white, and cold with sudden terror.

"Please … please put that away."

"But how is it that this lives in thy mind?" The American's gentle smile might have reassured, under different circumstances. "What seest thou else in the dark backward and abysm of time?"

Sigurdsun's mouth went desert-dry. The thing the American held, so nonchalantly, could blow them both to pieces in an instant. He had used them before, in the War, and found them so tricky and unpredictable he'd rather never touch one again. But there it was, in the palm of the American's hand, and one careless action could scatter them both like seed corn.

"You do not know what you have! Put it away, I beg you, or give it to me. I can keep it safe."

The American threw it to him, carelessly, as if it were a toy. Sigurdsun caught it with both hands, clutching. He put it in his belt; he almost threw it overboard, but caution stopped him. There might be a use for it later.

The American was busying himself with the ship's radio. Tuning it seemed to give him great pleasure, though the only result was a discordant hum. Sigurdsun knew it was pointless. There was nobody out there sending a signal, and nobody to hear one.

"I wish you would talk some sense," Sigurdsun sighed.

The American nodded sagely. "I find my zenith doth depend upon a most auspicious star, whose influence if now I court not but omit, my fortunes will ever after droop. Here cease more questions. Thou art inclined to sleep; 'tis a good dullness."

Sigurdsun coughed, great racking heaves that only ended when the American thumped him companionably on the back.

"Sleep!" said Sigurdsun, when he recovered. "One never sleeps in a dream, have you noticed that? There are times when my eyes swim, my mind falters, and I think I might be unconscious for a time, but sleep? Never.

"I used to have such wonderful dreams. I remember walking the streets of a great city, greater than any I have ever known. I knew it like I knew my birthplace. Its people were my people, and there was not one street, one house, I was not familiar with. Now? I don't sleep."

He looked at the American. Concern was all he saw there, a worried uncle looking after a sick nephew. The man was probably ten years his junior, too.

"Ach, it's probably better you don't talk. God knows, there have been times I wished I could go mad. It would make everything easy. But so long as we are together, I'll do the talking for both of us, hey?"

*

Sigurdsun never gave up. His hope, a distant dream, was that one day he would find a way out of the Sargasso, somehow, perhaps steal one of the more intact ships – a yacht for preference, like the ones he'd learned to sail on when he was a boy – and head for home. Food, water, would be problems, and the stars above were cold and unfamiliar, useless for navigation. But it was a good dream, and he believed in it.

He and the American spent days looking, each marked carefully on a tally stick. The American seemed content to follow in Sigurdsun's wake, chattering to himself, nosing around in the derelicts when they boarded them, looking for God alone knew what. Sigurdsun could not persuade the American to tell his name, so he kept on calling him Mister American, and the man did not seem to mind.

When they boarded a ship Mister American happily searched it, but seldom was interested in the things Sigurdsun found. He had no use for paper, and only a passing interest in food; the charts and navigation aids that sent Sigurdsun into raptures didn't interest him one bit. What captured his attention was clothing and books. He might sit for minutes at a time, gently stroking a piece of cloth, or mesmerised by a hat, a shoe, a jacket. He never took any of these things, and after the reverie he never paid them the least attention, but for that moment they were all the world to him.

Books, however waterlogged, always fascinated him. He would carry them for hours, read them obsessively, mumble under his breath as though the words meant something. It didn't seem to matter the language or the content. At one point he had fifteen of them in his arms, balanced precariously, and almost tumbled into the weed when he overbalanced. Most of his treasures eventually went straight into the drink, splashing one by one, lost. He wept like a baby and would not be comforted.

*

Black sails, off in the distance, and Sigurdsun halted, watching them.

He knew that ships had to join the weed-choked fleet all the time. That was how the *Boreas* had become part of the great waste; it had blundered out of a storm, its rudder jammed and heeling uncertainly to port, and nothing they could do stopped it from drifting, with ponderous slowness, into the heart of the Sargasso. Yet he did not often see a new ship. The little grey warship was still the best preserved of all the wrecks he'd discovered, and even that had been several days in the weed before they found it.

The black sails discomforted him in ways he couldn't explain, even to himself. It was as if ghosts were walking over his grave, dragging their chains, each cold link an unhappy memory.

Mister American bristled, eyes wide, teeth snapping. Sigurdsun had to grab him quickly, else he'd have gone dashing over the weed towards the sails. That, Sigurdsun knew without telling, would be disaster.

The sails billowed. Sigurdsun heard voices, but sound travelled far over water; there was no way to tell how close they were. The language was hauntingly familiar, but he could not place it.

"Come," he said, tugging at Mister American's arm.

"Go charge my goblins," he spat, "that they grind their joints with dry convulsions, shorten up their sinews with aged cramps, and more pinch-spotted make 'em than pard or cat-a-mountain!"

Sigurdsun dragged him away by force, kicking and spitting. Terror gave Sigurdsun wings; the black sails, whatever they might be, certainly could hear Mister American's shrieks and curses. Sigurdsun fancied he saw the weed move, search parties sent out.

He had to shove Mister American along. For all his rage he lacked strength, but so did Sigurdsun, and like two wandering tramps quarrelling over a rag and scrap of bone they proceeded, one pushing, one struggling. Sigurdsun, in a flash of inspiration, snatched one of Mister American's books out of his arms.

"Put thy sword up, traitor!" Mister American howled.

"For kings are clouts," was the reply, as Sigurdsun retreated hastily, "that every man shoots at, our crown the pin that thousands seek to cleave!" He had no idea what it meant. It was another fragment stolen from a near-empty storeroom, but it seemed enough, for Mister American came blundering after, and by good fortune or God's grace he did not shout again, needing all his breath for moving.

Even so, it wasn't enough. Mister American put a foot wrong. Running was treacherous in the weed, and before Sigurdsun could blink Mister American was half underwater, hands clutching. In a moment he would be all the way gone. It would be quiet, then; Sigurdsun could creep away.

He leapt forward, forgetting the book, which tumbled unconsidered to a watery finish. Grabbing Mister American by the jacket sleeve, he stopped him from going further under. Mister American's mouth gaped wide, so Sigurdsun stuffed his other arm into it, wincing with pain as teeth clamped shut.

Mister American's throat quivered. His eyes stared into Sigurdsun's.

The black sails, still just visible, moved away.

It was a long time after that before Sigurdsun felt safe enough to haul Mister American back up.

*

Sigurdsun and Mister American found refuge on a four master that had wallowed months in the Sargasso. It had been picked clean by other scavengers, but it was safe enough.

Sigurdsun took out some of his papers and began to sketch. For some time now he had been plotting out the weed, or as much of it as he could, and now he had one new data point. The black sails had moved. That meant clear ocean. It meant safety. The edge of the great expanse, from which point he and Mister American could, if they could find or make a means, escape.

Mister American moped by the ship's rail. It might have been the loss of most of his books that upset him, but Sigurdsun doubted it. Not that Sigurdsun really cared, not at that moment. The data was more important.

If they could just find the means. Most of the larger ships would have had lifeboats, rafts, something that they could use. Naturally, during whatever disaster had drawn these ships into the weed, the crews had taken to these boats and escaped, or tried to, so most of the weed-choked derelicts no longer had lifeboats. Most, but not all. Surely there would be some that did have them.

He sighed. The problem was, how to get the lifeboats to the edge of the weed? It wasn't as if they could just float through. Launched from here, where the weed was thick, any boat would soon be caught up in it. They needed something else.

The *Titanic,* he remembered, had carried collapsible boats. Would those be light enough for two men to carry across the weed? He suspected not. But perhaps there was something in the idea; perhaps they could carry the raft in bits. Oh, and then all the food they would want, he realised with disgust, and all the water too, and sails, and why not a pony, while they were about it? He could just see himself doing it. Puttering back and forth, somehow never getting lost, piling all the bits and pieces in one spot. All without being seen by the black sails. Or anyone else.

He shuddered. Mister American wasn't the only survivor lost in the weeds. He knew that through bitter experience. Weeks lost with no hope did strange things to people's minds. At least Mister American's madness was benign. But the others … he remembered what had happened to the crew of the *Boreas*. He knew he was the only survivor.

Charred, gnawed bones beside a suggestive pile of ash. He shivered.

Titanic, now, that had possibilities. She didn't carry enough boats – it would be difficult for any commercial liner; there wasn't the deck space for all those rigid-hulled boats. Lots of clever men mulling over the problem, clever men like Professor Extraordinarus Paulinus Sigurdsun, or like he had been once, before the beard and the grey-streaks, the relentless sun, the burns, the black sails and weed, weed, everywhere weed, as far as the eye could see and further, beyond imagining, beyond redemption, lost forever, never get out…

Cold water splashed in his face.

"You do look, my son," said Mister American, empty bucket in his hand, "in a moved sort, as if you were dismay'd; be cheerful, sir."

Sigurdsun lay still, blinking. "Thank you."

Vulcan. Vulcan, Roman god, Vulcan … vulcanised, that was it. Vulcanised rubber. There had been talk of making inflatable boats out of the stuff. Boats which would be more easily stored, and transported.

"Which we could carry over the weed," he said, as he pulled himself up to the railing. "See there, that smokestack? Perhaps a few hundred yards east of that point is the edge of the weed. All we need to do is keep that stack in view, all the time. Then we can find our way out of here. But we need one of those rubber boats first, and that means we need to forage. Take heart, Mister American! We're almost home free!"

*

She was exactly what they were looking for. Large, some kind of warship, she had been in the weed for perhaps a little over a year, judging by wear and tear. Sigurdsun did not recognise her design, nor yet the ragged flag which still flew at her stern – but that meant little. So many strange things could be seen in dreams that he no longer puzzled over details.

The problem was, she was large – mammoth, even – and that meant she'd be rich pickings. Anyone could see that, which meant she'd be a beacon for anyone who came near. And she was large enough that, if someone else found her first and was aboard her now, scavenging, Sigurdsun and Mister American wouldn't have the slightest idea, perhaps not until it was much too late.

The thing he'd taken from the smaller warship, still hanging from his belt, wouldn't be much use in defence. It could only be used once, and then they'd be stuck. They hadn't found anything more useful since then.

Sigurdsun helped Mister American board her, then crept up

himself.

He decks canted at an angle, and though mould hadn't eaten her yet, the metal was slick. They had to step cautiously. Mister American directed Sigurdsun's attention to an open hatch. Sigurdsun nodded. He reached out and grabbed the hatch rim, more to stabilise himself than anything, and leaned in for a closer look. Enough light streamed in from outside to tell him that this was some kind of communicating corridor.

On deck, there were peculiar seeming guns, all bloat and short barrel, off to his left, so he assumed that the corridor stretching away and turning left led to those weapons. That suggested that the stairs leading down, which he could just see from where he was, led to some kind of ammunition storage. So the corridor running further, back into the dark, presumably led somewhere more interesting.

The weed wouldn't burn, and he had no electric torch. All he had was paper, and some matches.

It had taken so long to find his paper. Much of it he'd written on, made his mark; he couldn't bear to burn it. He gazed longingly into the dark.

Mister American scrambled past him, and before he could do more than shout in surprise, had vanished into the bowels of the ship.

"Hoy!" He hastily rolled a spindle of paper, and prepared to light a match. "Wait!"

Noises, and this time, he felt, not from Mister American. He crouched down, trying to stay out of sight.

Three other survivors, one with an electric torch, were poking around. The light had come from the stairs Sigurdsun had seen, and then the first of them emerged. Sigurdsun watched closely.

The man was rags from shoulder to waist. One arm was burdened with something heavy, a bag or sack. He had a rifle strapped at his shoulder and the torch was in his free hand. His breeches looked like military dress uniform, long gone to rot.

The other two, a younger man and a woman, were dressed in baggy clothing Sigurdsun couldn't identify. Their clothes shone oddly when the light hit. One held an axe, the other a pistol.

It was their eyes and faces that made him stay hidden. He knew that near-permanent grimace, those staring, hopeless eyes. Stay too long in the weed and it caught at you, made your mind wander. Go too long without food, and you begin to think your neighbour's haunches are just the thing. Gnawed bones were the only remnants this sort left behind.

Mister American's footfall had startled them, but they seemed not to know which direction he'd taken. The one with the rifle grunted, and pointed back into the dark. The younger man took his torch and he and the girl set out. The rifleman made towards the hatch, to light.

Sigurdsun let go of the hatch and slid down the canting deck. His legs doubled under him when he hit the rail, tensing. It had been like this before. Throat dry, teeth rattling – would the other hear? – then, release.

When the one with the rifle emerged from the hatch Sigurdsun pushed up at him, arms out, closing round his neck and mouth. The survivor was in better shape than he, stronger, but the rifle round his neck and sack in his arm kept him from bringing all those advantages to bear. Sigurdsun grabbed that rifle, pulled the strap close around the survivor's neck. He pulled till his arms cracked, pulled till his hands went white, pulled till his muscles felt as if they'd split.

He was still doing that when Mister American emerged from the hatch. He was in a tearing hurry and not looking where he was going, so he fell forward, and but for luck would have tumbled over the rail and down to the weed-strewn water below.

Shaking hands pointed the rifle at the hatch just as the first of them, the younger man, emerged. The shot was an avalanche of sound, while the round spanged off the metal and went God alone knew where. The younger man screeched and fell back into the dark.

After what felt like an eternity and probably lasted less than a minute, Sigurdsun began to breathe again. He checked the rifle: that had been the only round. The sack was full of supplies, what seemed to be desiccated food of some kind, wrapped up in shining paper, water, even a medical kit.

The corpse stared up at him, empty eyes full of memories only Sigurdsun could see. Memories of mud and shell holes, terror-filled nights. Dreams he could only remember when he was dreaming, that splintered and vanished in daylight. Dreams of the moon, and what lived there, on its darkest side.

The drops running down his cheeks, he was amazed to discover, were tears, not blood.

*

Mister American carried the raft. It was light enough for that. Sigurdsun carried the food.

"Keep the stack on your right," he told Mister American. "That way we won't get lost."

He wondered how far they were from land. Surely it must be many miles away. They had paddles, and could probably put up some kind of sail. The stars were more familiar, now, after so many nights of study. The one which gleamed so bright was the Watchman, which warns men away from the now-accursed basalt city. The cluster near it was the Two Wanderers, marching across the sky arm-in-arm as winter follows summer. He remembered them now as he would old friends.

"I used to return to the city each night," he told Mister American, as they trudged across the weed. "I knew each street, each house. I was a fisherman, and happy, but I was only a boy; I couldn't know what was coming. Politics were for my parents.

"Then the Serbs betrayed us, and we had to go to war. My whole class stood up and, with one voice, cheered our Kaiser. I was fourteen, and had to wait, but in my mind, I was already a soldier.

"My dreams changed then. Danger was coming, and it would take the basalt city. The warnings began to pull at me, luring me away, telling me to flee. I didn't understand what it meant, only that I had to go, and when my friends tried to dissuade me I slipped aboard a ship by night, and stowed away. I remember being found by the captain, being beaten, then put to work.

"But the black sails…"

Mister American had stopped moving but Sigurdsun had not noticed. Now Mister American was some distance behind. Sigurdsun looked back.

"Why are you —"

Mister American silenced him with an angry glare. He pointed.

Far in the distance, but not so far that they were no danger, Sigurdsun could see the black sails.

He crouched, shivering. There had been stories, awful tales. Never go aboard, he was told, never go near, never have dealings with the hunched men who spoke for the ones who crewed those ships. At night, when in port, strange ululations came from the black sail ships, deep in the hold. Not even the hunched men went below decks, he noticed. Not even at night. They slept on deck, under the stars, and when the time came they would up anchor and vanish into the night. It was said that they took slaves, but he had never seen them do it.

Or, he realised, perhaps he'd never seen it then, but was seeing it now. For why else would the black sails come here, to the weed? True, they might be robbing the ships that found themselves caught here, but he thought not. There would be richer pickings further in, and so far at least he had not seen the black sails try to get any closer than the edges. But if they were fishing for survivors, then sticking to the edge of the weed was their best bet. All the survivors would want to make their way to the edge, to escape, just as he was doing now. Then they would be easy prey.

It couldn't be profitable for them, of course, but profit might not be their motive.

For a moment he entertained mad fantasies of boarding the black sails, slitting throats, prancing about like a cut-rate and starving Fairbanks, sliding down the sail with one dagger in his hand, another in his teeth.

Mister American wept.

So caught in his own thoughts was he that Sigurdsun did not notice, and it was only when he made to move away, back from the edge, that he realised. Discomfited, he wondered what to say, and then how to say it. "How now, spirit," he finally decided. "Wither wander you?"

He remembered the actor more than the character, a fat man, all charm, the kind who would never lack for friends. It was the only line of the play he could recall.

Mister American pointed at the black sails.

"A treacherous army levied," and his voice trembled. "One midnight fated to the purpose did Antonio open the gates of Milan, and, i'the dead of darkness, the ministers for the purpose…"

Tears choked him.

"You have been here before," Sigurdsun said. "You have seen those sails before."

Mister American nodded.

"They took something from you? Someone?"

Sigurdsun wrapped an arm around Mister American's shoulder, holding him close. It was incredible, he thought, how thin those shoulders were, how skin and bone he had become. It was time rushing past, famine standing on their shadows, and all around them, weed.

"They cannot stay forever. They can't afford to get too close either, or the black sails will be trapped here, same as everyone else. All we have to do is wait them out, you see? Wait until they go, and then we get out of here. We have food now, and shelter's easily had. If we're careful we can avoid them, and then, we're free!"

Mister American didn't take cheer from this. He stared out across the Sargasso, at the black sails, while his tears dried on his face in salty trails.

*

For the first time in a very long while, Sigurdsun dreamed. Or perhaps, he rationalised later, he believed that he dreamed, for it all muddled in his mind after he woke, and he could remember very little. It was like drowning, and when he stirred, it was to gasp and drag air back into his lungs.

Mister American had left.

It wasn't difficult to see where he had gone. The trail in the weed was plain, and led straight to the edge. Sigurdsun couldn't see the black sails, but in his bones he knew they were still out there, somewhere. Mister American had sought them out.

*

Sigurdsun stared across the water. Actual, clear water, lapping gently at the weed, and just a few hundred yards distant, it lay.

It was like a galley, with a lateen rig, but it had a longer hull, lay deeper in the water. It had oars for when the wind gave out, and it was using them now, as if its crew didn't trust the capricious breezes. It had not been difficult to track. Even if he hadn't seen the sail every so often, he would have followed the screams.

Mister American had arrived there before him. He had no idea what happened next, but Mister American's screams rang in his ears for a very long time. Perhaps the twisted men had caught him before he got close to their ship, perhaps he'd somehow crept aboard without being seen. It didn't matter which it was. Plainly the crew had caught him.

Sigurdsun wondered how long it would take him to reach land, if he launched his inflatable. Perhaps he never would. It was, at least, a chance.

He stood up waving his arms, and shouted. There was no response from the black sails, not so much as movement on deck. Was there a crew, he wondered? Or were the hunched men temporary faces, go-betweens for whatever hid below decks, unseen?

Launching the inflatable was easier than he had expected. He paddled over to the long hull. The sea lapped lazily, pulling him gently, as he stood, grabbed hold, and climbed aboard. The inflatable, without anything tying it to the black sail ship, drifted away.

No movement on deck. Like many another cargo ship, there wasn't room in the hold for all the cargo, so he had to pick his way past bales of trade goods. Several open, empty cages were also on deck. They reminded him of the crates the *Boreas* had kept chickens in, for fresh eggs, and later, when the hens stopped laying, fresh meat. But these were much larger, and by the stink had been occupied recently.

Mister American was nowhere to be found.

The shape of the ship seemed wrong, somehow. There were masts, rigging, a steering oar, and yet it felt as if what he saw, and what he felt, were two different things. His hands closed on objects that, though not visible to his eye, were plainly there. The steering oar did not feel right, at all, and he wondered if it made any difference to the ship's heading. The black sails he saw above him, hanging in lazy lateen, were oddly static. He could feel a breeze, but despite it the sails remained still and he began to wonder what force, if any existed, would fill that strange canvas. To his fingers the sail canvas felt delicate, like silk, but who would make a sail out of such fragile material?

He had explored the deck from stem to stern, and not only had he not found Mister American, he hadn't encountered a single crewman, or even a single living thing. Even the derelicts in the weed sometimes had rats, but this ship was completely abandoned.

The only place left to explore was below decks.

Unlike a dhow, which it greatly resembled, there were no cabins of any kind. Just a hatch, slightly aft of the mainmast. It was partly opened, which surprised Sigurdsun; a well-run ship would have its hatches secured. Perhaps Mister American had gone below.

He lifted the hatch, throwing daylight down into the ship's depths. He saw movement, something large, perhaps more than one something. It did not like the light, whatever it was.

There was no step or rope, so he hung from the hatch for a moment, feet dangling in the dark. Then he let go.

They were all around him. He could sense that without seeing them, for they preferred the shadows, only their shifting bulk betraying them. He could not guess how many. There was fresh blood in the air, and sweat, and something else, rank and tainted.

"It is said," he called out to the dark, "at the docks of Dylath -Leen, that the black galleys come from far distant lands, with goods to trade, fantastic rubies and other things, and that those who sail the black galleys will pay any price for slaves. I was there. I remember. Perhaps all dreamers who sail the sea remember Dylath-Leen, the great city, famed for its fleet, and its magnificent port, where all things are bought and sold. I have wandered down every track, each alley of that city. I knew the least shack in it, and the greatest houses. It was my city.

"Then you took it from me. You took it from all of us, I suppose, those who dream of the sea, and who travel over it, who explore its depths. Dylath-Leen, the basalt city, Dylath-Leen the jewel, the delight. You came to us by night and you...

"Is that why you spread your nets further? Why you planted this Sargasso? Or is it not your doing, just an unhappy accident, which you take advantage of?"

The creatures did not speak. Their grey bulk seemed to

quiver, or shift, in the darkness, so he could not know what they looked like. Each had a great, blunt muzzle, from which lighter-coloured tentacles or pseudopods quivered. It was like Scyphozoa, sea jellies, he reasoned; the nematocyst probably contained some nervous irritant, something it used to sedate or immobilise prey. Or it could be a sensory organ of some kind. It deserved further study, but that required time he did not have.

"My friend would have had something to say by now, but I don't have his talent. I don't know where he is, but I can guess what happened to him."

They were all around him now. With no rope or ladder there was no way out of the hold.

"Allow me to give you this, with my compliments."

He held out the Model 24 *Stielhandgranate* that Mister American had scavenged from the warship. He'd hated using them – the pull cord had a nasty habit of catching on things, setting off the grenades accidentally – but they had their uses.

"I have already primed it."

Moving Targets

Adrian Tchaikovsky

It kicked off when Derwent and Nzeogu gate-crashed the warehouse party in Edmonton aided and abetted by a handful of the Metropolitan's finest. The neighbours – meaning anyone in a mile of the place – had been complaining about the music, but Nzeogu'd had a reliable tipoff and was hoping a few dealers of their acquaintance might be caught red handed, not to mention all the new friends they might make in possession of substances contrary to the Misuse of Drugs Act 1971.

The tip-off had been some kind of crazy talk, though. Some small-time pot-grower they'd nicked had been all about the ultimate new high, and apparently a warehouse in Edmonton was the place to score it.

"Goddamn bath salts," Nzeogu decided, as they were waiting outside the warehouse doors. The boom and thunder of the music was loud enough that Derwent had to read his lips.

"Going to be nothing," she said in his ear. "Just the usual." It felt good to say it, even if she was far from convinced. The vice world was spinning faster than ever these days. People were finding new ways to blow their minds faster than the legislation could keep up.

"Goddamn Slumside," Nzeogu added bitterly.

Derwent nodded. They were within an easy step from the Surreyside Temporary Housing Project clusterfuck, the first of the trumpeted "transient estates" that Westminster had rolled out to great fanfare last year. Surreyside – aside from being nowhere near the affluent pastures of Surrey – had been opened as a stepping-off point for the homeless: transients, economic migrants, refugees, care-in-the-community patients and the just-plain poor. Spiralling property prices and a bullish rental market had driven unprecedented numbers onto the streets, and in the end even the current administration had accepted that some sort of action was needed. Their economic wisdom had decreed what was now mostly known as "slumside". The intent was that everyone in need would find temporary housing in the super-estate before being sent on to something more congenial. Derwent wondered whether work had even started on phase two of that plan. All that had really happened was that a widespread homelessness problem had been shunted out of sight into a hellhole now so overpopulated it was reaching some kind of critical mass. Derwent had been sufficiently vocal, when the white paper had gone out, that she'd put the brass's back up and missed on a promotion. Now, with the news crammed with the excesses and the horrible conditions of Slumside, she had the bitter satisfaction of knowing she'd been right.

And of course, those consigned to Slumside didn't stay there, but went out into neighbouring boroughs and got on with business. She'd lost count of how many of Vice's leads had led back to that maze of concrete towers and broken windows. The party they were about to bust would be full of the young and rootless off the estate, because they wanted to have fun just like everyone else.

Then the all clear came through and the team rammed down the doors onto a room packed with dancing, jumping, screaming teens. There was a mad light show going on, and the air practically shuddered with the beat. Nzeogu went for the DJ and started pulling plugs with brutal efficiency.

Before the music cut – while all the revellers were still trying to understand that the party was over, Derwent had a sudden turn. The UV lights had been cut, but the whites of the ravers' clothing were still glowing blue. For a moment she thought she saw some spectral not-quite-purple radiance that suffused the place. In that same instant it seemed to her that the walls of the warehouse were infinitely far away and receding still further, and the air around her was... Later, the only word she could think of was *busy*, as though it had been populated with some invisible throng.

But then Nzeogu had pulled enough jacks to shut it all down, and the work of the night began – picking out familiar faces and taking them away; taking details, confiscating evidence, doing their jobs. It was a long night. There were a lot of stoned teens stumbling about clutching at the air around them, wide-eyed and reeling, gabbling and pawing at each other. Nzeogu's tip-off had been good; someone had been dealing something new at the warehouse. Which meant someone over in Slumside had been doing some creative cooking.

There were two major upshots from that night, neither of them the kind to build a career on. Firstly, aside from a couple of small-time dealers, the vice bust really was a bust. Almost everyone Derwent and Nzeogu had taken in turned up clean when the lab tests came through. Most of them would even have been legal to drive.

The pair of them commiserated about it later. "You saw how they were, coming out of the place," Nzeogu said,. "The way they were moving, there's no way they weren't on something."

Derwent could only agree but, whatever it was, it had left no chemical traces in the users, nor noticeable after-effects. And by that time the few who had lawyers were talking about charges and time limits and compensation.

Which left Steni Osalawi.

Derwent got in one morning to nine voicemails, eleven emails and a text concerning the new-fledged internet campaign to release Steni Osalawi. The Chief Inspector wanted to see her ASAP to demand why there was no paperwork about the boy and why they hadn't let him go with the others. There was a Human Rights lawyer taking the whole business to the press for the publicity and there were friends of the incarcerated who were going to protest outside the station as though the kid was a latter-day Nelson Mandela.

Neither Derwent nor Nzeogu had ever heard the name before.

In that horrible panic unique to public servants who may have screwed up the admin, they went through all the records from the night, all the admissions, the names, the numbers. Nowhere did the name Steni Osalawi feature.

"False ID," Nzeogu decided, so they got a picture of the boy from www.freesteni.org and compared it to the mugshots of everyone they'd taken in.

By lunchtime that day they were able to stand before the Chief Inspector and say with certainty that they couldn't free Steni because they'd never had him.

Steni had been at the party, according to his apparent large number of friends. Steni hadn't been seen after the party. The Human Rights lawyer did her level best to draw the conclusion that he'd been nicked by the Met and spirited away to some secret interrogation site but the utter lack of evidence eventually defeated even her crusading desire for publicity. Steni, it was concluded, must have slipped out the back, and his current whereabouts were nothing to do with the Vice Squad. Presumably he was sunk somewhere in the morass that was Slumside.

PR disaster averted, therefore. Except…

Over the next week, Derwent and Nzeogu went over the footage they'd confiscated from various party-goers' cameras, hoping to see some indication of drugs being passed from hand to hand. They were both convinced that someone had been dealing *something* that night, even if the lab had drawn a blank.

And they would have gone with that phone footage as supporting evidence, if it hadn't been for the lack of anything else. They found plenty of people under the influence of *something* – blissed out, staring, reaching out to touch empty space, goggling in astonishment at their hands or at nothing at all.

And they found Steni. By then, they were familiar enough with his face that it leapt out at them. Steni had doubled down on whatever it was the crowd was taking and it looked like he was having a bad trip. Derwent and Nzeogu watched him flail and flinch and push madly through the crowd, only to come up short as though whatever he was fleeing was all around him. He was on three different videos.

In the third, he disappeared.

"Holy Mother of God, what just happened?" Nzeogu demanded, dragging back the video slider so that Steni re-emerged from thin air.

They watched it a dozen times, feeling more and more unnerved. There was Steni, pushing, running; there he was, stopping, staring *upwards*, arms flung to protect him from something that wasn't there. Then ... just gone. When they played it back frame by frame there was no intermediate stage: present to absent without transition.

But it was through a moving crowd and the image quality was poor, there were lights flashing and the hand holding the phone camera was shaky, probably the video was corrupted and, most persuasive of all arguments, people didn't just vanish. Vice washed its hands of Steni Osalawi just as soon as it could establish that his disappearance – either figurative or literal, hadn't happened on their watch.

*

There was another bust over near Camden. Derwent and Nzeogu weren't on that detail, but the organisers and the MC had all been out of Slumside. The report had an angry bafflement they recognised from their own. Plenty of party-goers stoned out of their minds, no sign of actual drug use. There was a word associated with the phenomenon, now:

"Ghasting". Nobody seemed to know who had coined it.

Nzeogu had gone over to have a word with the officer in charge of the Camden operation and, when he came back, he had a plastic-wrapped package under his arm.

"What's that?" Derwent asked him.

"Evidence, on loan."

They went to an interrogation room with it, and Nzeogu unwrapped the thing with the air of a stage magician demonstrating a trick.

"I don't get it." Derwent frowned. "Or … wait, wasn't there…?"

"They had a thing like this connected to the decks at Edmonton," Nzeogu confirmed. "I figured it was just a DIY amp or something."

"Looks like a licence to get yourself electrocuted." Derwent looked at the jury-rigged tangle, seeing a snarl of homebrew wiring mixed up with what might have been electromagnets and some projecting rods that were … antennae maybe? The whole had an oddly purposeful arrangement to it, as though the physical shape was as significant as the wires.

"Goddamn flux capacitor," was Nzeogu's expert assessment. "Only, what the Camden lot called it was a 'Ghast resonator'."

Derwent nodded. "So, we're going to turn it on, or what?"

After that, there was nothing for it. Derwent found a pair of insulated gloves and then cautiously plugged the whatever-it-was into the mains.

The Ghast resonator made a shuddering, screeching noise, like some sort of feedback gone feral, but just as Derwent was fumbling to yank the plug again it settled down to a barely audible hum. Nothing lit up or exploded or dispensed illegal pharmaceuticals.

"We've found a nasty noise machine," she concluded, and looked at Nzeogu. He was staring at her. She stared at him. They stared at each other. The world around them slowly began to glow with colours Derwent had no name for. She watched them creep out of the walls and ooze out of the air like condensation. Nzeogu's dark face was as infinitely detailed as God's thumb-print, his features a maze-like whorl that never ended. She could hear something, too, some great irregular rhythm coming to her from a distance she couldn't parse, the tide on an unnamed shore.

"Mother of God," Nzeogu got out. He slapped at the resonator but seemed to be separated from it by a colossal distance.

"Gak," Derwent said. Some part of her was *aware* of Nzeogu in a completely new way. She felt him as a physical construct in space and as a weight that was exerting a minute but perceptible gravity on all things around him. Mortifyingly, some part of her brain found this expression of physics and geometry intensely sexual, an inexplicable linking of the highest and most basal parts of the brain by a cracking electric bridge.

Right about then, a stranger burst into the room, ripped the resonator's plug out of the wall and took the pair of them into custody.

*

He gave his name as Falconer, which Derwent reckoned immediately as way too edgy to be true. He was very obviously someone who wanted to look like a dangerous government agent. He was a big man, taller than Nzeogu, who was topping six feet, and with the broad shoulders of someone who took their gym sessions seriously. He carried a gun.

Derwent – separated from Nzeogu at this point – refused to say a damn thing until someone told her why an officer of the Metropolitan Police Service was suddenly in a cell without charge or warning. That got her a phone call from the Chief Inspector who told her for God's sake to just cooperate. Apparently Falconer, in a blinding piece of reverse psychology, actually was a dangerous government agent working with

Counter-Terrorism.

He played hardball at first, all but accusing her of trying to bring down the monarchy. Derwent stuck to the facts, and in the end her annoyed bewilderment obviously got through because she was reunited with Nzeogu, sat down and given a stern talking to.

Falconer did his level best to tell them they didn't know what they were getting themselves into, and should just leave it alone. Derwent and Nzeogu, by unspoken agreement, told him that he was absolutely right they didn't know what they were getting themselves into, and that meant they were going to keep on unwittingly getting into it until someone – hint: Falconer – actually told them.

"Also," Derwent put in, "this is some sort of new drug culture thing. How does this get Counter-Terrorism on our case?"

"Funding," Nzeogu guessed. "Whoever's selling this shit's sending the cash to Saudi Arabia or something."

"Selling?" Falconer repeated incredulously. Derwent reckoned that was the moment he finally accepted they didn't know anything. She saw the pieces click together behind his eyes as he reclassified them from "threat" to "asset".

"Some kids are getting high off a transistor radio," Derwent told him. "How does that become a clear and present danger?"

So he showed them the video.

The footage came from a security camera – they were both more than familiar with the terrible picture resolution, which wasn't improved any by the flashing lights and constant bustle of motion. Someone had sent them a video of a party.

"Are they just taking the piss now, or what?" Nzeogu asked disgustedly.

"Maybe they want us to know what a good time they're having," agreed Derwent. The two of them stared at the grainy, jerky footage without much enthusiasm. If someone down there was dealing something, it was impossible to tell.

About two minutes in, the crowd began to get more than passionate about the gig, and Derwent's eyebrows went up past her fringe. "My, they *are* having a good time."

"Still don't see why it's our business," Nzeogu said prudishly. He didn't stop watching, though.

At four minutes in, Nzeogu asked, "Where are they going?"

"What?" Derwent glanced at him, then back at the screen. In that moment there were fewer people at the party. Those that remained were on their feet, couples breaking apart. They saw lots of waving arms, lots of wide-eyed faces, but for a moment it could still have been just a really wild party.

Then Nzeogu said, "Mother of God," and paused the video, flicking back a few seconds. "Guy there, in the stripy top."

It was Steni all over again. Derwent watched stripy-top guy vanish abruptly. Five seconds later and she'd forgotten him, because the condition was catching. The movement of the crowd was unmistakably panic by then, a fluid mob of people flurrying this way and that like sheep driven by an invisible dog. And fewer, always fewer, just vanishing away one by one until only a handful remained. They fled, but they never fled far. Whatever was on their heels was right before their faces as well, driving them around the room until they, too, were gone.

By five minutes the entire terrified crowd had been spirited away, and the floor of the club was covered with discarded clothing. Derwent thought it was from the impromptu orgy at first, but then she saw that distinctive stripy top and realised that the detritus had been left behind by its occupants. The thought turned her stomach.

The video continued to play, the camera's lifeless eye watching that impossible room. And, just as Derwent was about to rewind, something moved. Out of a corner came a young ... girl, Derwent thought, probably. She had hair cut short, and she was navigating carefully over the garment-strewn floor in a wheelchair. Halfway across the room she looked directly up into the camera. Then she slowly inched her way out of shot.

Derwent and Nzeogu exchanged glances.

"Faked," he decided, in a voice that shook a little. They both looked at Falconer.

"This was last week," he told them flatly. "This was when this became, like you say, a clear and present danger. And whatever the fuck these machines are, they're making them in Slumside."

He had a name from a previous bust, a supplier: Raymond Paoli. Perhaps they'd heard of someone by that name resident in Slumside?

Derwent and Nzeogu stared at him. "Do you have any idea just how many people they've crammed into that place?" she asked.

"Atacom," Nzeogu put in. "They're supposed to have records on everyone who got re-housed there."

Yeah right, was Derwent's thought on that, but Falconer had seized on the idea like his namesake, and that evening they went off to rattle the cages of the mighty.

*

The cheery red logo of Atacom was a familiar sight about Slumside. Atacom was the government's chosen public-private partner on the project, whose previous triumphs included running down the unemployment benefit system and overcharging the NHS. Now they were responsible for administering Slumside and moving its residents on to permanent housing elsewhere. So far, according to the more incisive news websites, they had been paid a whole swimming pool of public money but not actually hit any targets. People went into Slumside but it just got fuller.

Atacom's regional office was actually on the very edge of Slumside, a big concrete wart so heavily secured against the locals that Nzeogu reckoned he could see where all the money had gone right there. They were calling on Atacom's director of the Surreyside project, Hugh Hawkins. His alliterative name was already being muttered in the corridors at Westminster as the man who would take the fall when Atacom finally had to admit it couldn't process the vast numbers of people it had "temporarily" housed in Slumside.

The three of them went in at nine p.m. in the apparent hope of dragging Hawkins away from some soiree. To Falconer's obvious disappointment he found the director still at work, whilst all around him a hundred data entry clerks sorted through swathes of paperwork and wrung the most out of their zero hour contracts.

Hawkins didn't look well. His expensive suit was sweat-stained and unlaundered. The bags under his eyes had luggage of their own, set in a saggy, stubbly face. This was a man about to reap what Atacom had sown when it underbid all the competition to get the contract. At first he was dismissive, but Falconer showed him a warrant card and made a few pointed threats about extended powers. After that Hawkins placed Atacom's resources – such as they were – at Falconer's disposal, and probably promised him the moon on a string as well, given the company's propensity to write administrative cheques its personnel couldn't honour.

All for nothing: an exhaustive search failed to turn up Paoli's name anywhere in the database. No sign that Atacom had found the malefactor a home since Slumside had opened its gates to the masses. Of course, given that those gates never closed, there were plenty of denizens who hadn't come by official channels, mostly looking to hide in a crowd.

Afterwards, Derwent set about tapping the usual contacts and informants about the estate, taking in small-time dealers and leaning on them, hunting for any mention of a name. She was still in the early stages of this when Nzeogu leapt up with an exclamation and called her over. Moments later they were putting a call in to Falconer.

"How much did you like going to prod Hawkins, Mr Falconer?" Nzeogu asked. At the puzzled response he grinned at Derwent and explained, "Paoli is Atacom, or he was. I was going over their database, and there he is: not a resident – an employee."

Minutes later, Falconer picked them up and the three of them drove right back to Hawkins' offices.

*

Hawkins was plainly not overjoyed at their return. "Do you realise just how *busy* we are here?" he demanded. "I've…" He waved a hand about his office, which showed relatively little of the bureaucratic chaos reigning outside his door. "I've got the Home Secretary's office calling on a daily basis asking when I'm going to have Slu— Surreyside working as intended. I've got the press waiting to crucify me. I don't need some conspiracy theorist policeman trying to complicate my life."

Falconer was having none of it. "Raymond Paoli, Hawkins. I dropped the name before. You knew we were after him. Mind explaining why you didn't mention he works for you?"

Hawkins twitched. "I have no idea—" and then Falconer had shown him a photo, a blurry shot from someone's phone of a thin-faced, olive skinned man with a ponytail and a goatee.

"You know him," Falconer concluded.

"He doesn't work for us."

"But he used to, didn't he?"

Hawkins collapsed into his chair like someone decanting jelly. "Oh God," he moaned. "Yes, all right? But he was fired, terminated without notice. I'm sorry it's just … we've got enough worry right now without it getting out we had some kind of drug dealer on the payroll."

"Whatever he's dealing, it's not drugs," Nzeogu put in, thinking of the impossible security camera footage.

"I really have no idea." Hawkins put his head in his hands. "Security saw him going into Slum— damnit, into Surreyside. He was fraternising, you know. There's some kind of awful rave club business that goes on there, that we were trying to keep a lid on, but every time we sent the boys in to shut one down, they'd moved somewhere else, and it was because Paoli was just tipping them off. He was a … DJ or a dealer or, well, I didn't even care, right then. I gave him his marching orders. But, please – I don't need this to get to the press. They've got their teeth into enough of me, right now. I'm having to go before a Parliamentary committee in ten days' time. I don't need anything more."

"So where's Paoli now?" Falconer wanted to know.

"Oh God, you think I know? Somewhere in Slumside, probably. He had plenty of friends there." Hawkins didn't even try to correct himself this time.

Thankfully, by that time Derwent had shaken a little information loose from some of her regular informants.

"There's going to be a party in Slumside tonight," she told them. "Paoli's guest of honour."

*

Going into Slumside always gave Derwent the impression of a time-lapse film. The estate had officially opened the year before, but some of the work had been so much on the cheap that it was already falling down, while other parts were unfinished and still – equally on the cheap – being put up. Everywhere was the Atacom logo, in various stages of vandalisation. Falconer stared through the armoured glass of the big-ass four by four that was apparently standard issue for Dangerous Government Agents, taking in the graffiti, the squalor, the boarded up windows and gangs of surly adolescents glowering at their little convoy. "How do people live like this?" he demanded, no doubt thinking of his nice house somewhere in rural Berkshire.

Because we force them to, Derwent thought, but it wouldn't have been a popular opinion even amongst her colleagues, let alone with Mr Home Office here.

They met up with two dozen heavies in Atacom jackets on loan from Hawkins to help corral the crowd and stop Paoli slipping out the fire exit. Falconer had brought half a dozen of his crew as well, all armed, and Derwent was already guessing this would prove to be a poor mix of work ethics.

Surreyside Annex B Village Community Hall, said the sign on the least village-hall-like concrete bunker they had ever seen. The layer of gang signs and crude drawings of genitals had probably improved property prices in the neighbourhood. There was most certainly a community in residence, though. The pulse of the music was rattling Derwent's fillings and the windows were strobing with lights. The sensory impression was so overwhelming that it was a moment before Derwent identified the screaming from within.

"It's happening!" she snapped, whilst keeping her mind off just what *it* might be. In an instant she was off, Nzeogu behind her and the rest left in the dust. In retrospect the Chief Inspector would be right to chew her out over it, but she could hear people in trouble, real I'm-being-murdered trouble, and that sort of thing didn't wait for the paperwork.

The place was emptying at the seams even as she got close, a tumbling spew of panicking ravers gouting from the nearest door. She was looking at faces, hoping she'd know Paoli if he tried to get past her, but the more she looked, the more world there was. She was staring through the choked doorway and it seemed that there was infinite space and time contained within the room, and loops and tendrils of air moved past one another in a glassy haze, slithering like translucent fish.

Fugitive revellers were pelting past her then, and she was no longer looking for Paoli. Instead her eyes were following the oozing motion of the air before her – no, the air around her. Everywhere she looked, all the spaces were populated and repopulated, a bestiary of insubstantial things only detectable by their edges and outlines. They shuddered and pulsed like jellyfish, not merely packed one against the other but sliding effortlessly through a shared space, respecting no boundaries, not even each others'. She shuddered as their gelatinous borders intersected the party-goers, the walls, her own flesh.

They were blind and heedless, and yet she could sense something else, some vaster attention, and with a stab of utter fright knew that by that same medium it could sense her too. She felt as though she was aboard a tiny, tiny boat on an endless roiling sea, and some great maw was rising towards the surface, towards her, faster and faster until it would erupt all about her and —

Nzeogu cannoned into her, startling her from her trance. He was struggling with a skinny goateed guy in a Star Wars T-shirt: Paoli.

"Help me get him out of here!" he yelled. His face was taut, greyish, and she knew he'd seen it, some of it. He was fighting away the implications until he had a quiet room and a full bottle and the liberty to shout himself hoarse.

They lurched and manhandled Paoli towards the four-by-four, dragging him through a melee of shrieking ravers and Atacom thugs. Raymond Paoli wasn't fighting them, but he was putting up one hell of a fight against whatever invisible demons the Ghast resonator had hauled from his mind. Only when Nzeogu slammed him face-first into the car window to cuff him did they get his attention.

"I couldn't turn it off!" His face was twisted, wild. One eye was pressed to the car, the other swivelled to goggle at Derwent. "It's too strong, I made it too strong."

"Raymond Paoli, I am placing you under arrest under suspicion of I don't know the fuck what. I must warn you, you do not have to say anything —" Derwent started, and then gave up on the formal caution because there was no sign Paoli was listening to her. *Let's just say we said it.*

"It's not fun!" Paoli shrieked suddenly, as though recent events were suddenly catching up with him. "In the lab it was fun, but that was ten per cent. This is seventy! This is too much! You see *all the way* at seventy!" He convulsed backwards, throwing Nzeogu off him just as the cuffs clicked shut. Right into Derwent's face he screamed, "They'll go for *one hundred*!

Nobody wants to see what's at one hundred! Nobody wants it to see *you*!" and the last word just went on and became a hideous scream that rose above all the other chaos – a sound beyond anything a human throat should have produced. Derwent recoiled, and then Nzeogu slammed into Paoli again, ramming him against the car.

Paoli never made it, and Nzeogu jarred his shoulder against the bulletproof glass with nothing in his grasp but empty, fear-stinking clothes. In that moment Derwent had the sense of something vast streaming past her – *through* her. But by then she couldn't see any of the phantasmal monsters, the spaces around her were limited and measurable and mundane. Falconer had put seven bullets into the resonator and it had given up the ghost, execution accomplishing what simple unplugging had not.

*

Derwent knew Slumside, or she thought she had. On the drive back to the station, with a van-full of bewildered ravers and a box-full of Paoli's effects, she couldn't see it the same way. It wasn't just the hallucinations – they *had* been hallucinations – brought on by the resonator. It wasn't just the impossible fate that had overtaken Paoli, which she wasn't even bothering trying to characterise as an escape because God knew the man hadn't wanted to go. Even when she could unclog her mind of all of *that*, she could still see a terrible nervous energy everywhere in Slumside, as though the place was waiting for the storm to break. The locals were out on the streets, skittish and twitchy on corners. Dispatch reports over the radio revealed a rash of petty crimes, lost tempers, property damage. She wondered if word was spreading that Ghasting had gone from a diversion to a death sentence at 'seventy'.

Everywhere the Atacom logo loured from billboards and hoardings, and beneath them the contractors swarmed like ants, digging and building. *Too little too late, surely*, because the parliamentary hearings would kick off within the month, and then Hugh Hawkins' sweaty arse would be hanging in the breeze. She doubted his public pillorying would make conditions any better.

Nzeogu didn't say a word on the way back. His stare could reasonably be categorised as 'thousand yard.' His hands shook like they had the month after he had given up smoking. Back at his desk, he hunched over his keyboard, shaking his head.

"You didn't see it," he said, to himself, to Derwent.

"I saw," she told him shortly. "The resonator thing, it makes you see all kinds of stuff that's not there."

"No." He shivered. "Mother of God, Derwent, it's there. It's *still* there."

He was shivering, rubbing at his eyes with the heels of his hands as though he could scrub out the image of what they'd witnessed. "Clear and present danger," he said shakily. "Mother of God."

"It's not over," Falconer told them both. If he had seen anything, he wasn't saying. Perhaps he had seen it all before. Perhaps he just had no imagination.

"It's over for Paoli," Derwent pointed out.

"So he had associates, a supplier or people he supplied. The resonators are still out there. We don't even know if he was the one constructing them. I don't want to go online tomorrow and find the instructions up on YouTube."

Derwent powered up Paoli's phone. No PIN: he had apparently not trusted his own ability to remember a four digit number in the end, which meant that she didn't have to employ any ill-gotten skills that she wouldn't have admitted to possessing. Idly she flicked through whatever apps he had left open, learning more than she wanted about his predilections for pornography before finally locating Facebook.

He had a reminder. He had one event today. Paoli's final send-off had a Facebook Event devoted to it.

It was proudly announced as a Seventy Party: she got the impression that there were diminishing returns with Ghasting

and that Paoli and his fellows had been upping the specs to out
-do each other. She scrolled idly down all the vapidly positive
acceptances from what looked like half the population of
Slumside. And stopped.

"JoMa" had declined the invite, apparently. Like so many
people online, she had wanted Paoli to know exactly why he
wouldn't be graced by her company. Her reasons seemed more
reasonable than most, though.

*This isn't a toy. I've told you it's too dangerous. Seventy will go
beyond.*

And it had: Derwent could testify to that, sure enough. So
who was JoMa and how did she know so much about it? *Have I
just found Paoli's dealer?*

JoMa's avatar was a photo: a pale girl with short dark hair,
looking no more than eighteen. Derwent tried to get more
details, but her page was locked and there was little to find.
Except there was something familiar about that face.

Nzeogu looked over her shoulder and wordlessly called up
Falconer's security camera footage, freezing it towards the end
with the wheelchair centre screen.

Maybe it was the same individual, maybe it wasn't. The
similarities were striking, though.

"We should have been looking for her all the time, instead
of Paoli," Derwent growled, and plunged into the morass of
Atacom's files looking for any sign of mobility issues and
wheelchairs. That encompassed a whole category of Slumside's
residents, so the search should have been needle and haystack
territory. Atacom's own incompetence came to her rescue,
though. She found a dozen separate emailed complaints about
a broken lift at Venture Block, Ascension Row, from the
resident at Flat 37, one Josephine Mahler.

"You up for another jaunt into Slumside?" she asked.

Nzeogu's shoulders hunched. "Sure," he muttered, but he
didn't look at her and he didn't get up.

Derwent wanted to shout at him that she didn't exactly

fancy it either: that this was their lead, this was what they had to follow up. She didn't. She accepted that maybe whatever hallucinations he'd endured were worse than hers. After all, he had been holding Paoli when the man had been spirited away. Nzeogu didn't look like he was ready to go back.

"I'll go with Falconer," she told him. "You … see if there's anything more in Paoli's things."

*

The only accurate part of their target address was the word "block", which gave a suitably at-Her-Majesty's-Pleasure air. Ascension Row was going to have to wait a hell of a long time for any kind of upturn in its fortunes and the only "venture" involved in Venture Block would be the capitalists who had made off with the public funding.

The lift was not in working order, as advertised. Falconer and Derwent and two of the armed response team dutifully trooped up the stairs, while the rest watched the windows and the fire escape, and probably had a surprise in store for any sudden helicopter rescue from the roof. By this point, Derwent wasn't sure just *what* Falconer might end up doing.

"So this Mahler, crippled evil genius you reckon?" Derwent asked as they hit the second storey landing.

"Let's find out." Moments later they were going through the chipboard door of Flat 37 like it was papier-mâché.

In that moment, the expression on the face of Josephine Mahler was surely everything Falconer had hoped for. She had barely time to turn halfway from her computer, hands on the rims of her wheels, when the gunmen had her covered and were shouting at her to stay still. Falconer strode in after them with his warrant card out, exclaiming, "Gotcha!"

Mahler really was about eighteen. She wore a T-shirt showing a cube with a heart on it, and the legs inside her jeans were atrophied, stick-thin. She had her hands up but she was shaking her head, horrified. "What are you doing here?" she shouted over the demands of the response squad.

"Did you think we wouldn't find you?" Falconer asked her, idly twisting her computer round to look at the screen. "Tell me, what was Paoli? Just some underling who liked playing junkie with your tech? Because you know it's not about the legal highs, don't you?"

Mahler stared at him. "Who are you?" she demanded.

"I'm here to put a stop to these resonators before anyone else gets vanished. Before one of your friends decides that an army base or Prime Minister's Question Time needs livening up with a bit of Ghasting. I saw what you did before, Miss Mahler. I saw you wipe out a whole room full of people and then just calmly wheel yourself out of there. So how about you give me some answers?"

For a long moment Mahler said nothing, and Derwent finally realised it was because she was so very, very angry.

"What was I supposed to do?" she hissed at last. "Get up and dance around? Do you seriously think that was something *I* made happen?"

And Derwent had already been thinking that Falconer – in his need to put a lid on the whole impossible business – had been running too far ahead. Mahler's reactions were way off for someone who had been caught red-handed.

"What's this?" Falconer was squinting at Mahler's computer. Derwent could see what looked like a Google Earth view of Slumside, with lines and scribbles superimposed, highlighting where...

"Those are where Atacom's been working on the estate," she said automatically. It wasn't much, but Slumside was still her patch.

Falconer took that in, then stared at Mahler. "That's it, is it? Fed up of complaining about the lifts? Taking matters into your own hands?"

And Mahler laughed, a high and desperate sound. "Oh fuck, you really think it's *me?*"

Derwent's phone chimed and she clutched for it

automatically. Nzeogu had texted her *going to hawkins atacm urgent.*

She thumbed back *not alone also why???*

"You think I'm some criminal mastermind?" Mahler laughed again, though it was more like crying. "I've been trying to work this out ever since all my fucking friends got eaten at the party."

Another chime. Nzeogu had sent her a photo, skewed and slightly out of focus. It showed a business card.

Raymond Paoli. Atacom plc. Research and Development.

"You need to get out of here," Mahler told them. "At least you can take the stairs."

*

Just about everyone at Atacom had knocked off for the night, by now, except the big cheese himself. When Nzeogu burst into his office, Hawkins was in the middle of packing a briefcase. His expression, caught in the act, was one of utter denial.

"No," he got out. "No, I need to get to Westminster."

"You're not going anywhere." Nzeogu felt just as shaky and washed out as Hawkins looked, but maybe there was a reason for that. Maybe they had an experience in common "I will arrest you if I have to."

"On what charge?" Hawkins demanded.

"On any damn charge I feel like because I am going to hold onto you until you tell me why Atacom needs an R&D department." He slung down Paoli's card.

Hawkins' face twitched and quivered as though the man he'd once been, before taking on this job, was still trapped inside and trying to get out. "It's not my fault," he said faintly. "It's not what you think."

Nzeogu lunged forward and shoved him so that he slammed back down into his seat. "I do not even *know* what I think right now. I just know some guy you used to employ to *develop* things turns up on the street with some mind-fuck invention that's also a disintegrator ray or something. I want to know what's going on." He could hear his own voice going raw with exhaustion and accumulated trauma. "I want to know what happened to me."

Hawkins looked convulsively over his shoulder, out of the window at the sprawling eyesore of Slumside. "It's too late now anyway," he said, in a small voice. "It doesn't matter."

"Sure, sure, Parliamentary enquiry's going to tear you a new one," Nzeogu said, unsympathetically. "Look —"

Hawkins' smile was sickly, awful to behold. "Oh no, that's going to be just fine. We're going to hit all our targets." As though finally resigning himself to Nzeogu's presence, he settled back in the chair. "Paoli … Paoli thought it was all free love and opening the mind, but really hitting targets is the only thing."

"Explain," Nzeogu pushed.

"I had a great-great-uncle. Crawford was his name. He was a genius," Hawkins told him raggedly. "He invented something – his resonator. And it opens the mind, Paoli was right about that much. It opens the mind so far that *anything* can get in."

*

"We're not going anywhere until you give us some answers," Falconer told Mahler. "What have you done? What have your people planted here? When's it going to blow? What about your friend Raymond?"

Mahler looked from him to Derwent and obviously decided that she was the more reasonable of the two. "Raymond was an idiot. He got out of Atacom with their stuff and thought it was like designer drugs. He didn't believe me about them being dangerous. I mean, a hundred people just gone, and nobody cares. You tell the authorities, they say people disappear in Slumside all the time. But I saw Atacom's people go over the place, after. That's when I got onto Raymond, for all the good it did. That's when I started digging. Because the party I was at wasn't even one of Paoli's. That was a test, an official test." She made an abortive move for her computer, but Falconer was in the way. "I found papers – crackpot science, Fortean stuff, some crazy guy called Crawford Tillinghast. Tillinghast invented a machine."

"A machine that makes you hallucinate," Derwent prompted, because that was what she dearly wanted to believe.

"No," Mahler said simply. "It lets you see what's really there, all the time, around us. You've seen them, haven't you?"

"The things from out there," Derwent said unwillingly.

"Not out there." Mahler hugged herself. "In here, everywhere, touching us and inhabiting us all the time, except without the resonator we're irrelevant to each other. All those lights and sounds and sensations that Paoli got high off, they're the reality. They're an environment, an ecosystem. And when we're plugged into it, we're prey."

*

"Look out of the window," Hawkins invited. "Look at it. My legacy. They thought they could make me their scapegoat, you see, but I'll go before the pen pushers in Westminster and tell them it's all fine. Working as intended. I hadn't wanted to start things so soon, but you and your friends, you were asking too many questions. So I pushed the button." He shuddered, but a tiny giggle escaped him at the same time. "Score one for Uncle Crawford."

"What have you done?" Nzeogu demanded.

"Just following government policy," Hawkins said, trying for innocence. "I mean, let's not fool ourselves here. We both know the whole point behind putting all those people in Slumside is that it's out of sight, out of mind, yes? And it was obvious the whole temporary housing thing was never going to work. Too many people, too little planning, no budget at all. And then they dump the blame on me because they need someone to blame when it all fails." Hawkins' eyes were bloodshot, horrible: a man who had been staring at something terrible for a long time, without even needing a machine to help him see it. "But it won't fail," he confided. "Uncle Crawford came through for me. Too many people you see. Too little space. But what if there's always more space?"

*

"So you're trying to disrupt Atacom's works because they killed your friends?" Falconer grasped desperately, jabbing a hand at the map on Mahler's screen.

But Mahler was gripping the wheels of her chair. "Jesus," she said, "can you feel it?"

"What?" Falconer hissed, but Derwent could. The room around them seemed to be vibrating at some uncomfortable frequency and her eyes kept finding movement in empty space.

"There's a resonator," she got out. "Where is it? Turn it off!" She began running around the flat, opening drawers and scouring shelves to find the machine. Every step saw the walls of the world recede all around her, making space for other things.

"Stand still!" Mahler laughed again, that wretched, despairing sound. "Look at the map, you idiots! Look at what they've done!"

Derwent stared at the image, following all the lines and loops where Atacom had been digging up the road, her eyes tracking round and round about the violated streets until she stopped seeing the cramped confines of Slumside and saw instead a simple, familiar arrangement of wiring and structure.

"It's the whole estate," she whispered, even as the air around her began to shift and undulate. From beyond the walls of the flat – from beyond the walls of the world – she heard the first screams.

"Don't move," Mahler said, calm now the worst had come. "Movement attracts them."

*

Nzeogu looked out across Slumside and saw it all begin to leap out at him, detail by detail: the things that had always been there in the corner of his eye, but he'd never known to notice them. He saw their mindless, jellyfish forms blob and bloat through the air, through walls, through each other, trailing helices of tentacles. They devoured and were devoured like the world under a microscope suddenly writ impossible large. He saw the gulfs they swam in falling away in directions he didn't even have names for.

There were courses cut through that gelatinous sea of overlapping monsters, wakes left by the true killers. The streets were full of people fleeing back and forth, fighting the insubstantial hordes, tearing at their own eyes, but each moment those streets were less full. Nzeogu had held out hope that Paoli and Osalawi and the rest were just … *elsewhere*, waiting to be restored to the world. Now he knew that they had gone someplace where there was no coming back from.

He got his phone out with the intention of calling someone to cut off the power to all of Slumside, but instead of a dial tone came the echoing sound of the vast, liquid void into which all signals, all energy was vanishing.

Hawkins was at his elbow, staring. "Oh God," the executive gasped, but Nzeogu didn't hear horror in his voice, only the near-orgasmic glee of a bureaucrat who is going to hit his targets after all.

Nzeogu didn't think, really – not about his career, not about what Derwent might say – he just took Hawkins by the shoulder and the belt and threw him hard at the window. The executive burst through it in a radiating pattern of glass shards that seemed to fall away in every direction forever, fractalling into infinity. But then something rose up from the depths of nowhere and intercepted the arc of his body, and there was just an expensive suit gusting empty on the wind.

*

And within the boundless expanse that was Mahler's flat, three frail people held terribly still and waited to see if the newly-visible world would notice them.

The Play's the Thing

Keris McDonald

Northern England, 1902

The young man stepped out onto the wet cobbles and watched as the hansom pulled away down the street. The clop of hooves was audible for some time after the cab disappeared from view. Then the silence returned, the silence of a great city heard from its very edge, made up of the distant thrum of foundries and factories. Lights in the broad valley below painted a yellow smudge in the smog-tainted air.

He turned up the collar of his coat. It was drizzling and the deserted suburban road was not a pleasant place to linger, but the gate he sought was only a few paces away. From outside the walled grounds of Lithly House, little was visible except the bare branches of sycamores and the dark and dripping masses of the rhododendron bushes. Once away from the street's gas-lamps, only the pale glimmer of the crushed limestone drive suggested the route to follow through the darkness. It was clear that the track had not been swept since the start of winter – and clearer still, upon reaching the front of the house, that the place was suffering from some neglect. Ivy sprawled over the terrace and lank grass grew in the rose-beds. But smoke was issuing from two of the three great chimney stacks, and lamplight gleamed from the oriel window. It was a very substantial building with tall windows suggesting high-ceilinged rooms, built of yellowy-dun stone – though that was stained from the city's coal-smoke. Great black streaks hung down its façade from the eaves like shadowy stalactites.

He mounted the front steps and pulled upon the bell. The door was opened by a butler in an old-fashioned frock coat: a short, wizened man with a white fleece of hair and skin as black as burnt paper. The servant had to look up at the visitor, yet somehow gave the impression of staring down his nose as he enquired, "Yes? May I help you?"

"My name is Mr Arthur Richmond, of Roy and Johns Associates. Mr Thale requested my presence." So saying, Richmond produced his card for inspection. The butler took it in white-gloved hands and glanced searchingly at its owner, as if he suspected some fraud. What he saw was a young man of inoffensive demeanour and bland countenance, carrying a small leather case, his gold-rimmed spectacles glinting in the light that spilled from the door.

"I shall inform the master that you have arrived. Would you care to step inside, sir?"

Leaving the newcomer in the hall, the butler disappeared into the interior of the house. Richmond clasped his hands behind his back and wandered around the small circumference of light afforded by a single oil-lamp set on a side-table, but found little to rest his attention upon except for an ailing geranium in a Chinese pot and a tapestry depicting Jael about to drive the tent-peg into Sisera's head. He studied this scene abstractly.

Almost noiselessly, the butler returned. "Mr Thale will see you, sir. Might I take your coat and hat?" The disrobing accomplished, he took up the lamp and led Richmond into the depths of the house. The corridors and antechambers were richly furnished to the point of being cluttered, and only by following closely could the visitor avoid barking his shins upon the heavy furniture that lurked there. At length they came out into a room that was fully lit: the gas-mantles on the walls hissing gently, the huge fireplace occupied by blazing logs. A man of mature years reclined upon the *chaise longue* nearest the fireplace. Despite the heat and close atmosphere he wore a mustard-coloured dressing gown and his legs were draped in a tartan blanket. He was frowning.

"Mr Arthur Richmond, sir," said the butler.

Richmond came forward. "It is a pleasure to meet you, Mr Thale."

"Richmond?" said the master of Lithly House. "I was expecting Mr Johns. He has always represented your firm in the past." Thale was a heavy-set man with blunt, handsome features and a fleshy jaw line. He didn't rise to greet Richmond, and there was an edge of anxiety to his ill humour.

"Mr Johns is my uncle," said the young man mildly. "He passed on eighteen months ago."

Thale grunted, looking his visitor up and down while fiddling with the edge of his blanket. "I see. I'm sorry to hear it. But … you're a bit young, Richmond."

"I assure you, I am fully conversant with all the work of Roy and Johns Associates, and entirely competent to deal with any eventuality," he replied – adding after a slight pause: "With, of course, the discretion and care for which that company is renowned."

Thale gave him a long, considering look and then reached for the brandy glass on the small table at his side. "And are you familiar with the unique circumstances of this house?"

"The … unusual properties of Lithly House have always been of particular interest to me, sir."

Thale raised one eyebrow. "Very well. Naotalba, fetch a sherry for the young man."

The butler, who had been waiting motionless with hands folded, dropped a slight bow and flitted from the room.

"Excellent fellow," Thale muttered, relaxing a little. "Bought him in Havana. Long time ago now, of course." He didn't seem to notice his visitor's studiously blank expression. "Richmond, is it? What do you think of the house, now you've seen it?"

"The exterior is most impressive," Richmond answered carefully.

"Yes, it does have a picturesque facade. Did you know Mr Atkinson Grimshaw has painted it as one of his 'moonlight' series? He could not be persuaded to take an interest in the rooms within, unfortunately – there was an unhappy disagreement between us on certain matters of taste. However, I understand that he found even the front elevation quite inspirational."

"Yes, I can imagine that."

A smile pulled at Thale's lips. "This house has quite an effect upon the sensitive temperament," he confided. "I am only an amateur collector of art, but I pride myself that I am an expert collector of artists. I do my best to play host here to those creative souls who will appreciate its special atmosphere. The dear late Mr Beardsley was particularly fond of Lithly House, and was always a favourite of the family – he and his lovely sister. He conceived his *Salome* pieces during a holiday here, did you realise? Wonderful, aren't they?"

"I am familiar with the illustrations," the younger man said guardedly. "They are quite striking."

"He had to tone down the final prints for public consumption, of course. The original sketches were ... unsuitable." Thale's tone was casual, but his eyes were fixed upon his guest with a curious gleam.

The object of his scrutiny did not react. "Might I ask," he said, "the nature of your particular problem on this occasion?"

The older man grunted and regarded the folds of tartan before him with some gloom. "It's my own fault," he said. "I went out hunting. I don't leave the house much, as a rule, but there was a wonderful harvest moon and it was far too tempting an opportunity to miss. Had a splendid time. Unfortunately I took a fall which left me confined to my bed for some weeks."

At this point Naotalba reappeared bearing a tray with a single glass of sherry. Richmond accepted the drink and sipped it gingerly, still standing.

Thale sighed. "I am still a prisoner of this poor body. There is no prospect that I will be able to walk properly again." He swirled the brandy in his glass. "So you will understand that I have not been able to fulfil my duties as master of the house properly for some little time. I have not been able to inspect all the rooms, even with servants to carry me. Things have become muddled. I have lost control of some areas. There have been intrusions. That is why I called in your firm; Roy and Johns have dealt well with this family, and I am afraid I will need you to confront this situation for me."

"Specifically?"

"The Library has gone missing. And some other rooms. The Conservatory and the Clock Room, among others."

"How many?" Richmond asked, pulling a small notebook from his pocket and starting to make notes with a gilt pencil. His mild voice had become firm.

"Naotalba?"

"Seven, sir." Naotalba addressed Richmond directly. "There are eighty-one rooms in the house normally. Though some are frequently elusive, Miss Camilla has been trying to track them down in her father's absence. But there are seven we cannot find."

"There is normally a reliable route to the Library through the Picture Gallery," Thale added, "but a harpy seems to have taken up residence there and we cannot make our way past. All the other doors are missing. You may have to establish new routes."

Richmond put his sherry glass down on the mantelpiece, having found it too difficult to juggle both that and the notepad. "You wish me to dispose of the harpy as well?"

"Well, as you see fit. So long as the rooms are found, I can tolerate some vermin within the wainscoting."

Richmond nodded thoughtfully and chewed at his lower lip.

"You feel you are up to the task, then?" Thale asked.

There was barely a moment's hesitation. "Yes, sir. You may put your entire trust in me. Of course … it would be of great assistance to me if your butler could supply a full list of the rooms, extant and missing, if such a thing exists. It would save me a lot of time to begin with."

"Certainly." Thale waved a nonchalant hand. "Naotalba will bring you a list first thing in the morning. You won't be starting tonight at any rate – it's so much easier to find the doors by daylight."

"I will begin with the dawn," Richmond assured him, "but it may take some time to complete the entire inventory."

"I understand. Naotalba will show you to your room. I believe you will be sleeping in the Red Bedchamber. Is that correct, Naotalba?"

"Sir."

"Hmm. That room is not entirely reliable, I'm afraid – bit of a borderline case; you could have a disturbed night if you're unlucky. But then, Richmond, if you're not capable of dealing with that little eccentricity then you'll have very little chance of coping with the rest of the house. Fair's fair, eh?"

Richmond dipped a small, stiff bow. "I'm sure I shall be quite satisfied with the sleeping arrangements."

He was led out through the far door of the Drawing Room, through a pillared hall from which two great semi-circular flights of stairs swept up to the higher floors of the house, and beneath one of those cascades of steps toward a long corridor. As they passed through, a movement on the balcony above caught Richmond's eye, and he looked up sharply. A woman was leaning over the balustrade, staring at him with an expression that was certainly not indifferent but was otherwise ambiguous. As far as he could make out in that brief glimpse, she was young and informally dressed, the white of her blouse contrasting with her intensely dark hair. That was all he was able to determine before Naotalba's lamp passed under the stair and darkness engulfed the scene. Richmond was forced to hurry after him to keep up with the circle of light.

They reached a door, one of many ranged along an oak-panelled stretch of corridor. "Fifth door on the left after the tapestry of *Saturn and His Children*, sir," Naotalba said. "Usually."

The walls of the chamber were papered scarlet, the hangings of the old-fashioned bed made of blood-coloured velvet. A fire burned brightly in the grate, and laid out upon the counterpane was a silk nightshirt. Naotalba lit a taper and processed about the room, lighting candles in silver sconces. "I trust you will be comfortable here, sir. The bed has been thoroughly aired. There is a bathroom on the other side of the corridor, one or two doors to the right. If you require a bath tomorrow I shall be pleased to have hot water brought for you. Breakfast will be served at seven. Is everything to your satisfaction?"

"Perfectly," Richmond said, putting his case down on the bed. "Thank you."

"Then I shall wish you a good night, sir." Noiseless as a ghost, Naotalba bowed and withdrew. Richmond strolled to the window, pushed open the curtain and wooden shutter, and looked briefly down into the garden. The rain must have ceased at some point since he had entered the house; now a strong wash of moonlight lay over the panorama. He judged he was at the back of the building because he could make out the stable-block and a lake. He drew the curtain once more. Then he turned back to the bed, opened his case and took out a pistol, a box of ammunition, a large gold fob watch and a cheap novel.

He placed the first of these items under the bolster at his bed-head. After washing at the bowl and ewer on the side-table, he undressed, slipped into the nightshirt provided and climbed into bed. He sat up for some minutes reading, but was interrupted when the candles by his side went out, quite suddenly, without flickering or guttering. He looked about him sharply at that point. One by one the other candles in the room extinguished themselves, darkness swelling to fill the vacated space. Finally the fire itself dimmed, sank and went out.

Richmond sat in the dark for a few moments, then shrugged, put aside his book and spectacles, and lay down for a night of dreamless slumber.

*

When Naotalba arrived the next morning, bearing breakfast on a tray, Richmond was already up and dressed and gazing out of the window at the lake in the garden below.

"Did you sleep well, sir?"

"Perfectly," said Richmond. "There does seem to be a problem with the lighting, but it was only a minor inconvenience."

Naotalba's white brows rose. "You were not … troubled … by the phenomenon then, sir?"

"Not particularly."

"I'm very glad to hear it. Some of our past guests have found it quite distressing."

"Clearly I am possessed of a less sensitive nature," Richmond said, sitting down and looking at the breakfast. "Do you have the list I requested?"

"Certainly," Naotalba said, lifting a folded document from the tray and tucking it under Richmond's saucer. "Will there be anything else, sir?"

Richmond speared a mustard-basted kidney with his fork. "Umm … I won't be sitting down to luncheon. If you could provide me with some sandwiches that would be fine, thank you."

"Of course, sir. The master has requested that you join him for dinner tonight at seven."

"Hmm." Richmond nodded over a mouthful of kidney. He unfolded the paper with the hand not wielding the fork and glanced down the list. "Do you have any information that would help me get started?"

Naotalba inclined his head. "Only in the general sense, sir. The corridors are reliable, as is the great staircase. Other stairs, except the ones from the kitchen, are liable to get one lost. The second floor is considerably more intricate than the ground or the first. The attic rooms are largely servants' quarters or empty, or at least that is the intended situation. If you wish to enter the cellars you will have to ask myself or Mrs Taylor, the housekeeper, to unlock the gates. The Picture Gallery, should you intend to investigate that avenue of approach, is on the first floor."

"Thank you."

"If that is all, sir, I shall go and see that your sandwiches are prepared. And if you will permit me the liberty, I should like to wish you the best of luck."

With a bow, he retired. Richmond, absorbed in the list of rooms, forgot to keep chewing and simply read.

*

After breakfast, he began to compile something which, while it could never be a map of the house, might be a guide. With sheaves of paper in his arm, he began a systematic search of every room, starting from his own. In each chamber he recorded the orientation, the features, the exits and any signs of occupancy. In each room, too, once he was satisfied of its position, he would pull from his waistcoat pocket that object that might be taken for a gold watch, and make a series of delicate adjustments to the mechanism. Complex cross-referenced diagrams became a necessity. He discovered that there were two interior light-wells in the centre of the house, complicating the ground-plan. Even if Lithly House had been entirely mundane and passive it would have been easy to lose one's way between rooms.

But of course, the house was not passive. Richmond stumbled across the first anomaly almost at once: whilst there was a connecting door between the bedroom with the bamboo wallpaper and the small chamber with the harpsichord, it was not possible to move back from the latter to the former once the sneck had clicked shut, for the same door only opened into a cupboard full of broken violins. Instead one had to take the roundabout route back into the corridor, past the bust of Pan, and into the Bamboo Room that way.

Whilst a little unnerving, that particular manifestation of the house's nature was harmless and, it seemed, fairly stable. Richmond rapidly came across other, more extreme, examples. Walking up a narrow flight of stairs from the second floor, before the morning was even half over, he came out through the pantry door into the basement kitchen. The cook looked up, startled, from the meat she was chopping, while two scullery-maids idling by the fire glanced at each other and giggled. Richmond blinked, turned around and retreated down the stairs – only to emerge at once through a narrow door onto a balcony space right at the edge of the roof of the house, three storeys up, the cold wind whipping at his hair. At his back the door blew shut with a crash, and seemed to have wedged by the time he turned to open it. Richmond was forced to stumble fifty yards along the edge of the roof with his feet in the lead trough of the gutter, leaning on the bank of slates for fear of falling off to his death. He held on to his papers only through the utmost determination. Reaching a gabled attic window, he was unable to force the frame and resorted at last to smashing the glass and dropping through into the room below.

That chamber turned out to be filled with swathes of yellow sand, draped and banked right up to the rough wooden walls. A few cacti were growing among the small dunes. Richmond floundered to his feet and watched a lizard dart away under a rafter. He pulled a handkerchief from an inside pocket, wiped his spectacles carefully upon it and made more notes on his papers. Then he scrambled over to the door of the room, which thankfully opened outward onto the corridor, and emerged in a small landslide onto the uncarpeted attic passageway.

It took a certain amount of perseverance to regain the

ground floor, and then more to retrace his route via kitchen and rooftop while doggedly working out easier lines of access to the rooms in question. This once done, he reset his watch in each room. The scullery maids sniggered and whispered at each of his reappearances. Having satisfied himself that there was no more need to make the journey along the guttering and through the broken window, Richmond decided to concentrate on the suite of rooms around the westernmost light-well, which seemed determined to resist mapping. It took him the rest of the morning to work out that the Linen Cupboard could be accessed from the Billiard Room, but only if that chamber was originally entered from the Chinese Parlour.

When some distant bell tolled one, Richmond sat down and ate his ham sandwiches and a hard-boiled egg in the back row of the small Theatre at the extreme west end of the house. Although the auditorium, lit by gas mantles, was filled almost to capacity, his companions were not talkative. Each and every member of the audience – most of them on their feet in attitudes of extreme excitement and delight – was composed of fine Delian marble, intricately sculpted down to the last curl on the last periwig. Their appreciative attention was focused on the stage, whereon resided a black-lacquered Japanese box with brassbound doors. Richmond munched his sandwiches and stared thoughtfully at the box, but left the room without investigating its contents.

His work went well during the afternoon, and by the time Naotalba came to find him, carrying an oil lamp against the gathering dusk, he had managed to tick off a third of the rooms on the butler's list. He had glimpsed the Egyptian Bedchamber through a connecting door but had been unable to locate it subsequently. In the Trophy Chamber he had remarked upon the mounted heads of a number of mythical beasts. The Candle Room had turned out to be painted entirely black, and to indeed contain nothing but a softly burning candle of greyish tallow.

Naotalba found him seated on a horsehair sofa, writing. The pages were covered in the young man's tiny neat handwriting: cross-referenced, arrowed, asterisked and underlined.

"Dinner will be served in an hour, sir," the butler announced. "Your evening attire has been laid out, and I have drawn you a bath."

"Very well," Richmond murmured, not raising his face. "What room is this?"

"The Charlett Room, sir," Naotalba replied, drawing the long curtains across the bay window. The heavy material, patterned like chestnut hair sprigged with blue ribbons, stirred in a draught. "Named after a friend of the family."

Richmond ticked off another line with an air of satisfaction. "Excellent."

In his own chamber he found the formal evening attire provided by his host. It fitted passably well. When the dinner gong rang he proceeded to the Dining Room – a well-trodden and therefore entirely mundane route – where Thale was already seated at a highly polished table. On his right-hand side sat a dark-eyed young woman, the one Richmond had seen last night leaning over the banister. Beyond her sat a slender man with a Mediterranean complexion.

"Ha – no problem finding the dinner table then?" Thale joked. "Sit down, Richmond. May I introduce you to my daughter, Camilla? And this is Nikolaos Aldones, my personal secretary."

Richmond bowed shortly across the table to each in turn. Camilla met his eyes with a dark stare, but did not respond to his greeting and Richmond's polite smile broke upon the walls of her reserve. She was a strikingly handsome woman, dressed very formally in pearl-grey silk, and she carried herself with a contemptuously proud air, but despite this her pallor and the black smudges under her eyes betrayed a lack of ease.

"Very pleased to meet you," Aldones said silkily, rising and shaking Richmond's hand. His grasp was slightly too warm.

"How goes your task?" Thale asked.

"Quite well," said Richmond as a heavy china bowl was placed in front of him by a servant. The soup was meaty and rather pungent. He unfurled his linen napkin. "I did find one locked door on the first floor that I wished to ask you about."

"The one at the top of the stairs? That is my own chamber," Thale explained. "Behind that door lie the Master Bedroom and the Agamemnon Bathroom only, I can assure you."

"Thank-you," said Richmond, making a mental note. "I should also report that I have found the Clock Room, which I believe had previously been mislaid."

"Oh really? Splendid! Where?"

"Through the Silk Dragon Bedchamber. Perhaps you have noticed the large mirror on the door? If you press upon the mirror-frame instead of the door handle, it opens an entirely different egress from the room, and the Clock Room is down a short corridor."

Aldones raised one eyebrow and applauded archly: "Congratulations."

Camilla stared down at her untouched soup.

"Goodness me! Well done, Richmond – that was smart work. The Clock Room has never been down that end of the house that I can remember. Hmm. Well, that must be noisy on the hour. We must make sure not to put guests in that bedroom if we can help it."

"It was the chiming that alerted me," Richmond admitted.

"Ha! Well, good show. Have you been up to the Picture Gallery yet?"

"Not yet, sir. I had planned a reconnaissance trip after dinner."

"Well, don't take too long about it," said Thale. "Aldones here was hoping you'd match him in a game of billiards."

Richmond didn't miss the smile on Aldones' face, nor the sneer that curved Camilla's full, purplish lips. He allowed himself a non-committal nod. The rest of the soup-course was finished in silence. Richmond just had time to take in the glazed picture on the bottom of his dish – a satyr of quite improbable proportions chasing a nymph – before it was cleared away and a plate of veal in a sour cherry sauce substituted before him.

"Ah," said Thale as the many side-dishes were arranged upon the tablecloth and Naotalba served all the diners with a rich Burgundy. "The gastronomic pleasures, the one appetite that one never outgrows, and the only delight left to me these sad days."

Aldones sniggered openly.

"Hardly, father," said Camilla. Richmond nearly dropped a spoonful of peas upon hearing her speak. She had a lush, deep voice like the purr of some jungle cat.

"Indulge me, child," Thale sighed. "If you cannot respect my advanced years, then pity the fate that has left me a cripple."

"Your own pity is quite sufficient," Camilla replied. "And you brought your current state upon yourself." She impaled a piece of veal with a kind of indifferent savagery.

Aldones coughed and reminded her, "It was an accident," but she didn't bother to indulge him with so much as a glance. Her brooding gaze kept returning to Richmond's face, which was putting him off his own meal.

Thale laughed a thin-lipped laugh. "Of course you are right, my dear. I should not have gone out hunting. I should not have been tempted to desert my post." He considered Richmond for a moment and then seemed to reach a decision to elucidate. "But I've been almost a recluse since the death of dear Mrs Beaumont – so heartbreaking, that was, and the London season has hardly been worthwhile without her parties – and it has been too long since I've felt the blood really stirring. I was probably a little reckless in taking the fences, and certainly am not as fit as I used to be. It turned out I had broken my leg..." Thale sighed and regarded the folds of tartan blanket laid over his lower body. "The limb would not mend, despite the best care. I was obliged to have it amputated, and chose to do so without ether. You might suppose that I would have been an enthusiast for that sort of thing, but although the experience was … intense … I do find that the inconvenience of mobility I am now labouring under rather outweighs the interest afforded by the extremity of sensation."

There was a long silence.

"More wine, sir?" Naotalba asked, gliding up to Richmond's elbow.

"What? Ah— No, thank you." Richmond became aware that all the other diners were watching him; Aldones with a crooked smile, Camilla with a glare sharper than a scalpel, and Thale purse-lipped, appraising, attentive. Each in their own way, Richmond realised, was savouring the moment. He put his fork down with an audible clink.

"A very fine veal," he said, "most delicious. My compliments to your cook."

Camilla began to laugh, her head thrown back so that it could bubble unimpeded from the long pale length of her throat. It was not a kindly sound. Then she folded her napkin and stood, smiling for the first time at Richmond. Without asking her father's leave or bidding anyone farewell she strode from the dining room.

Thale watched her retreating figure while toying idly with an asparagus stalk soused in melted butter.

"*Whence comest thou, Beauty? Heaven, or the Abyss?*" he quoted. "My daughter is a very fine young lady, do you not think so, Richmond? She has been the muse to many a poet. Monsieur Baudelaire was smitten in his day. And I believe Mr Swinburne is currently most dreadfully in love with her. There is certainly competition for my Camilla's favour." His words dropped like small stones into the pool of silence.

*

Leaving that company was like coming out into fresh air from a closed room. Richmond changed into his working suit and then marched up the curved staircase. But when he reached the door to the Picture Gallery he was not reckless enough to rush in; he halted outside and put one ear to the oak.

There was no sound from within.

Very softly, Richmond placed his lamp down and eased the door open. The Gallery was not entirely in darkness: ranks of mullioned windows to his right admitted a wave of moonlight. The wall on his left appeared to be hung with paintings, but he couldn't see far because the long cloister was barred by a multitude of naked tree-branches jammed in between floor and ceiling, their jagged snags piercing the broken panes of glass. The whole space was transformed into a crosshatched mess of moonlight and grey wood and black shadow that could not be deciphered by the human eye. An acrid smell tainted the air.

Richmond took one step into the room. The bare floorboards were polished where they were not besmirched with huge white splashes of bird-mess, or hidden under drifts of broken twigs. He looked at the first picture on the wall: an oil-portrait of Thale, depicted as an emperor robed and crowned.

There was the crunch of movement deep within the Gallery. Richmond started and peered down the hall. The sound was repeated, getting louder; the noise of some large body moving from branch to branch, flapping heavy wings, shoving though brittle barriers of dead twigs – getting much closer. Richmond blinked. Just as something suddenly emerged from the tangle and swooped shrieking upon him, he lunged backwards and threw the door shut. A solid weight thudded against the wood, scratching and scuffling, but though Richmond gripped the doorknob tightly there was no attempt made on that from the other side.

Breathing heavily, he retreated a couple of steps from the door. He had received a blurred glimpse as he'd fled of a fanged female face, withered breasts and outstretched crow-wings. He pressed his hands to his temples.

"That made you jump, I see," said a voice behind him. "So you are not entirely a plaster saint."

Richmond turned and found Aldones smirking at him. The personal secretary had changed out of his dinner garb and now wore a yellow silk dressing gown, beneath which his legs were bare but for a pair of Turkish slippers. "You were looking for me?" Richmond said.

"Of course. Come with me." Aldones crooked a finger playfully and then saw Richmond's face grow blank and masklike. "I can show you the Library," he explained.

Richmond followed him along the passage to a door he had not previously entered.

"This is my bedchamber," Aldones murmured. "I'm sure you'd have got round to it sooner or later. The Sebastian Room, on your little list."

The room's appellation was immediately apparent: the chamber, notable as it was for the huge four-poster bed and a central iron chandelier on a massive chain, was dominated by a painting of the martyrdom of St Sebastian, twice as large as life. The woeful ecstasy upon the youth's face and the arrow-shafts jutting from his bloody flesh had been painted with loving detail.

"A charming picture, don't you think?"

"If you say so," Richmond replied. "Most people would find it difficult to sleep in the same room as that."

"I don't *sleep* here," Aldones sniggered. "Nor anywhere in this house – I wouldn't dare. After a few weeks you find you don't need it. I have a pipeful every so often in the Smoking Room and that suffices. Now – you will want to be over here." So saying, he went round the side of the bed and pulled away a small but heavy glass table from next to the headboard. Lifting the drape he disclosed a little door about twelve inches high set into the wall. There was a tiny gold key in the lock. "There," he announced.

Richmond knelt before the door. He could only grip the key between thumb and one finger, but it turned easily.

"Has this always been a door to the Library?" he asked. Through the tiny archway he could make out a large room lined from floor to ceiling with bookshelves. Firelight from some unseen source played on morocco-bound spines and gilt lettering. A cast-iron spiral staircase was just visible in one corner, rising up to a balcony above.

"No, it was a little cupboard for wine bottles when I first came here," Aldones said.

Richmond pressed himself flatter against the floor and chanced pushing one arm into the room. His fingers just brushed the edge of the Persian carpet, but it was clear that his shoulders couldn't follow though that small entrance.

"No way in," he muttered, brushing the dust from his clothes as he stood again. He turned. The other man was seated upon the glass table, dressing-gown spread wide.

"Eat me," Aldones suggested.

Richmond pulled in a sharp breath. "I think not," he said coolly. He produced his pocket-watch, flipped it open, then reset one of the dials and walked away.

Aldones leapt to his feet, pursued him across the room and grabbed his arm just as he reached the door. "You wait one moment," he hissed. His face was creased with spite. "Now sir, do get it into your head that this house is not a place for innocents. You, with your little cloud of sanctity – do you think you're safe? Do you think you'll emerge unscathed? You are wading through a swamp, and any step now it will close over your head."

Richmond stared back at him, not flinching from the face thrust within inches of his own.

"You don't have a clue, do you?" Aldones sneered. "You don't know where you are. You think you're mapping this place, but you haven't the faintest idea. This is *his*. And he has lost his grip: he isn't in control any more. What do you think will happen if you finish? He's not going to get to his feet and reclaim the territory! Are you going to come back every month and find it for him all over again? His nerve is gone – his heart is not in it. After all these years, his grip is failing. Have you seen the things that are coming out into the light? Do you know that after midnight the Jabberwock stalks these corridors? And in the Roman Room something flounders across the floor in the dark and wails Thale's secrets? I have heard it. They are his ghosts. He is too old. He cannot cope. He should be lifted of the burden – and replaced."

Aldones drew back. His eyes were heavy-lidded. Slowly his grip on Richmond's arm loosened. "You, he will use," he muttered. "He is clinging to his power, and he is using you, but he will not admit how much he needs you. He will break you to prove he is still the master here."

Richmond turned away and stepped through the door. As it swung shut behind him he heard Aldones' last words: "No one can leave this place untainted."

He walked slowly back down the dark passage to the staircase, and from there into more familiar territory. His own room was much as he had left it, except that it had been tidied in his absence. On the pillow was a small book: *One Hundred and Twenty Days of Sodom*, with hand-coloured illustrations. Richmond closed the volume, laid it aside and went to stare out of the window. The moon glared down over the darkened gardens, turning the still waters of the lake to glass. It was at the absolute peak of fullness, round as an orange, just as it had been on the previous night.

He pushed open the window and leaned out, craning his neck to see the house above and to either side of him. Here at the back, the house was less uniform; he could dimly make out various architectural protrusions. To his left – a good distance away, almost at the far end of the building – the moonlight glinted upon a glass extension that jutted out into the kitchen garden. This, he guessed, was the missing Conservatory.

Richmond considered seizing this unexpected opportunity and climbing out through the window to come directly at his goal, but thought better of it. Thale was unlikely to be pleased if he established a route that involved clambering out of the building and through the shrubbery after dark. He shrugged and closed the window.

He woke in the small hours, hearing outside his door something huge scrape and shuffle its way down the panelled corridor, whining to itself and scratching at the woodwork. The stink of carrion filtered into the bedroom. Richmond felt for the pistol under his pillow and lay very still until the noises died away.

*

On his second day of work at Lithly House, Richmond established the location of the rest of the known rooms. These included the Steam Room – a gallery occupied almost to the walls by the hissing black bulk of a huge locomotive engine, tank still hot and firebox still stoked, but with no visible doorway in the room large enough to have afforded entrance to such a behemoth. And the Ebony Bedchamber, which was full of flies; and the Parisian Bedchamber, which housed a terribly strange bed; and the Toy Room, which was filled with grinning, twitching, misshapen marionettes. And the Chapel, whose designer in a fit of ecumenical fervour had included not only an altar to the crucified Christ, but also to the dismembered Osiris, the castrated Attis, the decapitated Orpheus, the hanged Wotan and the disembowelled Prometheus. He mapped the Nile Study, wallpapered entirely in crocodile-skin; the Smoking Room, filled with a haze of opium; the Whistling Room, which suffered from an alarming defect in the stonework; and the Ballroom, which was empty of everything but echoes.

He gained access to the bottom of both the light-wells, just to be thorough. In one, dry and sandy, there was rooted a leafless tree as tall as himself, carved from a single seamless piece of ivory. In the other a fountain splashed among mossy rocks. He might have thought the liquid was water had not the acrid smell informed him that it was urine.

He inspected the servants' quarters and the kitchens, whose fittings turned out to be entirely conventional, and then under Naotalba's supervision he surveyed the cellars – whose fittings, although not at all conventional, were not the slightest surprise to him by this point. The stable layout of both areas informed him that they were regularly used.

Some time after his luncheon of ox-tongue sandwiches, Richmond entered the Egyptian Bedchamber. The room was filled with light from the south-facing windows and a cool afternoon silence had settled upon the house. Richmond reset his watch and then glanced at the fittings, but his interest was taken by the murals painted upon the walls: stylised in the Egyptian manner, they depicted ranks of vassals presenting their offerings to an enthroned woman. Richmond spotted the cartouche over the queen's head and idly stepped closer to read the hieroglyphics.

"Nitocris," he murmured to himself. "Of course." At that moment his foot caught on something. He bent to pick it up. A twelve-foot length of chain dangled from his hand, one end attached to an empty leather collar, the other shackled to the foot of the bed.

He was still staring at it when Camilla purred, "You go hunting through the Labyrinth, Theseus. Do you have a clue to guide you?"

He turned. The four-poster bed, which he had barely registered, was completely enclosed by tulle hangings. But the light was shining through the thin material and within the enclosure he could now make out the darker form of his questioner. He approached the foot of the bed slowly and she stepped forward to meet him.

"Do you know what waits at the heart of the Labyrinth?" she asked. She stood with her arms raised to the posts at either side. Her breath stirred the silk curtain between them. He could see through the translucent cloth that she was naked, and he didn't answer.

"In the heart of the Labyrinth, which is the soul," she murmured, drawing back the curtain with a languid movement, "is the beast. Royal, yet a monster. The devourer. Inhuman. The source of all fear and all power, trapped. That is why we build the maze in the first place: for fear that the beast might rampage free."

She paused, watching him to see what his reaction to her might be. Her creamy skin seemed to glow against the dark gloss of her unbound hair.

"Camilla," he said, as if trying the name out. His gaze skidded up her lush body, finally resting on her face.

"Where is your beast?" she asked. "You keep it well hidden. See, I offer it a new landscape to roam, if only it would show itself."

"It is Lithly House that I have been engaged to explore," Richmond reminded her.

"Ah. In my Father's house are many mansions. How true."

Richmond's spectacles glinted. "Tell me, where is the heart of his Labyrinth?"

She smiled slowly, eyes glittering under long dark lashes. "The Library," she whispered.

"Ah."

"Will you dare face the Minotaur there?"

"I am not afraid of Thale's beast," he replied mildly. "Nor yours." He had neither flinched from her nor made any move toward her, and his face was calm. Something in that expression made her smile fade.

"You're a strange man," she whispered.

"What," he asked, "is your basis for comparison?"

She pulled back slightly, lips pursed, and was silent.

"If you'll excuse me?"

He got halfway across the room before she said in a low

voice, "My sister…"

This brought him to a halt. He looked back.

She hadn't moved. "My sister. She is in one of the lost rooms. Which ones have you still left to find?"

He consulted his papers, needlessly. "The Library, Nursery, Elizabethan Bedchamber, Conservatory, Mirror Room and Pomegranate Bedchamber. I have located all the others."

"The Pomegranate Chamber: that is hers. The night my father went out hunting, he was displeased with Cassilda and sent her without supper to her room. He instructed her not to come out until he fetched her." Camilla's eyes looked like black pits in the white mask of her face. "We have not seen her in weeks. He was ashamed to tell you."

Richmond blinked. "Will she still be alive?"

"That depends whether she disobeyed him and left her room, and what others she might have access to. There was brandy in the Library, as I remember."

"I see."

Camilla's hardened mouth pulled creases in her face. "You should look at your list and ask yourself: 'Why these rooms? Why did he lose these ones first?' They are not random. The Elizabethan Bedchamber was our mother's. I can guess some of the rest… Did you know that he smashed all the mirrors in his own room after his accident? Mr Richmond, he does not desire you to succeed in your task. Whatever he says to you, he wanted to lose those rooms. He does not want them back. He does not care if Cassilda is dead." With those words she dragged the curtain back around herself and the bed, the rings rattling like bones against the pole.

"Thank you," Richmond said as he turned to the door. "I think you have after all, my Ariadne, given me the clue I needed to find the way."

*

He made his way to the Palm Bathroom on the second floor. It had seemed an unremarkable chamber when he'd first catalogued it: tiled in white with a sunken marble bath and brass fittings, the air smelling faintly of carbolic soap. A statue of Priapus was the only ornamentation except for the half-dozen palm-trees that gave it its name, standing about in glazed pots, their heads bowed against the ceiling. But set into the white floor-tiles were pale green ones that made up the spiralling shape of a Troy maze.

He had to drag some of the palms aside in order to reveal the entire pattern. Wiping his hands on a towel, he trod the winding path into the centre. There he paused. No noticeable alteration had occurred in the room. Slowly he paced his way out to the edge again, where he was directly facing the door to the bathroom. Two steps took him to it and he laid his hand upon the porcelain doorknob, glancing back around him. Nothing had changed. He pulled the door open.

There was no corridor outside the room, only a void of total blackness – and in the distance the doorway into some further room, through which light was streaming. A figure was silhouetted in that doorway. Richmond pulled the pistol from inside his jacket and stepped forward into the dark passage.

Both doors swung shut simultaneously and at once he was plunged into absolute darkness. He crouched and froze, ears straining. He could hear nothing but the rustle of his own clothes. A smooth, hard surface, very cold to the touch, was beneath his feet and his fingertips. No hint of any light reached his eyes; he might as well have been blind. No breeze stirred against his cheek, no scent came to his nostrils. Nothing told him he was not entirely alone.

At last Richmond laid down the pistol at his feet – it chinked audibly, though he was trying to be soundless – and felt around in his jacket pockets, to retrieve the stub of a candle and a box of lucifers. He struck a match and light erupted in the room; without looking about him he lit the candle.

He hung in the void. Around him candle flames burned like stars. He looked down and stared into his own pale face; he looked about him and a hundred Richmonds gaped back, light flashing from their spectacles. He stood up; an upside-down Richmond hung from his soles. All the other Richmonds were paired too, and they stood as he did and spun around as he did in perfect silent synchrony, an infinite darkening series of candle-bearers receded on every side into blackness. He shut his eyes and tried to reclaim himself.

He was in a room made entirely from mirrors. What the shape of that room might be he couldn't guess. The only light source was his candle and its glimmering reflections. He couldn't even see the ground he stood on; that was a transparent skin over the crawling depths of infinity. Richmond put away his gun, fished out the fob-watch, and reset it. All around him the reflections aped his motions. He raised his candle and they joined him a silent toast. He turned about and they spun like moons.

All but one.

One of the reflections did not move. Standing with its back to him: in every detail it was a perfect reflection of him, except that it was motionless. Fixing his gaze upon this, Richmond started across the abyss, ignoring the phantoms, lurching toward that one static point. His free hand reached out and thumped against a solid surface: wood. It was a painting on a wooden panel. Richmond more or less fell against it and it crashed outward, pitching him face down on a floor made of slats. His head spun and his stomach heaved as the candle slipped from his hands and went out.

Richmond found himself clinging to a vertical wooden ladder. That much he could tell, but blackness was absolute once more; there was no guessing how far he would fall, should he let go. The ladder was pinned to a brick wall. He eased himself up two rungs, and at once the top of his head met a hard surface. Raising one hand he felt wood that yielded to pressure. A line of light opened horizontally in front of his face.

Richmond crawled out of the big toy-chest onto the floor of the Nursery and then stayed on hands and knees for some time until he was sure of his bearings. His first action upon standing was to brush the dust from his clothes.

The Nursery clock ticked softly in one corner. Richmond looked carefully around him. Two small beds, a table covered in a worn candlewick throw, a dresser, and a huge rocking-horse made up the furnishings. There was a door in one corner. The walls were painted with a mural depicting, in all the glorious colour and realistic detail of a Pre-Raphaelite master, a processional Dance of Death.

After a few minutes' work Richmond went over to the door. Behind it was a flight of worn stone steps and, ascending these, he emerged into the great fire-lit belly of the Library.

*

Shortly after the bell had rung nine o'clock, Naotalba knocked quietly upon the door of the Drawing Room and slipped within. Thale lay on his couch before the fire, fiddling with a beautifully carved pornographic Chinese chess-set. Aldones was pacing up and down the room, reading a book of Sappho's poems. Camilla was in a window seat, staring out into the dark beyond the pane.

Naotalba coughed softly. "Sir. Mr Richmond has returned."

The young man entered the room as he spoke and took up a place on the carpet at a polite distance from his host. Naotalba's eyes were anxious, but he got no further chance to speak.

"Ah – splendid, Richmond," Thale said, stretching. "Do you play chess? We are expecting guests very shortly, so it will not be a long game. Mr Machen and some of his thespian friends are coming over for a few days. Are you fond of the performing arts?"

"I regret I will not be staying to meet them," Richmond said. "I have finished my work here and will be going at once."

"What?" exclaimed Aldones. Camilla looked around.

"Finished?" Thale said thickly. The colour was draining from his cheeks. "You found the Library then?"

"Yes, sir."

At that moment the door opened further and a young woman in a filthy dress stumbled into the room. She brushed past Naotalba and, without paying the slightest attention to anyone else, hurried over to the window seat, threw herself to her knees and buried her face in Camilla's lap.

Camilla gave a gasp and sank her hand into the other woman's hair. "Cassilda!" she whispered.

"You found her," observed Aldones, eyebrows raised.

Richmond inclined his head. But Thale was not looking at his daughter; he was staring at the book in Richmond's hand.

"Ah, yes," said Richmond, noticing his gaze. "There is also the matter of this volume, and my instructions."

"The book has nothing to do with this," said Thale. His face was so pale now that it looked as if it had been carved from bone. "I have been master of this house for many decades. The book was only written a few years ago. There was a Frenchman, a playwright…"

"Castaigne?" Aldones offered, frowning.

Thale shot him an agonised look. "Yes. A nothing. He never wrote anything else of significance. He stayed here a few weeks, and he was inspired, as so many. He wrote a play. When it was printed in Paris he sent me a copy. Then he — " But Thale swallowed the rest of his sentence.

"He killed himself," said Richmond. "Yes, I know."

"What is going on here?" asked Aldones.

"The play," said Richmond, laying the book on the table next to him, "you read it."

"Ah. Hh. Yes," Thale said. "It is…"

"It is a mirror. Castaigne wrote a play that was a mirror that you could hold up to yourself. Lithly House is a prism for the soul, but it splits and distorts and enlarges and hints; you can so easily pretend that what you see is not you. But the play –

ah, the magic of the written word. It showed you your soul, and reflected over and over to infinity, in perfect clarity, your despair and your emptiness and your unmeaning. Isn't that so?" Richmond's fingertips brushed the book's binding.

Thale squirmed in his chair, fists clenching. "I put it away," he groaned.

"Yes. I imagine you tried your best to forget it. But you could not, could you? You had to reread it. How often, I wonder? Your self-loathing has permeated this entire house. Your nightmares stalk the corridors."

Thale shut his eyes, to stop himself staring at the slim volume on the table. Across the room, Camilla said in a low voice, "You disobeyed our father and left your room, did you not? I shall have to punish you, Cassilda."

And Cassilda, sobbing, replied, "Please. Oh yes, please."

"In the end," said Richmond mildly, "your fear became so strong, and your compulsion to read so strong, that the only way out was to lose it somewhere you could never return to. So you crippled yourself, and lost the Library."

"That was an accident," Aldones protested. "He sent for you."

Richmond spared him a glance. "Oh yes. He still desired the book. He wanted to retrieve it, just as much as he wanted to lose it. It is like finding a picture so shocking that one cannot help but look at it again and again, until one's nerves are cauterised and one becomes hardened to the pain. You should know how that is. But with this play one cannot become numb."

"It changes things," Thale said. "With every reading, it changes the world; the house; the people. They draw closer to the world in the book. He has written us into his play, and now it closes around us. Lithly House did not always stand beside a lake. Camilla was not always my daughter. Cassilda had another name – I don't remember now what it was... I stood in the Conservatory and watched the moon rise in front of the chimneys. Oh God. My dreams are broken … I behold the tatters of the King." He seemed then to recollect his mind from its wanderings and finished weakly, "That – that play feeds off reality; truth is shredding away under my hands."

"Truth?" said Richmond. "Truth is a phantom."

"What are we to do?" Camilla asked in a low voice.

"Read the book," said Richmond, "and find out."

"You bastard," said Aldones with something like awe.

"I am not joking." Richmond fixed Thale's drained and sweating countenance with a cold stare. "I have recovered your rooms, but I will not be back to repeat the operation. Read the book. Read it once a month, every month. It will shape and hold the house. Those are your instructions."

"I don't understand!" Thale protested. "I have always done as I was bid… What have I…? Why will you not aid me?"

Richmond folded his hands. "You have fulfilled your role admirably. We have no complaints at Roy and Johns about your tenure. But we have now entered a new phase of our work and you must all adapt to these changed conditions. Castaigne wrote the play at our instigation. You will read it. Others will come; you must play host to them as you have always done and you must encourage them to read it too."

"But," said Thale weakly, pushing himself up in his seat, "I am the Last King, in the play. And at the start of Act Two – "

"Cowardice is hardly an acceptable trait in the employees of Roy and Johns Associates," Richmond reminded him. "You know your contract." He pulled the gold watch from his pocket and flicked it open. "Now, much as I have enjoyed my stay here, I am afraid I must be going…"

"Hold him!" Aldones yelled, springing forward. His hand closed around the watch and he wrenched it out of Richmond's grasp. The gold chain ripped free and tiny links rattled across the furniture. At almost the same moment Naotalba jumped in, locked an arm around Richmond's neck, grabbed his right hand and shoved it hard up between his shoulder blades.

Richmond collapsed. His head came off in Naotalba's arm and fell to the floor. His trapped hand tore from the sleeve and the limb within and the young man's body slumped to the ground. For a moment everyone froze. Then out from the crumpled shape of the corpse began to flood a hoard of glittering insects, yellow dung-beetles, heaving and scuttling across the floor. Naotalba stepped back in horror. Aldones writhed onto a chair, green with revulsion. The beetles poured across the room, disappearing into cracks between floorboards and into the dark shadows beneath furniture. In a few moments they had dispersed and vanished. They left only an empty suit of clothes and the flimsy remnants of Richmond's face and two hands, white and papery like the chewed pulp of wasps' nests.

"Bastard!" Aldones shrieked. He tore open the gold watch cover and the contents went flying across the carpet: a few loose springs, a dead moth, a piece of crumpled paper bearing the words *More Light!* and the spinal column of a mouse. On the back of the watch-case was engraved a curious sign, identical to that embossed on the cover of the play.

"Shit!" cried Aldones, throwing the case across the room. "Shit! Shit!"

Thale, voiceless, started to shake as if with tears or laughter, though neither emerged. Blood began to trickle from between his lips. Naotalba dropped the grisly trophies of his would-be captive, covered his eyes with his hands and shook his head back and forth, back and forth. Camilla threw open her throat and howled with empty mirth, knotting her hands in her sister's golden hair. For a while there was pandemonium, and then slowly the inhabitants of the room grew still.

Dust settled in the breathless air.

Into the silence of the drawing room stole the distant chime of the doorbell.

Naotalba suddenly stood up and bowed.

"Your Majesty," he said. "Mr Machen and his entourage

have arrived for their audience with you."

Thale raised a composed face and empty, empty eyes. He wiped the line of blood from his chin. "My royal daughters," he said, his voice somehow cracked, somehow different. "Our vassals stand at the palace gate. You should go forth to receive them, and convey our welcome."

Story Notes

Donald

"The Shadow over Innsmouth" is one of Lovecraft's later stories and generally regarded as "core Mythos". The Deep Ones are perhaps the "race" most often drawn upon for Lovecraftiana, and also the most common recipients of a sympathetic eye. One reason for this is that "Innsmouth" is a story about race. There's no avoiding the admission that a lot of HPL's stories are intensely racist and, while the worst of these belong to his earlier New York period, he remains fixated on issues of racial mixing and purity which are significant in "Innsmouth". The idea of the poor Innsmouth denizens rounded up in camps at the end of the story, however, strikes a different note to the modern reader than it might have done to Lovecraft. Even the final section of the story does not go as far as to ask "who are the real monsters" but the question arises out of the story whether HPL intended it or not. Deep Ones become less unfathomable entities and more another people with whom we share the planet, and with whom some manner of détente must eventually be brokered.

AT

Pitter Patter

I used to work for the Reserve Forces and Cadets Association. I remember Holloway TAC, and how we tried to keep it going. I was sorry to hear about its sale.

At one point when I was between apartments I was allowed to stay temporarily in a TAC's guest accommodation. There's no lonelier feeling on earth than when you're wandering in the darkened halls of a building intended for several hundred people and you the only one in it. You can hear traffic, and you know that only a short distance away one of the busiest intersections in all of London is going about its nightly routine. For you, it might as well not exist. It's just a muffled, far-off noise. You're all alone with your thoughts. Your thoughts, and whatever else might be out there in the dark.

If you're wondering whether the building in this tale is meant to be Exham Priory, I deliberately leave the question open.

AG

Special Needs Child

I fell in love with ghouls thirty years ago when I read the scenario "Paper Chase" in the third edition *Call of Cthulhu* rulebook. It was the lines: "As a ghoul, his life is great. He does not need money. He does not have to dress for dinner. He does not have to meet people ... except at meal-times." That ice-cold Addams-esque humour delighted me. Ghouls are proof that being a blasphemous abomination doesn't mean you have to be miserable about it; much like the Addams Family, they are merrily oblivious to how horrific they are. (Brian McNaughton's ghoul stories showcase this, though they are *not* for the faint of heart.) Ghouls are so nearly human – mocking caricatures of ourselves – that as long as you can overlook the putrescence, the cannibalism and the necrophilia, they are good company. Of course, if you *can* overlook those things you're already on the slippery slope downhill into the dark, as my protagonist Gina discovers...

KM

Irrational Numbers

Here are the Fungi from Yuggoth, aka the Mi-go, which apparently continue whatever operation they were conducting in Vermont in "The Whisperer in Darkness". They make an odd contribution to the Mythos non-canon. They are scientifically advanced, but their science is very science-y – brains in jars and tools to augment their physical capabilities, very much the stuff of alien-invasion creature features. They don't show up on film, and they work closely with human servants whom they claim to reward by allowing them (or their brains) to ride along on interstellar voyages. And they're unusually fragile for Lovecraftian entities.

With "Irrational Numbers" I confess to having taken liberties with the breed as presented in "Whisperer". There is a definite malice, or at least callousness, in the original, but at the same time they plainly value what they can use, which in this case includes my narrator. Still, I have ventured to cast the mysticism of the cult rituals from "Whisperer" as the crustaceous aliens bringing their idiom down to a level the superstitious Vermontian hill people could follow, inferior to the pan-dimensional mathematics of the narrator ("Dreams in the Witch House" again?) More, the reintroduction of our old friend Noyes at this late remove suggests a veracity to their claims of rewarding loyalty that is probably beyond the original intent. But I can honestly say, as a writer whose oeuvre has mostly concerned the doings of the chitinous, who wouldn't want to work for intergalactic crab-mushrooms if they've a jar with your brain's name on it?

AT

New Build

In Frank Belknap Long's "The Hound of Tindalos", the last thing would-be explorer of the fourth dimension Halpin Chalmers does before expiring messily is write "Their *tongues* – ahhhh—" Speaking for myself, I've always felt that if you have time to actually write down, with an honest to God pen, the word "ahhhh", you're not in as much danger as you'd like me to believe. However, a phone call works just fine, he says guiltily.

There's something mesmeric about Long's original. I

strongly suspect it once mesmerised Stephen King, and as evidence I submit his short fiction "Sun Dog" from the *Four Past Midnight* novella collection. That one has juice. The idea that you can't see a thing, but that you can look into its world; that a creature might inhabit a world parallel to and yet utterly unlike ours, and wants to break through, all that sounds remarkably like Long to me.

That, and I happen to like Victorian pubs. If you get the chance, the Princess Louise at High Holborn is the one I had principally in mind. Long may it stand, and mine's a bitter, thanks.

AG

Branch Line Repairman

The Old Ones or Elder Things are Lovecraft's most explicitly described monsters, historically and literally anatomised in "At the Mountains of Madness" where we also meet their counterparts, the Shoggoths. In that book their intricately detailed civilization is long dead, overthrown by their own creations. However, we also meet them in "Dreams in the Witch House", not because HPL was engaged in intentional, Mythos-building, but because he hadn't found a publisher for "Mountains" and so had the creatures lying unused on his conceptual cutting room floor. In that story the Old Ones are alive and well in some extraterrestrial city of their own, and from there it was a short step to wonder what those well-to-do alien magnates might make of their horrifically failed Earth colony. The Old Ones were also very much the inspiration for this collection. "They were men," HPL writes of them in "Mountains". They are his very best line in creatures simultaneously alien, and yet logical enough for humans to halfway understand and even sympathise with. Like humans, they are capable of great achievements and great excesses. Their reliance on slavery brings on their ruin, although I don't know that HPL, even at his most socialist, would have conceded such a left-wing narrative to the Shoggoths and their ilk. After all, it's hard to be a good Marxist when you *are* the means of production...

AT

Devo Nodenti
I'm a big fan of the *Dreamlands* stories, though it annoys me when the setting is treated as just another fantasy world. I strongly lean to keeping the Dreamlands as surreal and symbolic and as rife with avatars and metaphor as the dreams they are supposed to be; a part of the shared subconscious of humanity. I'm also interested in how HPL picked Nodens as a Dreamlands god – clearly he'd done his research into the Lydney dig even without benefit of Wikipedia, since the description of Nodens is based on a mosaic from that site, and I'm assuming he knew all about the incubation chambers there. What I wanted to do was make Nodens (and his Nightgaunts) as creepy as possible: "hoary", "gray" and "awful" with a "wizened hand" are descriptors I take to be more significant than the cheesy dolphins. The Lydney digs in the 1920s and 1980s really happened (and yes, Tolkien wrote on the meaning of Nodens' name), though there wasn't one in the 1960s as in the story. Rory DeAngelo is roughly based on Mortimer Wheeler though, who was by all accounts constantly embroiled in adulterous affairs with his assistants. I can't find *any details* on the 1980s dig at all. Not even which organisation carried it out. Weird, that...

KM

Season of Sacrifice and Resurrection
The Great Race of Yith, like several of the other HPL critters I've drawn on, are products of his later writings, and of a more science-fictional frame of mind: the horror is less all-encompassingly cosmic and more immediate and in many ways comprehensible. The Yith always fascinated me. They are

a race of scholars, they seem to possess empathy towards creatures of other species, and – again like several of the other races I've used – they occupy a place on the food chain far closer to pitiful humanity than the gods of the outer darkness. Like many other Lovecraftian beasties, the Great Race bear us no active malice. Unlike many, they are actively interested in us, or at least in what we know. They live amongst us, awkwardly inhabiting our clumsy bodies, and they do their best to put everything back where they found it when their lease is up.

And yet they are also coldly genocidal when they need to be, their entire species flinging its consciousness forwards to evict the minds of some other civilization and doom them to the fate the Great Race themselves are escaping. Even the bodies they are best known for, those conical, tentacled *things*, are not their own, just the fashionable wardrobe for that season of their eternal time-hopping existence.

Faced with extinction or sufficient profit, we'd do just the same, if we could.

AT

Prospero and Caliban

Trail of Cthulhu fans may be suffering from déjà vu right about now. To them I say, why not?

Being Bermudian, I've heard all the stories about the Triangle you can possibly think of, but rarely have I heard one told by a Bermudian. It's you lot outside who keep insisting that aliens from beyond Pluto's taint, or whatever it may be, whisk aircraft, ships and people off into the great beyond should they ever dare intrude in that vast expanse of water between Bermuda, Florida and Puerto Rico. Frankly, Vincent Gaddis needed a solid kick in the pants, at least once every seven days. But perhaps I'm biased.

Shakespeare's supposed to have based his *Tempest* on our still-vex'd Bermooths. Wikipedia helpfully informs me that much of the plot may derive from the *commedia dell'arte*, and I suppose it's comforting to know that much of Bermuda's current political and social climate also derives inspiration from the *commedia*. Be that as it may, I've often felt that we live in a fever dream down here, one from which we have little chance of awakening.

The towns, the majestic cities, the landscapes and seascapes we create thereby; may they not consume us. Or, if you'd prefer a little Latin at this juncture, *Quo Fata Ferunt*. It's as good a motto as any, I suppose.

AG

Moving Targets
"From Beyond" is an early HPL story, one where the real impact is not so much in the specific telling as the wider implication. The monsters are not conjured out of deep space or the past or the sea; they're not conjured from anywhere at all. They are with us constantly, overlapping our everyday lives, and we and they both live in blissful ignorance of one another until Tillinghast switches on his resonator and expands our senses until we can see them, and they, in turn, can see us. And whilst most of the inhabitants of that concurrent world are harmless save to each other, there are worse things, and simply to lay eyes on them is to risk dissolution. The story usually turns up as one of his minor canon and yet the idea in itself is perhaps the most Lovecraftian of all. The mind-(and body-) destroying other is *right there*, constantly around and between and within us, and a chance resonance can draw back the veil and expose us to that wider universe. The apparent mindless nature of the denizens of that shared space – very like things seen under a microscope – only goes to emphasise how little we and our vaunted powers actually matter in the grander scheme of things. They don't send us dreams or want us to worship the Daemon Sultan; they won't use us or teach us magic or even try to cleanse the world of us. Even when they

obliterate us, there's no guarantee they have any conception of what we are.

AT

The Play's the Thing

If Hill House was famously "not sane", then Lithly House is down to 0-SAN and gibbering maniacally in the corner. Two of my favourite things in horror: The *King in Yellow* sub-Mythos and spatial impossibility. I'm thrilled by police boxes bigger on the inside, ghosts crawling out of videos, shops that *just aren't there* when you come back to complain a week later about the dodgy cursed antique they sold you, people trapped in mirrors … all that stuff that makes you mistrust the basic material fabric of the world.

"The Play's the Thing" was originally a challenge tale written for our story-writing group, The Deadliners – I think we all had to include certain random sentences and objects (like the tartan blanket) culled from other books. It grew into a massive homage to as many classic supernatural authors as I could think of, as I tried to write a story about a liminal house that had traumatised every horror-story writer who'd stayed there as a guest. The Charlett Room is from M R James, the Whistling Room is William Hope Hodgson, the Red Room is H.G. Wells, etc. Arthur Machen really was a travelling actor at one time. Extravagant tips of the hat to Robert W. Chambers and James Blish of course, as well as the 1970s TV series *Sapphire and Steel*, of which this is sort of an evil version.

KM

Also published by The Alchemy Press

Rumours of the Marvellous by Peter Atkins

Doors to Elsewhere by Mike Barrett

Evocations by James Brogden

Give Me These Moments Back by Mike Chinn

The Paladin Mandates by Mike Chinn

Nick Nightmare Investigates by Adrian Cole

Leinster Gardens and Other Subtleties by Jan Edwards

Shadows of Light and Dark by Jo Fletcher

Merry-Go-Round and Other Words by Bryn Fortey

Tell No Lies by John Grant

Touchstones by John Howard

Monsters by Paul Kane

Something Remains by Joel Lane and Friends

Where the Bodies are Buried by Kim Newman

Music From the Fifth Planet by Anne Nicholls

Music in the Bone by Marion Pitman

Invent-10n by Rod Rees

The Complete Weird Epistles of Penelope Pettiweather, Ghost Hunter by Jessica Amanda Salmonson

Dead Water and Other Weird Tales by David A. Sutton

Check out www.alchemypress.co.uk
for further details of these and our anthologies